THE DAYS WITH RAIN

ALSO FROM RITA A. GORDON

Standalone Novel

30 Days in Belfast

Let It Rain Series

Seven Days in Seattle (Book 1)

The Days with Rain (Book 2)

The Fall of Us (Book 3, coming soon)

"The greatest happiness of life is the conviction that
we are loved; loved for ourselves, or rather,
loved in spite of ourselves."

— VICTOR HUGO

Passion wasn't enough.

THE DAYS WITH RAIN

A Novel

RITA A. GORDON

12:56 a.m.

California

The Days With Rain

www.ritaagordon.com

May contain sexual situations, sensitive and offensive language, and mature topics. Recommended for ages 18 years and up.

Cover design by Rita A. Gordon
Author's photo by Abigail Huller
Interior design by Olivier Darbonville

First Edition May 2024

Library of Congress Control Number: 2024906041

ISBN: 979-8-9853566-7-0 (hardcover)
ISBN: 979-8-9853566-8-7 (paperback)
ISBN: 979-8-9853566-9-4 (ebook)

Published in the USA by 12:56 a.m.
www.twelvefiftysixam.com

CONTENTS

PART 3

PART 4

PART 5

DEDICATION

This book is dedicated to all those who dared to fall in love.

AUTHOR'S NOTE

The Days with Rain is a story of passion between two people and how sometimes passion is not enough to survive the pain life throws their way. When we meet Raven and Parker, they are twelve years into their journey, trying to find their way back to a promise they made to one another. This story tells how they got to this point.

Some passages describe difficulties, including a condition that is similar to Hyperthymesia, cases of dissociation, sleep terrors, and a miscarriage. With that in mind, I advise you to consider your health and well-being before diving into Raven and Parker's story.

I also want to take a moment to remind you that this is just part of the twelve-year story of Raven and Parker. As in *Seven Days in Seattle*, Book 1 of the *Let It Rain* series, there are no conclusions or happy endings in this book. There will be some happy endings in the future and some happy-for-now scenarios. For now, let's continue the journey as the story unfolds, and we'll get there…together.

PROLOGUE

Heaven

Parker Page

Two weeks ago.

It's hard to focus with her around. Traces of jasmine and honey linger in the air like lust long after she leaves my arms. Although I informed her during dinner that I needed to retire to my study to prepare for tomorrow's brief, I anticipated her following me here. And despite the fact she has her own home and even though there are fifteen other rooms in my house, she's here. In a city the size of San Francisco, she should be somewhere else. She should be resting somewhere soft, not splayed sideways, sleeping on a sofa in my study. Still, somehow, she's here…with me.

I've resigned myself to the fact that this is how we are with each other, forever bound by a single thread, sending signals between us. This has been the soundtrack to our relationship for as long as I can remember. We've been apart, hanging by a thread on the fringes of each other's lives, separated by distance, and at other times together, tangled and messy, but always connected.

Now, I sit behind my desk and study her across the room, watching silently as she slumbers on the sofa. I sigh. She's beautiful. Her brown hair spills wildly across the pillow and falls in waves over the side of the couch. Light from the lamp casts a soft hue on her warm golden-brown skin. Her slender fingers curl and tug at the fur throw that covers her long, lean body. She won't sleep soundly until I put her to bed. I know that from experience. Because after twelve years of living and breathing in a world where she exists, there's not much I haven't learned about the woman who's become my best friend.

The click on my Rolex signifies it's midnight. Monday is here all too soon, and in a few hours, I must put her on a plane, and she'll be gone. I close my laptop, stand, and go to where she's lying on the sofa. I kneel before her, brush a curl from her face, and tuck it behind her ear.

"Hey," I say softly.

She stirs slightly, but her eyes stay closed. And like I've done a thousand times before, I scoop her into my arms. I carry her upstairs, through the house, down the hall, and place her in my bed. I step into my closet, remove my clothes, drop them in a basket, and then pull on a pair of silk pajama pants she got me. When I walk back to the bed, I slide in beside her, wrap my arms around her, and pull her into me. She could be anywhere in the world now, but she's not. She's here with me. And at this moment, holding her in my arms, inhaling her essence, *this* feels like heaven.

CHAPTER I

A Dream

Rain

Present Day

Floating in a sea of blackness, my body feels hollow, like a barren tree after a winter's rain, its branches bare—lacking life. Struggling, the tree's roots dig their fragile wooden nails beneath the final vestiges of sodden soil surrounding it. There's a chill in the air. I'm cold, wet, frightened. And like the tree, I'm seconds from folding. Moments before I fall, I feel warm pressure on my limb. There's a ringing in my ears, a subtle siren signaling me to wake.

Someone calls my name. "Rain." The darkness lifts, becoming grey, and slowly light filters in. *I'm here.* Somewhere. The illumination from what seems to be an operation light scatters across the room, revealing bare, beige walls. "Babe." In the distance, I hear the sound of Parker's voice. *Am I at the hospital?* "Rain, babe. Open your eyes. Please," Parker pleads. *Can't he see me looking at him?* We're in a room—but I don't know where... "Rain, babe, I'm here." I feel the press of his lips at the corner of mine. I inhale the familiar, deep, sweet, woodsy scent I love. My eyes flutter open, and I see his beautiful face. I feel the warmth of his touch. In the backdrop are the familiar surroundings of a place that's become my second home. It *is* him.

"Parker?"

"Yes, Rain, it's me." He pulls me into his arms. "You're dreaming. It's okay, you're safe. I got you. Give it a minute. Breathe. You'll be all right." His words calm me.

I rest my head against his chest, focusing on the rise and fall, timing my breath with his. It's a tactic he taught me nine years ago, the morning I had a sleep terror—our first time together. To this day, he's the only one that can comfort me. When my breathing relaxes, I touch his face, and he covers my hand with his. *Was I dreaming?*

"It…f-felt real." My voice falters.

"*This* is real. Right here. Right now." He lifts my hand and slides it across his face. Feeling the rough texture of his beard reminds me of how tingly it made me feel when he used to trail kisses along my body. That was so long ago. When my fingers reach his lips, he kisses the palm of my hand. "Are you okay?"

"I think so."

"You haven't had one like this in a while. You want to talk about it?"

"Not now." I exhale. "We have a lot of talking to do later. We probably should save it for then."

"Sure, but I'm here if you change your mind."

"We need to get ready, don't we?" I ask, pretending to be okay. I sit up, and Parker sits up, too.

Turning to him, my knees drawn, pressing into his side, I stare at the man I've known half my life. It's hard to believe that sometimes the sum of our lives can be condensed into a few simple words forming pages in a book. Chapter One, the pages are crisp, and anticipation rides high as the reader learns how we came together. By Chapter Twenty, the pages are bent, and there is an unnatural break where the pages seem to separate from the seams, signifying how we came apart. By Chapter Thirty, the reader's fanning the pages, trying to figure out how much more two people can withstand before they're reduced to just friends, and then there's *this*? Whatever *this* is—the space in between. How will it end? Was it all a dream? Am I here, or did I imagine the past twelve years with my constant companion, former lover, my friend?

It's a lot to take in—all the moving pieces of my life. My recent trip to Seattle left me with more questions than answers. The revelation from my sister and the shock of seeing Nik walk into my meeting left me feeling overwhelmed and confused. Exhausted, I was never so ready to leave a city. I couldn't exit the building fast enough when my meeting was over. The flight back gave me time to think and reevaluate what's important. One conclusion I've come to is that I need to use the time before I dive into my next project to get help. To arm myself with the tools to better handle the complexities of my life mentally. Because I finally realize I can't do this without the right support.

"We have time to get ready and have breakfast before we leave," Parker tells me.

"I got dibs on your shower. You can use the one down the hall," I say, rolling over him and off the bed. But I don't get far before he grabs my wrist.

"Babe. You sure you're okay?"

I look at Parker and hold his gaze so he's sure of my words. "Because of you, the steps we're taking, I will be."

It doesn't take long for Parker and me to get ready. As usual, he reminded me that I'm the only one he gives up his shower for—not that he invites other women to his house. That's not who he is—nor what he wants. But I suppose his point is that there was a time when we always showered together—that was our thing. But that seems like a lifetime ago—four years, to be exact. I know he wants that back. I know he's biding his time—waiting for me to stop straddling the line—and return to him…to us.

Then there's breakfast—I usually make that for him. Especially on days we need to leave on time to get somewhere. He's methodical when cooking and likes to take his time. I'm meticulous, too. However, I know how to prepare something substantial that takes less time. Which is why we are out of the house in record time.

The drive seems to go in slow motion as I anticipate what lies ahead. I stare out the window and watch the city I love so much as it passes in the background, like a scene from a movie. But this isn't a movie—this is my life. Not just mine—my life with Parker is filled with moments…of firsts. The first time I saw his face, our first date, our first kiss, the first time we made and professed our love, our first laugh, our first loss, our first goodbye. I see everything, the countless memories, running like a movie reel, proof forever etched like commemorative glass in my mind. I see our life.

"Parker."

"Yeah, Rain."

"Can I hold your hand?" I don't have to wait for a response.

He stretches his hand out, palm up for me to take. When I do, he raises it to his lips and kisses my fingers before returning our hands to the space between us. How apropos. For other former couples, there's water under the bridge, auld lang syne, a "that's all for now." But for us, it's the space in between—it's not over, we'll figure it out, find our way through, a "we're getting to the good part"…hopefully. And maybe, just maybe, if we're lucky, a chance at finding forever.

"I'll never be tired of holding your hand," he assures me.

CHAPTER 2

She Is the Sun

Parker

Present day

SHE'S BEAUTIFUL. SITTING BESIDE ME IN THE BACK SEAT OF THE CAR, holding my hand, she turns to me and stares, and I can't help but smile. And like she's done a thousand times before, she studies my face—one she's intimately acquainted with after twelve years. I've known this woman for practically half my life. Even more amazing is that she's still here. The way she looks at me, I know she's memorizing how different I am from last night, last week, last year, the last decade, and every day since that first day in class—the first time I saw her face. That was a long time ago, before she professed her love for me. We've had a long journey getting to this point, but still, she's here, holding my hand, beside me. She's the one constant in my life, the one true love of my life, the one I hope to make my wife. She is the sun that circles my planet, warming me from the surface to my core. And she's all I can ever ask for. The one I can count on every day—because I know the sun will rise, the seasons will change, we will grow old, yet still, I'll have all the days with Rain.

"Are we really doing this?" Rain shakes my hand in nervous anticipation as we near our destination.

"Yeah. We're doing this. You good?"

She purses her lips and nods reluctantly. "I think so."

The car stops, and the driver comes around the vehicle to open my door. Rain doesn't let go of my hand, but I feel her hesitate as I try to exit.

"Rain, we have to go inside."

"I know." Her words come out in a breathy sigh.

Instead of waiting to get out from her side of the car, she scoots across the seat toward me. With her hand still clutching mine, I help her exit the car. The sun is shining, but like most days in San Francisco, the air is crisp. Rain stands directly in front of me, looking up.

"I'm scared, Parker."

I brush her hair over her shoulder and give her a reassuring smile. "We'll be okay."

"You promise?"

"You have my heart. Nothing can change that." I pull her into me and hold her tight. I remain like that, wrapped in jasmine and honey, while the world fleetingly falls away. Then, I take her hand and lead her into the unassuming one-story structure to an appointment to help us navigate our future together.

As I suspected, Rain returned from Seattle changed—determined to do whatever it took to get her life together. No more "I can do this on my own" self-help scenarios. She finally agreed to go to therapy but didn't want to do it alone—so we decided on couple's therapy. This is suitable since we've spent so much of our lives together, although we're not a couple. I hope that will soon resolve itself. That is, whenever she's ready. Because I will wait a lifetime for Rain.

We enter the lobby and are shown to our appointment right away.

Rain, still holding my hand, sits next to me on the couch in a room that has a modern aesthetic. She looks at me with a nervous smile, and I want to kiss her to make it all better...but I don't. I squeeze her hand, hold it on my thigh, and feel her fingers relax. Our therapist discusses some preliminary items, our re-occurring sessions, how emotionally focused therapy works, what we should expect during sessions, and gets reacquainted with Rain and I, since she had one video call with us before this visit. Unlike Rain, following our breakup, I've had several sessions with a therapist over the past four years. It's through those sessions that I was able to find the strength to navigate memories of our past pain and separation.

The doctor jumps right in. "Well, it's good to have you both here finally. Let's get started. Rain, can you tell me how you two first met?"

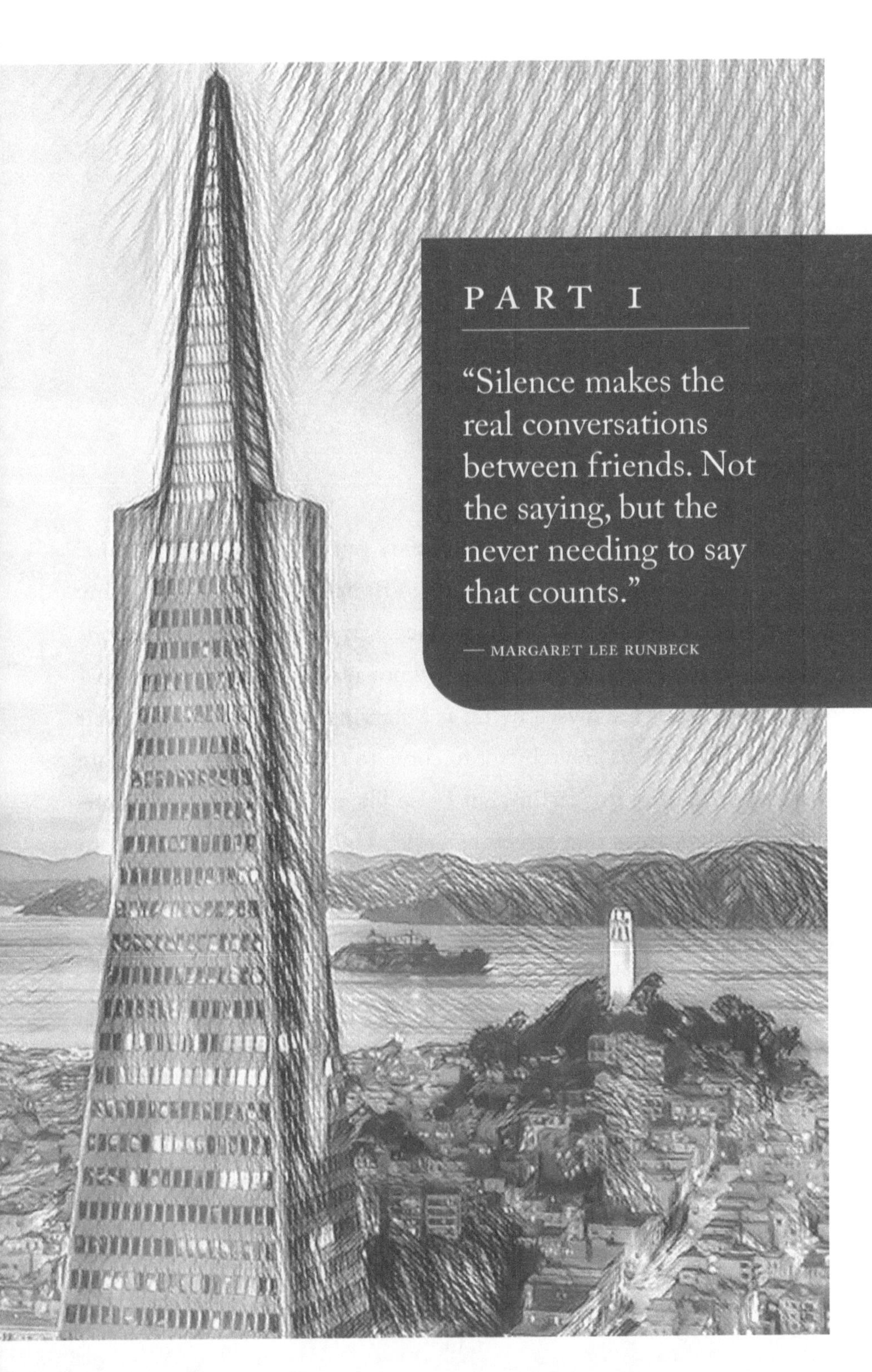

PART I

"Silence makes the real conversations between friends. Not the saying, but the never needing to say that counts."

— MARGARET LEE RUNBECK

CHAPTER 3

Silver Lining

Rain

Eleven Years Ago

I CAN'T BELIEVE I'M HERE, FOLLOWING MY DREAMS. IT FEELS SURREAL. When I sat down and mapped out the things I wanted to do in my career, three passions rose to the surface: art, architecture, and actions prescribed as otherwise binding, also known as…the law. Although I can draw, I didn't see myself living as a starving artist or having to wait years for my work as an architect to come to fruition. I like immediate results—to control my destiny, but I also like a good debate and establishing ground rules that structure a deal. Unlike my father, I want to ensure people stick to their commitments. So, I decided to combine it all and become a real estate attorney, which is why I'm on my way to my political science, justice course at Stanford University.

I need to get coffee before heading to class. For whatever reason, when I say no foam, the barista thinks it's code for filling it to the brim. When I take my cup, some sloshes out of the sip hole.

"Chai tea," he calls out. The next person is vying for my spot, so I head out the door. The movement of me nudging the door with my shoulder makes more liquid pop from the hole, so I put my mouth on the lid to lick it up.

"Excuse me." I feel someone's body bump my shoulder before I hear the words. The lid to my coffee crashes into my lips, then pops off, releasing a stream of hot coffee down my face and shirt.

"What the—" I look down at the mess that was my outfit. "What the ever-loving…. Oh my god." I rush back inside and grab a handful of paper towels to soak up the hot liquid. There's nothing I can do. I have a class. Huffing, I grab another lid, zip my jacket, and head to class, smelling like hot coffee.

When I arrive, my peers are still filing in. I sit, take out my laptop, and prepare for the lecture. Our professor walks in looking thoroughly irritated, which is not unusual for him, but today, like my coffee, he looks like he might flip a lid.

"Class." His deep baritone German accent booms off the walls, silencing us. He picks up a stack of papers I recognize as our recent exams and waves them furiously. "I'm very disappointed in you. I stand before you weekly, imparting all the knowledge you need to succeed. Yet, it doesn't stick." He begins a monologue about how unintelligent we are.

The entire class is so quiet that I hear Dane breathing through his nose in the front row. I suppress a laugh. He must have a cold. There's a thing that's been going around lately. Everyone is wide-eyed, watching the teacher. I can't believe my money is going to a man essentially calling us stupid.

"You're not going to get this by divine inspiration. If only I were a brain surgeon." Our professor's voice booms throughout the lecture hall.

Sensing someone staring, I turn to my left. The most beautiful aquamarine eyes stare back at me, and I immediately forget where I am. I imagine blue waves at Ocean Beach rolling to shore across the sand as the sun warms my face. I get lost in the lovely memories of hanging out on the beach with my parents in my childhood. *Focus, focus, girlfriend. You're in class,* I tell myself, so I don't lose it. Pushing past the memories, I focus on the ocean reflecting in his eyes. I study his perfectly shaped lips with a hint of pink in the middle—lips I imagine kissing. I smile, and he smiles back. His hair is a tousled mess of dirty blond waves with sun-kissed tips. His skin is tanned like he's been jogging in the sun.

"You have to do better," our professor commands.

I purse my lips, no longer wanting to listen to the bile spewing from our professor. I want to stand and walk out, but don't. I focus on Ocean Eyes, and it calms me. My colleague raises his eyebrows and shakes his head. I close my eyes, take a deep breath, then open them. He smiles like it will be okay, and I shrug. Then he lifts his chin toward the front of the class, and I break eye contact to focus on the teacher, who is moving toward the front row to hand out the papers.

When my paper finally makes its way to me, I look at it briefly even though I already know I'm getting a good grade. I still remember all the questions, answers, books I've read, and exams I've had in class. Having a good memory is a blessing and curse wrapped in one, and I feel my mind start to spiral. Then I remember how easy it was to calm myself by looking at the guy to my left. I turn, and his eyes hold mine, and I swear I will stay that way until class is over. I'm surprised to realize we had a whole conversation without saying a word, using only body language, as our professor continued ranting in the background.

Finally, class is over. When he stands, I do the same, and as if an invisible thread connects us, we follow each other out of the room. By the time I reach the door, I'm laughing. Once we are out of the class, we huddle outside the door and laugh like old friends.

"I'm Parker." He holds his hand out to me between laughs. I take it and feel an immediate wave of electricity pass between us.

"I'm Raven. People call me Rae."

"What's your full name, Raven?"

"Raven Rain Nichols."

"Rain. I love the sound of that. It reminds me how essential it is to all life. Can I call you Rain?"

"Yeah. You can call me Rain."

"Do you have another class after this one, Rain?"

"Unfortunately, yes."

"Same. I'll see you at the same time next week."

"Sure. Oh, hey, Parker."

"Yeah, Rain."

"What's your full name?"

"Parker Page."

"Parker Page, Esquire. It has a good ring to it."

"Let's not get ahead of ourselves. But thanks."

SITTING IN MY NEXT CLASS, I REFLECT ON MY INTERACTION WITH Parker. I think of the phrase silver lining—the something good that comes from something bad. I never really thought about its meaning before now.

Parker was surprisingly capable of pulling me out of my head when I needed it. As lovely as he was to look at, I had to focus on my studies and direct my attention to my professor. Nailing this and all my other classes to graduate at the top of the class is my top priority. Still, I can't wait to see him again.

After all the day's classes and group studies are over, I hook up with Breck Baker, another law student whom I met at lunch a month ago. He struck up a conversation, and we talked every week since then, but I wouldn't go as far as to call him my boyfriend. I'm still feeling him out.

"Rae." Breck grabs me around the waist and pulls me to his side. I pull back a little. We haven't been around each other long enough to be that affectionate. "How was class?"

"Same as usual. Except for one snarky teacher today who went on a tangent."

"You need to get used to that shit."

"What?" I pull out of his arms, knowing my face reflects my confusion.

"Suck it up. That's how it is here."

"Uhm. I don't think so."

"Which part don't you agree with."

"Both."

"Come on, Rae."

I purse my lips. My initial thought is not to say anything more, but then I think better of it and say what I feel—because I don't know how to be any other way.

"Listen, Breck. I need to study for the class I'm supposed to 'suck it up' for, so I won't be able to eat with you." I tip my head in a "you get my drift?" look.

Breck has a stunned look. I don't wait for his response. I walk off. I don't know what the hell he was thinking when he said what he did or if he even was thinking. For him to question me only to dismiss my response is beyond disrespectful. I deserve better.

CHAPTER 4

If You Know, You Know

Parker

RAIN. HER NAME CONJURES UP BRIEF WINTERS IN SAN FRANCISCO when the days with rain are few and far between. The days when you want to stay inside, sit in front of the fireplace and read a book, watch a movie, or make love.

Her beauty caught my attention the first time I saw her in class. Her warm golden-brown skin seemed to glow as the sun streaming in from the windows caressed her face. The way her perfectly shaped kissable lips were slightly parted made me want to pull her into my arms and press my lips to hers. Mesmerized, I watched as she strolled in, took her seat, then scanned the room. I was a few rows directly behind, but she didn't turn her head to find me that day. It was a move she repeated over the past few weeks, so I decided to sit within her eyesight.

Today, when our teacher went on a rampage, Rain turned, and we locked eyes. I held my breath, not knowing what to expect. There was a chance she could've been offended, turned off, or worse. From my previous observations, she seemed friendly in all the interactions with students in class. Annoyed, maybe that was what I thought she'd be, but surprisingly, when she looked at me, I felt she could read my mind. The way she smiled at me, I felt it at my core. Thinking back, I don't remember saying much in class: a smile here, a glance there, a shrug, a nod. Then, after class, our interaction felt so natural. Like she already knew me. When she placed her delicate hand in mine to shake it, I felt something pass between us, like a jolt of energy permanently boding us. All I know is that I can't wait to see her again.

My phone rings, and I already know who it is.

"Hey, Mom, Dad. How's it going?"

"Parker, honey. Things are good. How's school?"

"Good."

"Any issues?"

Besides my angry contract law teacher? "No."

I don't tell them about my teacher because he's not worth them placing a call to get him fired. I know they're a call away if I need their help—they always are. But it is not the time. Besides, he has to look at himself every day, not me, at least not after this semester. And I don't think Rain would want that, either. Like me, she's acing the class.

"That's good. Will you have a chance to head into the city this weekend? I'd love to have you home."

"Sure, Mom. I can be home."

"Great. Then we can discuss some upcoming events you'll need to attend with your dad and me."

"He doesn't need to attend. Let him focus on his studies."

"It's okay, Dad. I'll be fine."

"Tina will be at a few of the events."

"I'm not into Tina, Mom. Remember that fizzled out in our first year in high school."

"Janis. Don't meddle," my dad tells her.

"What?"

"You know what."

"Okay, Mom, Dad. Was there anything else? I need to study."

"No, son," my dad says.

"Honey, think about what I said."

"I will, Mom. I love you both. See you this weekend."

"Bye," they say in unison.

Tina Bahler. Even back in high school, I realized we weren't a match. That's why I ended things after a few months. Why Mom would want me to hook up with her is beyond me. The most important thing to Tina is her social media presence and how many likes she gets. The last time I saw her, that's all she talked about. She wanted to take a selfie with me, and I refused. I always refuse. That's not a thing amongst our crowd, so I'm unsure why she does it.

I know why Mom is pushing for me to date. When I get my JD, she wants me to be settled and think about a family. Not because I'm wild by any means. It's how she was raised and how those like us are expected to live our lives. The "if you know, you know" people.

You won't find us in the news or get glimpses of us in magazines. That's not how we exist in society. We're the ones that, with a wink and a nod, could erect a hundred skyscrapers and not make a dent in our wealth. With a handshake, we could eradicate the city of all technology companies. The city exists the way it is because we don't interfere unless we need to...unless one of our own needs something. We're the people behind the words "it's done." We're paying the salaries of those who pay the one percent. It doesn't get any higher than us.

With this type of status comes duty and honor, and first amongst all of that is family. That's what I want—what my parents have...a family. To have the love of my life by my side. There is nothing I want more than that.

CHAPTER 5

But First, Coffee...

Rain

God, I need some coffee, I tell myself, reaching into my tote for my wallet. I move up in the coffee line. Instead of six people deep, I'm now five. I'm so glad the weekend is over. Although I had hopes of building a better relationship with my family, I didn't accomplish much. When I picked up the last of my belongings from Mom's house, she didn't have much to say, which is the same reaction I got a few months ago after I moved into my first apartment. I thought she would be excited for me to demonstrate my independence. What parent wouldn't?

"Chai tea," I hear the barista call out. Probably the same damn person that bumped into me on the way out the door the last time.

I've held summer jobs every year since I was old enough to work and built up my savings. I had my pick of schools to attend without worrying about money due to the scholarship I received. I earn extra cash by making watercolor paintings, prints, and cards to sell at local art shows and online.

I step up to the register and say, "Double latte. No foam. Thanks." I open my wallet to get cash, even though I really should use mobile pay.

"I'll have the same. Thanks." I hear a deep, familiar voice from behind me. Parker reaches over and holds his phone under the scanner. "I got this."

"Parker, it's nice to see you again." The barista beams at him. Who wouldn't? He looks like a model in his dark-washed jeans, a Henley shirt, and a suede bomber draped over his arm. Parker smiles and nods, then focuses his attention on me.

"Thank you. You didn't have to do that."

"I know," he says. Lowering his hand, he guides me to step aside so I don't crash into anyone like I did before. I look up at him, and yup, still handsome as ever. "You have a habit of staring at me."

"I guess I can't help it. You're a handsome man. You should be used to it."

"And you're bold. I should get used to that."

I smile because he's right. When you come from a family that doesn't pay much attention to you, you have to do things to be seen. For me, that means I speak my mind unfiltered. I'm known for being direct and honest.

"Since we're getting used to each other, does that make us friends?" I ask.

The corners of his lips curve into a smile that warms my insides. "Yes, Rain. I can be your friend."

"I don't usually see you here at this time."

"I skipped out on a study group early."

"You knew I'd be here."

"The coffee in your hand last week was a giveaway."

"Are you stalking me, Parker Page?"

"Friends don't stalk. They're there for each other." His eyes shift from me over my shoulder, then he extends his arm past me, and someone bumps into him. "Like that," he adds.

"Sorry, man," I hear someone say behind me.

"Two lattes for Parker," the barista calls out.

"We're up," he announces, stepping up to the counter. He grabs both our drinks and hands me mine. "After you." He gestures. He holds the door open for me, and we head to class.

As we walk, the sun shines down on us, and we talk about what mood our teacher's going to be in today. Parker thinks the class will go smoothly. I'm sure he's right. He said he aced the last test—we both did. I love it. He's smart, so I won't have to explain myself. I tend to use big words—some of the many things my brain can hold due to my condition. Watching Parker, I note how natural it is for him to open doors and touch my back, guiding me. I've never had a man be this attentive. It's nice. When we get to class, I sit in the same spot near the center of the room. This time, Parker sits next to me, and I sense this is the start of how we'll be the rest of the semester.

"You mentioned you had a study group this morning. Is that normal for you?"

"We try to do what works for the majority. Mornings tend to work best. On rare occasions we meet in the evening. We don't meet every day."

"Don't let me interfere with your studies."

"You're not. If you want, you can join us, or…." He gestures between us. "We can arrange a time to study together when it's convenient for you."

"I prefer studying after class. My brain's not fully functioning in the mornings. You know…coffee first." I hold up my cup and then take a sip.

"Then, it's settled. My new friend and I have study time after school. Whenever you want—I'm there." He lifts his cup, taps it to mine, then sips his coffee.

Parker and I exchange numbers in class, meet after school, and study at the library. We discuss the different disciplines in law we plan to focus on and discover that although different, we'll likely have more classes together over the next few years.

When we finish studying, he tells me about some of the crazy stuff he and his best friend Josh got into when they were younger. We fall into a fit of laughter and I think we may get kicked out of the library. Parker has a funny side, and I find it unexpected for someone who's also slightly commanding and serious.

The next few days are uneventful. I decide I'm busy whenever Breck wants to meet after class. Our last conversation left a bad taste in my mouth, and I still haven't gotten over it. Who am I fooling? The way my brain works, I never get over anything. If something triggers the memory, like an unwanted guest, it lives rent-free in my head. But unlike a guest—I can't kick it out.

The best way to push things from the forefront of my thoughts is to focus on something else. So, I double down on my studies and think about how I will get through the week without seeing Breck and how nice it'll be to see Parker in class again.

By Thursday, I suspect Breck must be frustrated, and to my disappointment, he finally catches up to me on my way out of my last class.

"Rae, it's been a while since I've seen you. What's up?" Breck asks.

"School. Trying to stay on top of my studies. Working on my degree. You?"

"You know what I'm talking about, Rae."

"Enlighten me, Breck. What are you talking about?"

"I haven't seen you since our last conversation. You can't be upset about anything I said."

"What makes you think you know what I feel about anything? It's a bit presumptuous of you, don't you think? Especially someone who's supposedly studying to be an attorney. I'd expect you to stick to the facts. To ask a direct question."

"You're right, Rae. I –."

"I'm not done, Breck, which brings me to a question I have for you. If you wanted to dismiss me so easily, telling me things like suck it up, why did you ever approach me?"

"I didn't mean anything by telling you to—."

"Breck, that's not my question."

"I never dated someone like you before. I thought it could be interesting."

When he says "interesting," it takes all of my energy not to punch him in the throat. Instead, I laugh in his face. "Interesting? Like trying the flavor of the week interesting?" I ask, and the wide-eyed look on his face tells me I hit the bullseye. "Listen, Breck, in case you haven't heard, people of African descent aren't freaking toys. We are people—descendants of kings and queens. Look it up. So, in the future, if you want to try an experiment—try touching yourself with a live wire. Let me know how that goes. In the meantime, I suggest you lose my number because...." I take out my phone and block him. "Because I just blocked you. I don't want you to waste your time trying to reach me since you'll be busy *doing* experiments."

Then, I do something I'm all too familiar with—I walk away, leaving Breck with his mouth hanging open. I don't have time for this.

CHAPTER 6

Fingerprints

Rain

PARKER PAGE IS A BEAUTIFUL MAN: TALL, SUN-KISSED, TANNED SKIN, rocking the dreamiest aquamarine eyes I can get lost in. Even the sound of his name rolls off my tongue like butter. Parker. Connecting with him in class felt so easy. I never had that with anyone…ever. I wonder if this is what a real connection with someone feels like.

I didn't feel anything around Breck other than irritation. He has a pretty face but is nothing more than a jock. He's another bad decision on my part, like Andre before him, or like that time when I thought I could handle more than three glasses of wine and threw up all over Molly's toilet. All bad decisions that you live and learn from. Whether these are things that generally happen when you're my age or if they have something to do with my screwed-up family life, I don't know. What I do know is that sometimes I'm a mess, but the simple act of being around Parker makes me feel better. His calming presence makes me feel that no matter how big the mess, I'll get through it and come out clean on the other side.

I hear footsteps behind me before I hear my name. "Rain." I turn around to see what I've conjured.

"Parker. Are you walking me to class?"

"Now I am." He looks down at me and smiles. I wonder how tall he is. I'm five feet six. He must be about six feet….

"Rain?" His smooth, silky voice coaxes me out of my head. "You're calculating something." How does he even know that? "You keep looking me up and down. I'm six-four, in case you were wondering." A slow, sexy smile forms on his face. Oh my god, he's fucking "fill me up fine." Just being near him sends my pulse racing.

"You caught me ogling again. It's a good height."

He raises an eyebrow, looking at me curiously, but doesn't share whatever mischievousness is on his mind. Instead, he says, "We should get to class. After you." He gestures for me to move forward.

He sits next to me like he has the past two weeks. I like that. He smells woodsy, sweet…good, and I imagine nestling my nose in his neck.

As we wait for class to start, we discuss our studies and plans for the weekend. Talking with him feels natural. He's different than all the other guys I've hung out with. He seems genuinely interested in what I say and asks clarifying questions that show he's listening. Parker is also thoughtful, knowledgeable, and easy to get along with.

We give our professor our full attention as class begins. When I say full, I mean I'm memorizing everything the teacher says. My hands happen to be doodling a drawing of the Transamerica Pyramid building. I remember drawing skyscrapers that looked more like a series of staggered rectangles when I was younger. My dad saw it and said, *"I'll take you to see cool-shaped buildings."* He was like that—he took an interest in whatever I was doing and expanded upon it. That weekend, he drove my sister and me around town to all the iconic buildings like Coit Tower and the Bank of America Center, finally ending at the Transamerica Pyramid. I'd never seen a building shaped like a triangle before. I was hooked. When we got home, I drew them all.

I finish my drawing, take it from my notebook, and slide it across to Parker. At first, his eyebrows furrow. Then, a slow smile forms. He lifts his chin to the front of the class. I get it. He's redirecting me back to the instructor. I return his smile, he winks, and I focus back on the lecture. Occasionally, we pass silent glances, but for the most part, we stay focused until class is over. Then, we go our separate ways and reconnect later in the day.

"Hey, you want to study together this afternoon?" Parker asks after we file out of our last class.

"Library?"

"Sure," he agrees. We walk together. "Thank you for the drawing. I was surprised. I didn't know you could draw."

"One of my many talents."

"Why Transamerica?"

"It's my favorite iconic building."

"It is a fantastic structure. There's a park at the base of the building. We should go for a walk there one day," he says. I need to change the subject before I get lost in memories from when I was a kid.

"Are your parents lawyers, Parker?"

"No. My parents run a foundation."

"What made you want to be a lawyer?"

"I read my parents' legal documents, and they seemed interesting. They let me sit in on their transactions with our attorneys. I found it fascinating, and I interceded during some of their conversations when I was younger. My parents wanted me to continue their work with the foundation, which I do, but law is my passion. It comes easy to me."

"Is it the words?"

"That, and everything else about it: integrity, protection, structure, the specificity," he says.

We enter the library and locate a spot to sit. It's lovely and quiet, and I feel motivated by the brilliance of being amongst all the books. Parker pulls out a chair for me as usual, and I sit.

"What about you?" he asks, sitting beside me. "Why did you choose law?"

"Passion. I also have a way with words and don't mind a debate. Oh, and in case you haven't noticed, I'm extremely opinionated."

"Me too. What's wrong with having a brain and showcasing it?"

"Nothing," I say, relieved we're on the same wavelength.

"Rain, the guy I saw you with the other day…Breck. What's the deal with him?"

"Are you asking me if I'm seeing someone?"

"I am."

"We've been seeing each other." I didn't tell him that I broke up with Breck. I want to see where this conversation goes. Parker nods, taking it all in. I wonder what's going on behind those dreamy eyes.

"He's in a few of my classes. How'd you meet?"

"Cafeteria."

"You don't seem like the type who's into jocks."

I open my backpack, pull out my laptop, and open it. "Really?"

"Really. I've watched you in class. Your questions are insightful. You recall things most of us don't remember. Then, you challenge the teacher with what you've learned. The banter back and forth is amazing to watch."

"You've been studying me."

"Paying attention."

"What are you looking for when you watch me?"

"Trying to figure you out. You take notes but not a lot, and I wondered how you retain everything. Every time you speak up in class, I'm fascinated by how you cite things verbatim that our instructor said weeks before. To do this work, we all need to remember former court decisions rendered to apply to the current case, but it's almost like you have a photographic memory."

He knows. Oh shoot, Parker figured it out. I hope to god he doesn't think I'm a freak. That's what most people think. When I was in grade school, the teacher asked us who could remind the class what we discussed last week, and I told everyone what she'd said. I repeated everything she said verbatim, including when she paused discussing the lesson to say, *"Jimmy, pay attention."*

I was mortified when someone said, *"Wow, Raven, did you memorize every class?"*

Jimmy Smith started chanting, *"freak, freak, freak."*

I pulled myself together and said, *"Sounds like Jimmy's paying attention now."*

Although the teacher also appeared mortified, she straightened her face, playing it off, and said, *"That's right, Raven. Thank you."*

Parker is sitting beside me, studying my face, waiting for a response. I take a deep breath. *Here goes.*

"I have perfect recall."

"I'm impressed and a little jealous."

"You seem to be doing fine in class."

"I've been told I'm a natural, but wow. I learn something new every day." He shakes his head, and I know he's thinking about what I just told him.

"It's a blessing and curse." Primarily, for me, it's a curse. But I don't tell him that, because I don't want to freak him out more by telling him how not being able to forget means replaying my worst memories on repeat. I don't tell him that sometimes I get so lost in my thoughts that I temporarily lose all sense of self and time. I can sit in a room full of people and, like a time machine, be transported somewhere else in the past. I can't tell him that the bad memories come with bad feelings that bring an uncontrollable wave of bile to my throat while reliving scenes from my past.

"Rain? You okay?" I allow his voice to pull me from the precipice of a drop into the abyss. I look down, realizing he's holding my hand. He pulls away. I place my hand on the table, palm up, offering it back to him. He puts his hand on top. His hand swallows mine, but it's nice, warm, and he makes me feel safe.

"Yeah. I'm okay. Does it bother you?"

"What? That you can remember things I can't?" I nod. His eyebrows furrow in confusion. "Why would it?"

"I don't know. Some people get freaked out about it once they figure it out."

"No, Rain. It's just another part that makes you unique, like a fingerprint. We all have them."

"What's yours? You know, the thing that's uniquely you."

"I'll have to think about that and get back to you." He smiles at me, lets my hand go, opens his laptop, and we study, shoulder to shoulder, his leg touching mine, until the sun drops below the horizon.

CHAPTER 7

The Most Important

Parker

Ten years ago

My first year at Stanford wasn't as bad as I expected. I thought the constraints of university might stifle me. I like control. To ensure things are moving in the direction I want. Maybe that's why I want to be an attorney: to gather all the facts and create a scenario that gets me to where I want to go. To control the narrative. I like it when I have the power to shape the future of something. I'm fueled by passion. Passion for family, law, and to shape things and make them better.

When we first started hanging out a year ago, Rain wanted to know which characteristics I considered unique—my fingerprints. I didn't answer her then. I thought I might scare her away. I don't want her to misinterpret this as a negative, but rather my desire to see others safe and healthy, to want for nothing, to be able to move through life wrapped in love.

Rain. Wow, it's hard to believe there was ever a time that she wasn't in my life. Over the past year, we've gotten to know each other well enough to finish each other's sentences. We spent almost every evening studying together, and this year, we had most of our classes together, which is great because I get to see her every day. Having her around seems as natural as breathing, and I don't see a time when I would want something different. She is the air that I breathe.

Thinking about her reminds me of a time when I was about eight. I went with my parents to one of the society events they often attended. The room must have held about three hundred people. They called my dad's name, and I watched him take the stage. All eyes were on him, as were mine. My mom always talked about how handsome my dad was, so I thought that's what they thought when they saw him. I watched in awe as he gave a person an award for some technical innovation. Everyone clapped and was excited for this individual. When my dad returned to the table, he put his arm around my chair, sat back, and watched the scene like usual.

In the car on the way home, I told him, "Maybe one day you'll be giving me a cool reward like that."

He didn't say anything, but after settling in the house, with a glass of whiskey in his hand and me sitting beside him, he said, "Parker, I don't want you to think I didn't hear you in the car. I just wanted to be home when I responded." Mom was sitting across from us, her eyes bouncing between us. She nodded, and then he continued. "You mentioned getting one of those rewards would be nice. But you didn't realize that the award was just a token of appreciation and that as soon as that man left the stage, the award was out of the audience's memory."

"Preston, my baby didn't see all that."

"I know, honey, that's my point. Parker, all eyes were on me when I returned to my seat. But even that was brief because the second I leaned back in my chair and put my arm around your seat, all eyes dropped to you. Then they shifted to your mom sitting next to you."

"I don't understand, Dad. Why? Why me? Why mom?"

"Because, Parker, the most powerful man in the room was me. Sitting beside me were the most important people in my world. People watch every move I make to see what I'll do next. They want to know what interests me—what's important to me. So, no shiny object, no accolades, nothing can compete with having you two loves of my life by my side. Your mom and I have built a life that ensures you'll never need a shiny object to satisfy you. You have everything you can ever ask for at your fingertips. My reward is here in this room, and one day in the future, in another room sitting beside you, will be your child, whom you'll be telling the same thing to. And beside that child will be a wife you adore. That's all I could ever ask for, all you should ever want. Family. Love."

He went on to tell me why the people were staring, why he was so important...why *we* were so important. He explained what it meant to be part of the elite few on this planet and that, in the future, he'd introduce me to my peers around the globe. He told me that we were all connected by our status, that the people I saw coming and going from buildings when we went downtown were all people who worked for us.

That conversation was stored away in my mind until the end of the school year when I had to say goodbye to Rain. It's summer, and I will be traveling with my family and participating in numerous obligations. During these times, I wish she were my woman, so we could experience these things together. When I get back—I'm going to take a chance and ask her out. I hope she feels the same about me.

PART 2

“Love is composed of a single soul inhabiting two bodies.”

— ARISTOTLE

CHAPTER 8

Be Mine

Rain

Nine Years Ago

GETTING TO THIS POINT IN MY JUNIOR YEAR HAS BEEN A LONG JOURNEY. I still spent the summer working as a legal clerk. On the weekends, I volunteered at an art gallery, where I met my friend Jade, an art history student. Law and art are my two passions. They kept me focused on my career goals and less on my dysfunctional family—well, what family I have left. My mom hasn't paid much attention to the fact that her daughter is attending one of the most prestigious universities while studying to be an attorney. Sometimes, I wonder what happened in her life that made her so detached. Actually, that's not an accurate portrayal. She seems more interested in her man and has a closer relationship with my sister, Robin, who moved to Seattle after graduation. As for me, I sometimes feel like a fish out of water—trying to find my way back to something that feels normal. But what is normal? Momentary conversations with your mom? Phantom memories of a father? God, my life is a mess.

When I arrive at class, I take my usual seat, and within moments, I'm joined by Parker, bringing with him the woodsy, sweet scent I enjoy so much.

"Hey, Rain. How's your day so far?"

"My computer crashed and I lost half the paper I was writing, but aside from that it's okay, I suppose."

"You remember what you wrote, right?"

"Yeah, but—."

"You don't want to rewrite it. I get it," he says, finishing my sentence as usual.

"Exactly."

The class fills with people falling into their usual seats, opening their laptops, and getting ready to absorb whatever knowledgeable nuggets our professor plans to impart. As the professor speaks, my eyes stroll to Parker, who's staring at me. A slow smile sweeps over my face. This is typically the part where he winks, but his leg bounces, and I nod toward it. His eyebrows lift, he purses his lips, and his leg stops. He bites the inside of his lips, and I frown. Parker has something to say aloud that he can't because we're amid a lecture. I touch his hand briefly and then turn my attention to the instructor. Whatever he has to say will have to wait.

The class seems to drag on forever. It goes to the point that I'll have to run for my next class, which, unfortunately, won't leave me much time to talk with Parker. Just before we stand to go, he peeks at his watch. Parker and I are both sticklers for time and are serious about our studies. I'm always impressed by how focused he is. Other wealthy students treat this all as a game. On the other hand, although his potential to succeed in life is guaranteed due to his family status, Parker doesn't act like it is. The level of discipline and focus he places on his academic achievement is unmatched by other than my own.

"Hey, I know you don't have time now, but can I meet you after your next class?"

"Sure. I planned to study afterward, but I'll wait for you."

"Great," his words come in a nervous huff. Then he heads toward one side of the building, and I exit for my next class.

To say I dread my American Law class is an understatement. Not because it's hard, but because this guy Kevin is in my class. He's always looking at me like a predator, and I'm the prey. His shifty eyes make my stomach turn, and I purposely sit on the opposite side of the room, away from him, out of his view, which is what I do today.

Once seated, our professor references a recently collapsed bridge and subsequent train derailment disaster in Colorado. One I saw on a social media news feed. I pay close attention to his retrospective, so I know what key things to consider when writing my research paper. Noting all the points on my laptop helps me keep my brain from wandering about similar disasters over the years that were plastered across the headlines. If I let my mind wander, I could easily get lost in a trance as information flashes across my eyes like a news segment. This is the part that sucks about my condition—the constant mind games. I need to keep myself in check so no one walks up on me while I'm lost, like a child in the woods trying to find my way out of the maze in my mind. Before I realize it, the lecture is over, and as I head toward the door, I hear my name.

"Raven." Damnit, Kevin. He couldn't resist. I can't seem to get away from him. My first inclination is to keep walking like I don't hear him, hoping in vain that he'll forget about whatever he wants to say to me. "Raven," he repeats louder this time, and someone taps my shoulder to get my attention. I turn around. Another student interfering with my peace slides past me, giving Kevin the access to me that he so desperately wants. "Hold up a minute."

By the time I stop, he's already beside me. "I'm meeting someone. I need to go."

"About that, I was wondering if we could—."

"I need to go." My pronunciation of each word is laced with irritation, which, if he is as smart as this school thinks he is, will hopefully register with him. He shuts his mouth, then, like a guppy, he opens and closes it again. I step into the hallway, relieved to find Parker's smiling face greeting me.

"Parker," I say a little louder than necessary. Parker holds his hand out to take my book bag. Witnessing the scene, Kevin leaves visibly irritated.

"Oh." I hear him say as I walk away with Parker.

"Rain, was Kevin bothering you?"

"He tried to get my attention. I don't know what he wanted. The way he looks at me is creepy," I say, following Parker until we reach a commemorative bench. Parker prompts me to sit. His expression goes dark briefly, but he checks it when I frown.

"Is he bothering you? I can have a conversation with him."

"It's okay."

"You sure? I can handle it."

"Really, Parker, I'm fine. Anyway, let's not dwell on him. How was your class?"

"Class was good. I discovered who'll be in my study group and the timeline for the final paper."

"Same. What was up in class this morning? You seemed a little anxious."

"You don't miss a thing."

"I thought we established that when we met."

A series of expressions form on his face, and for the first time, I'm not sure how to read what he's thinking.

"About that. When we first met, you were seeing Breck."

"Yeah, he turned out to be a major loser. He was treating me like a social experiment."

"Dating outside his race, you mean."

"Yeah. How'd you know? I'm glad I figured that out before—."

"You don't have to tell me. It doesn't matter how I found out—this campus is a bubble."

"Nothing happened anyway."

"Rain. I'm sorry. We're getting off track. I'm not here to talk about Kevin or Breck. I'm here to discuss us."

"Us?"

"Yeah. We've been spending a lot of time together. Almost every day." He turns so that his knees are touching mine. That's our thing. We always seem to have some part of our bodies touching when we talk. We're either holding hands, leaning into each other, or, like now, our legs are touching.

"It's been nice."

"More than nice, Rain. I look forward to our time together. It's my favorite part of the day."

"Same. It's like I've known you all my life," I tell him, and his smile widens as he flicks invisible lint off his knee.

"That makes what I want to say a little easier." He stops fidgeting. "I've been attracted to you since I first saw you on campus. When I realized we had several classes together, I was thrilled because I didn't have to wonder where you were or when I'd see you again."

"What are you saying, Parker? You've been stalking me?" My

comment earns me a tentative laugh. "Hey, you know that was a joke, right?" I smile at him. "In all the time I've known you, I've never seen you to be unsure of yourself. Whatever it is making you feel that way—let it go. It's me. I'm the one you can talk to without words. So, show me."

Parker looks at me. His face softens as his eyes search mine. He holds his hand out to me, and without breaking my gaze, I place my hand in his. It's warm and strong and feels like he's hugging my soul. He leans forward and gently dusts his lips to mine. I smile against his lips. It's soft yet brief, but his kiss signals everything he wants to say.

"Hey, handsome," I whisper against his lips.

"Hey, beautiful."

"Was that so scary?"

"Not at all." He presses his lips to mine and kisses me again, and I never want the moment to end. "Mmm. This is my new favorite thing to do."

"Sealed with a kiss," I say, knowing this moment changes who we are to each other forever.

"Rain, there's more. I want to follow our kiss up with a verbal contract."

"Okay, Parker Page, Esquire. I'm ready."

"Future esquire."

"Future esquire," I correct myself.

"Rain, the day I met you, I became whole. Until then, I was simply existing—moving through life, hoping I'd eventually find the other half of me, hoping I could finally breathe. Then I saw you sitting in class, and I knew—we were meant to be. You're so beautiful. I couldn't take my eyes off you. I didn't want to be too far from you. I felt like I finally started living, and now, I can't imagine living a day without you. I understand we have studies to focus on, but I'd like to spend more time with you. To get to know you deeper. I want to do more than to see you in class, on lunch breaks, or during study time. I want all the moments with you—to wake up with you in my arms, not just because we fell asleep studying, although those times are great, too. I want to experience all of you. Will you be my woman, the one I promise to cherish daily?"

I blink to hold back my tears. "That was beautiful, Parker. You've put a lot of thought into this."

"I've been thinking about you for a while. Hell, you're all I think about."

The circles Parker's fingers are rubbing on my wrist remind me I'm still holding his hand. His eyes are locked on mine, waiting for me to articulate the answer he sees reflected in them. Because unlike anyone else I've met before, Parker can read me like a book.

"Can I have another kiss?" I ask.

"Will you be mine?"

"Yes."

Parker doesn't hesitate. He uses his free hand to cup my cheek and presses his lips to mine. This time he takes his time tasting me, sucking my bottom lip into his mouth. It's our first real kiss, fresh and new, everything a first kiss should be. He pulls back slightly, licks his lip, and smiles.

"You taste like candy."

"It's probably my lip gloss." We both laugh, and relief washes over his face. "So, does this mean you'll take me out on a date? Because you know my schedule is tight. As you said, I have all these classes and a secret rendezvous with a cute guy named Parker I met in Justice class." I wink at him.

"As a matter of fact, I am. I know you like planning, so how about we schedule the next month together, then we can improvise the rest from there?"

I touch his face and trace his lips with my fingers. Parker is handsome, kind, and everything I hoped for but never expected to find. I can see forever in his eyes.

CHAPTER 9

A Special Kind of Love

Parker

EARLIER THIS WEEK, WHEN I ASKED RAIN TO BE MY WOMAN, IT WAS the most nerve-racking thing I've ever done because I never wanted anything more than her. Having what my parents have—a loving relationship with the person they adore, is everything to me.

My memories of growing up in San Francisco are filled with family, love, activities, and the sorts of things that come with being part of the elite. There was always something going on. Although my parents had an endless list of people on their payroll—cooks, drivers, you name it—they were always hands-on concerning me. My mom or dad took me to school, soccer practice, debate team, and other activities. Most of the time, they took me to and from wherever I needed to go together, and I sat between them in the back seat. Sometimes, Dad would stretch his hand across me and take Mom's hand, then raise it to his lips and kiss it. She'd look at him and smile, then look down at me, take the same hand, and muss my hair. It always felt like she was anointing me with their love. I remember thinking I wanted that—a special kind of love. Whatever that was, it passed a spark of electricity from Dad to Mom to me. I was too young to understand that moment for what it was—deep love. Then, as I got older, I got it.

All these years later, I can't recall a time when my mom and dad haven't looked at each other with love in their eyes. Growing up, I had a great life, good schools, cool friends like Josh and our buddy Ethan, and a loving home where I never had to ask for anything. Because I've never wanted anything except that one person to look at the way my dad looks at my mom. There was never a doubt in my mind that one day I would have that—that I would find her. I just didn't know it would be so soon. Then I met Rain.

I'm taking Rain out this afternoon for our first official date, and I can't wait. Focusing on my studies this week has been difficult, knowing I'd eventually make it to today—when I can take my girl out. Rain wanted to spend this morning getting prepped for our date, so I had breakfast delivered to her apartment and sent a car for her to run her errands in.

When I arrive at her apartment, I go up to get her. When she opens the door, I'm stunned. Standing in front of me wearing a blue ombre silk dress with white pearl straps, she's even more beautiful than ever before. She's holding an oversized deep blue Angora sweater that matches the darkest shade of ombre. Her hair is defined in large ringlets that cascade over her shoulders. She's such a vision of beauty; I don't know how we'll make it past this moment without me devouring her.

"Rain, you look spectacular." I slide my hands around her waist and pull her into me. I dip my head and kiss her perfectly shaped lips. She tastes so good. I moan into her mouth, savoring the moment. "Wow, so beautiful." I pull away slightly, feeling my body respond to her closeness. I've been this way since our first kiss and each one since then. I want this woman. My woman.

"Thank you. And you're handsome as always," she says, stepping out of my arms to get a look at me. "Turn around, handsome." I turn, giving her a three-sixty view. When I'm facing her again, I take her back into my arms. I look down and catch her gaze. She's staring at me like I'm all she's ever wanted, and I'm tempted to devour her right there, but I dust my lips against hers. Because if I do more, we won't make it out the door.

"We should get going." I take her hand and walk toward the door.

During the drive to the city, Rain talks to me about her family. Her sister, Robin, lives in Seattle but has no plans to visit San Francisco. She's frustrated that they're not close and has been proactively reaching out to engage Robin in dialogue.

"What about your mom? How's that going?"

"Nothing has changed. I tried to get her to talk about what happened with Dad, but she clams up as soon as I broach the subject." I reach over and hold her hand.

"I'm sorry to hear that, Rain. You're trying, and that's all you can do. If I can be of any help, let me know. Can other family members help you fill in the missing pieces?"

"No, none I'm close to—it's not who I am."

"To let others into your circle?"

"Something like that. If only I knew what happened with my dad, maybe it could help us all open up a dialogue and begin to heal. His absence feels like a huge catalyst for everything that's wrong with us."

I grab her hand, lift her fingers to my lips, and kiss them. "It may take time, but things can be worked out if your family is willing. I'm here for you, Rain. Whatever you need, just let me know." She looks at me and smiles, warming my insides.

Our ride downtown is typical—people running through the crosswalks to get to the other side before the countdown ends.

Skyscrapers blocking out the sun and casting shadows over the streets—all the things we love about the city. Suddenly, Rain pulls at my hand.

She's looking out the window. "Stop the car," she yells.

"Pull over," I tell the driver.

Once we're stopped, Rain scoots closer to me. "I want to take a picture of the building from this viewpoint," she says, referring to the Transamerica building standing tall like a modern white pyramid with two wings in the distance. The forty-eight-story iconic building is impressive by any standards. The driver opens my door. I take Rain's hand, and we exit my side of the car.

"Do you want to be in the picture?" I ask as I brush a curl out of her face. She hands me her phone.

"Just one, but I want to get a shot of the building by itself. It's so beautiful at this angle, centered at the end of the street."

I take a picture with her and the building in the backdrop, and then, while the driver watches behind me for cars, I step into the center of the road and get the perfect shot. When I'm done, we return to the car and head down the road.

When we arrive at the Transamerica Building, I hold Rain's hand as we're met by a representative who takes us to the members-only bar floor near the top of the building. Being raised in San Francisco, we're both familiar with the building's history, but neither of us has been inside. I know the building's owner, who contracted with a team to redesign the interior into a luxury space. The newly renovated building has a light, airy, modern aesthetic, full of neutral beige and white tones and natural wood. I pull Rain into my side as we ride the elevator, which is fast and smooth, and within seconds, we arrive at our floor. When the elevator doors open, we are welcomed by another staff member. We're led into a beautifully designed room with similarly modern aesthetics but accented in dark trims. It has an impressive bar with an accordion-type backdrop with angles mirroring the building façade.

"Parker, wow, this is stunning," Rain says, walking toward the windows overlooking a spectacular view of San Francisco. Luther Vandross' rendition of *Always and Forever* plays in the background.

"Not as beautiful as you." I pull her to face me, dip my head, and kiss her. Rain slides her hands up my shoulders, neck, and through my hair, deepening the kiss. She tastes like love and honey all wrapped into one. I break the kiss. "Hey, what do you think? I have a meal planned for us, but if you want to stand here and make out, we can do that too." I brush her hair over her shoulders.

"This is nice, but you taste like more." She dusts her lips against mine, and I want to lick right back into her, but I don't.

"Rain, honey, keep that up, and I might have to take you home."

She smiles against my lips. "Okay. Let's have a drink?"

"You're too young to drink."

"Sparkling water in a champagne flute."

"That'll do."

I turn toward a staff member waiting by a table they have set up for us. I take Rain's hand, lead her to the table, and pull out a chair for her. The server pours two sparkling waters and then returns to the bar area.

"Let's toast." I raise my glass. "To our first date and many more to follow. I've waited two years for this moment. You made me the happiest man when you said yes to dating me."

"Parker, you're the most handsome man I know, my best friend, and the one who makes me feel special every day. You're so wonderful. Saying yes to you was my only option."

We touch our glasses and then sip our drinks. The staff begin bringing out portions of our meal. Rain tries a piece of caviar-topped roasted potato and then sips her sparkling water. Watching her savor the moment in this iconic setting she loves so much, enjoying herself away from the hustle of school and the pressures of life, is all I could ever want for Rain. She's so beautiful, I can imagine spending my life with her. During our meal, we discuss how we met and decide we should try and celebrate every anniversary here at the building.

I stand, reach a hand to Rain, and help her up. We walk to the clearing near the bar. I pull her into me, slip my hand around her waist, and we dance to *Lady* by Lionel Richie. I look into her eyes and let the music express how I've felt over the past two years. Rain's body feels hot next to mine—I can't wait to have her fully. The look she's giving me, like she's exactly where she wants to be, makes me want to kiss her, so I do. It's gentle at first as I taste her soft lips, a mix of her sweetness and chocolate from our dessert. Then I part her lips and lick into her, and our kiss becomes needy and urgent, and we get lost in each other. My body responds to the nearness of her, and it's all I can do to control myself.

Rain pulls away breathlessly. "Parker."

"Too much?" I touch my forehead to hers, my chest rising and falling against her body.

"It's everything."

"Remember what I told you earlier?"

"I never forget a thing."

I kiss her briefly, then whisper against her lips. "We're going home, beautiful."

"It better be to make love to me."

Rain doesn't need to say anything else. I give her a chaste kiss, a staff member hands me her sweater and purse, and we head out of the building to the car. When we get in the back seat, Rain sits in my lap and holds me tight, one hand roaming through my hair, making me heated with desire. I swear I'm hard the entire ride home to my house.

Traffic delays us. Once we're at my home, I lead Rain to the kitchen, where I grab us bottled water before taking her straight to the bedroom. Rain puts her purse on the dresser in my walk-in closet, and I join her there. I hold my hand to her, and she takes it.

"Let me help you with this," I say, sliding her sweater off of her shoulders and laying it on the dresser. "And this." I lower a strap on her slip dress and kiss her shoulder, then do the same on the other side. The gown falls to the floor, pooling around her feet. She's wearing a pair of blue silk panties but no bra. "You're beautiful, Rain." I pull her close, dip my head, and kiss her. Leaning her body slightly over my arm, I kiss down her neck, then cup her breast in my hand, then lower my mouth to suck the other one. God, she feels so good. Her skin is soft, her nipples hard in response to my touch. My dick presses against my slacks, straining to be set free. I lower my hands and slide her underwear down her legs. I straighten, pulling her with me. Covering her lips with mine, I kiss her with every ounce of passion I've been holding back. It's urgent, needy, and wet, and I want her so bad. I pull back. "Rain. We need to talk."

"Now?" she asks, breathless.

"Yeah, Rain, now." I grab one of my t-shirts and lay it on the dresser, lift Rain, sit her on top, and stand between her legs. "Kiss me," I tell her, and she dips her head and kisses me, and I love every minute of it. She's so soft and sensual. I caress her legs and pull her closer to me.

I break the kiss. "Tonight is special for a number of reasons. I've never said this to any woman because you're the only woman to capture my heart. After knowing you for the past few years, I know I'll never want anyone but you." Rain reaches out and caresses my face. I smile in her hands. "Rain, I've never slept with a woman without protection, but I don't want any barriers between us. I want to feel all of you. Are you on contraception?"

"I am. And I'm clean."

"I'm clean too. I don't want you to think this is just about the feeling. I want you to be the only woman who carries my seed in their body in the way a man and woman are meant to be together. Do you understand what I'm saying?"

"I think so. I'd be the only woman you come inside and claim as yours."

"That's right, Rain. But it's not just that. I'm committed to you—my love, my life, my body. I don't want anyone but you." I reach over, pull out the top drawer where I keep my watches, and retrieve a box. I open the box and pull out a diamond infinity ring band. Rain gasps.

"Oh my god, Parker, what is that?"

"This is a promise ring. You can wear it on whichever hand you choose. This ring is my promise to make you my wife one day when you're ready."

"This seems sudden."

"It's a promise for the future. I already know I want a future with you."

"How can you be so sure?"

"What I know at this moment is being with you feels right. It has since the day I met you. I know I don't want anyone else."

"This is so deep. I never considered being married or being ready for something like that."

I chuckle and stroke her arms to put her at ease. "I get it. This is not a wedding ring, and I'm not proposing. But it is a promise. With it, we'll commit ourselves to each other. I promise to always be there for you, no matter what. My body belongs only to you. I'll wait as long as it takes for you to say yes, even if it's a lifetime. I love you, Rain. Will you wear my ring?"

Rain's eyes well with tears. "Parker, you would have me all naked, wouldn't you?" She laughs. I hug her, grab her sweater, and cover her body.

"Sorry, babe. You're just so beautiful."

She sighs. "I want to kiss you right now, but I want to address your question. Since that first day in class, something drew me like a magnet to you. Like a thread, I've been tied to you since. Now that you're in my life, I never want to experience a day without you. Parker, I don't fully understand what I feel, but it feels right to be with you. I haven't had the best examples of what a healthy relationship should be, so I'm bound to make mistakes along the way. But I'm willing to take a chance on us."

"That's all I can ask for."

"You'll be the first and only man I experience fully. My body is yours. My heart is yours. If this is love, I accept it and you. Wearing your ring is an honor, and in doing so, I commit myself to you."

I put the ring on Rain's finger, then kiss her. It's gentle. As I take my time tasting her, I savor the feel of her body pressed against mine. My hands wander her body beneath the sweater until I break the kiss.

"Rain, honey. I'm going to take you to bed now and show you what I feel for you. Can you handle that?"

"I can handle that."

I push the sweater off her shoulders and pull Rain so that she's straddling me. I lift her, and she tightens her legs around my waist as I walk out of the closet to the bed. I gently lower her and kneel over her on the bed, caging her in with my arms.

"You're so beautiful." I lower a hand and slide my fingers between her folds, and she's wet. I dip my head and kiss her long and deep. I suck and lick into her as my fingers massage her sensitive skin, then I slide my fingers in and out of her body as my thumb circles her sweet spot.

"Ahh, Parker, that feels so good." She moans, and I swallow them with another kiss. I can feel her walls contract around my fingers as I work her body.

"Come for me, honey," I whisper, adding more pressure, and my girl comes hard on my hand, calling my name.

"Oh, God, Parker."

Continuing to move my fingers in and out, I pull her release from her until her contractions subside. I kiss her deeply, and she reaches between us to grab the hardened length in my pants. It takes everything within me not to lose control.

"Parker. I need you," she pleads, and I smile because she's mine, and I love her so much. I can't wait to be inside my love.

I straighten, step to the floor, and remove my clothes one piece at a time while staring down at Rain, who's all flushed with desire. Looking at her, I see my future wife. Watching me, she reaches her hands out, making a come here motion. I drop my underwear, and my rod is at full attention. She bites her lip.

"You're cute, babe. We need to get you to those pillows up there." I tip my head toward the top of the bed. Rain pulls herself toward them.

I crawl into the bed and hover over her. Dipping my head, I claim her lips. As I deepen the kiss, I feel her hand wrap around my length, guiding me to her body. I slip a hand beneath her hip and pull her into me. Slowly, I penetrate her walls and pump into her. In and out with slow movements, I take in all that is her. Enjoying the feel of my body in her walls. Allowing her juices to coat me. I move with ease like I belong just like this—connected to Rain. I don't understand the feeling, but it feels like heaven and more.

"Rain. You feel so good, honey. Ohhh," I moan into her neck. Increasing the pace, I feel her walls contract around my shaft, and I move with a steady rhythm, giving her what she needs to come again.

"Parker," she calls out, coming again. "You feel so good."

"That's right, love. I'm here. Give it all to me." I continue pumping through her orgasm, and I can feel my body tighten as I begin chasing my release. Covering her mouth with mine, I give her wet, sloppy kisses—my tongue darting in and out like my dick into her. I feel myself falling.

"Oh, God, Rain," I grunt, pumping into her. "Come for me again, babe. Come with me." I tell her, and she does, and amidst tears, sweat, and love, we come together, calling to our souls with my seed coating her insides, claiming her.

CHAPTER 10

When Morning Comes

Parker

"No!" RAIN'S SCREAM PIERCES MY EARS AS THE WORD RICOCHETS between us.

The bed shakes and her body pulls away from my side before I hear her scream "No" again at the top of her lungs. I've never seen her in distress, and I don't know what's happening to her as she reaches out. All I know is that I need to help her.

"Rain, honey." I reach across and touch her arm. She's hot, and I pull back the blanket to lower her temperature until she stops tossing. She settles some, and her arm drops back down.

"Honey, what's wrong? Tell me what's happening," I plead with Rain as I pull her into my arms.

I brush her hair away from her face. I cup her cheeks to see her face better. She's awake, but her eyes are pressed closed.

"Honey, are you hurt?" I kiss her eyelid. "Talk to me." I pull Rain onto my lap so she's astride me. She puts her head into my neck. "Rain, talk to me. Let me help you," I whisper in her ear. "I'll ask you a question, and you can nod or shake your head. Did I do something to hurt you?" Rain doesn't immediately respond. "Honey, did I hurt you?" She shakes her head. "Are you in pain, babe?" She shakes her head again. "Ok, babe, okay. I'm going to lift your head. Then I need you to open your eyes and talk to me."

I lift her head and wipe her tears with my thumb. Rain keeps her eyes closed, so I kiss her eyes, cheeks, and the corner of her lips. "Rain, it's Parker. I'm right here. You're safe. You can tell me anything, and I promise to help you through whatever this is." I kiss her lips. It's brief. "Babe, you taste salty and sweet at the same time. Kind of like salted caramel." My words earn me a slight smile. "Ok, there's my girl. I don't want you to cry anymore, so you'll have to try to open your eyes, focus on me, and tell me what you see. On the count of three, Rain. One. Two. Three." She opens her eyes. "Breathe for me, nice and steady. What do you see when you look at me? Just say whatever comes to your mind." I once read about this calming technique in class, and I hope it works for Rain. "Focus on my voice and tell me what you see." She looks up.

"Your hair is a mess." Her voice is tentative and soft.

"Show me, babe." Rain reaches up and brushes my hair back with her fingers. "What else do you see, honey?"

"Your eyes are dark like the ocean at night in a storm."

"There's not enough light in here. What else?" She reaches out and touches my cheek and curls her fingers like she's combing the hair.

"The stubble I like so much," she admits. I lean into her and rub my cheek against hers so she can feel I'm real.

"Kiss me, Rain," I tell her. Her lips hover over mine for a second before she dusts a kiss on my lips. I kiss her in return, then pull away. "You ready to tell me what happened?"

"I had a sleep terror. It's the same one I have every morning at this time. More like a memory," she says. Her eyes glaze over as if looking past me to something else. "I woke up early one day when I was eight because I heard a noise. I didn't know where it came from, so I went downstairs and listened in the living room. It was quiet for a while, then

I heard rustling. I was sitting in an oversized lounge chair with my feet and knees tucked close to my chest. The noise got closer, and I saw my dad heading toward the door. He had a bunch of things with him, like a duffle back and a piece of luggage. I didn't know what was happening because he didn't travel much for work. 'Dad,' I said, and I don't know if he heard me because I don't know if I was thinking I said the word or I actually called out to him. He hesitated a second, then continued out the door. He turned back after all his belongings were on the other side of the threshold. I thought our eyes locked briefly, but I'm not sure if he saw me. It was so dark. It looked like he shook his head, turned, closed the door, and left. That was the last time I saw him."

"Rain, honey." I pull her into a tight hug. I can't believe she's been going through this alone.

"For the longest time, I thought I had done something to cause him to leave. I thought if I had called louder to him, he'd recognize what he was doing and come back. For years, I believed I could have prevented him from leaving. But now I'm just stuck with this vivid memory repeating like Groundhog Day in my head."

"It wasn't your fault."

"I don't know whose fault it is, but I can't forget the pain of losing him that day. It's stamped like the mark of hot iron on hide."

"Every morning these feelings overcome you?"

"Every single day."

"How long does it take before you feel like yourself again?"

"Usually about thirty minutes to an hour, sometimes longer. But somehow—I don't know, your voice pulled me out of it. This is the shortest time it ever took me to pull myself together. Parker, I've never told anyone this story. My mother doesn't even know."

"It's ok, babe, I got you," I tell her, holding her tight against me. "Your secret's safe with me. But I'm not going to let you deal with this alone. If my voice helps pull you out of this, then that's what I'll do when I'm near. And when we are apart, we'll set an alarm with my voice as the ringtone or something. Then you can call me when you wake up. No matter where or what I'm doing, call me. I don't care if it's via video call when we're apart or if I'm sleeping next to you. Get me up. Let me help you through it."

"You can't."

"I can. I will. Did you see the memory in your head when you heard me call out to you?"

"No. By then, I was feeling the aftermath of my emotions. When it happens, my stomach churns, and I feel like throwing up."

"Nausea."

"Yeah. But over the years, trying to hide this, I learned how to suppress it."

I reach over to the nightstand and grab water. "Drink this." Rain drinks the water, and I watch the movement of her throat. She's so delicate, and I want to wrap her up and protect her from the world.

"Thank you," she says, handing me back the bottle.

"Tell me. When you opened your eyes and I asked you to describe what you saw, what was the first thing that came to mind?"

"You. I was thinking about you. How good it was making love to you last night," she says. It's unexpected, and I smile. I'm sure she can feel me grow hard against her.

"You're so beautiful, honey." I dust my lips against hers. "Then it's settled. Every morning, no matter where we are, we'll have this time together because I only want beautiful memories in your head. Every woman should wake up feeling good about their day and what lies ahead. Not lost in memories of the past. Not frightened and alone. Promise that you'll wake me as soon as you're up."

Rain nods. "Yeah. I promise, Parker Page, Esquire," she says, and I don't correct her this time. We kiss, and it's deep and needy. I roll her on her back, and she reaches between us to stroke my shaft, which is now granite. I position myself between her folds, push in, and make love to my beautiful woman.

CHAPTER 11

After the Storm

Rain

I DIDN'T KNOW WHAT TO EXPECT WHEN PARKER LEARNED ABOUT MY sleep terrors. It's a lot for me. Recalling that single moment every day. My dad was my world, and I was his baby girl. When I asked why he always called me that, he said, "*It doesn't matter how old you get, you'll always be my baby girl.*" That's what makes this hard. If I was that important to him, why did he leave the way he did? Why hasn't he reached out? My mom was so different after that day. She seemed more focused on things and people outside the house, and I felt like a stepchild. It also felt like there was a rift between my sister and me.

Now Parker knows my secret. He's the only one who knows what I've concealed from others. I've only slept with a few other guys—none of whom I stayed the night with. I've never trusted anyone with my secret until now. I certainly didn't expect him to want to help me work through them every morning. I didn't want to burden him with this. Yet here I am, lying beside the man who committed to help me with my trouble.

"Parker."

"Babe, you up already?"

"Yeah." He props himself up on the pillow and then pulls me to him. He pushes my hair back over my shoulders and studies my face. I look at him, trying to read his thoughts through his eyes. I trace his lips with my fingers, then rub my hands on the five-day stubble on his face until I reach the smooth skin on his cheeks, around his eyes, and on his forehead. I run my hands through his hair. Parker doesn't say anything as I explore his features and take in his essence. I get what he's doing. He's allowing me to focus on something other than my memories.

"You're lovely to look at. Do you know that, Parker?"

"I know what you tell me. And we promised to tell each other the truth."

"Kiss me, and then let's get some breakfast." He kisses me. It's lovely and warm, and I can't get enough of this man as I groan into his mouth.

"Rain..." He growls into me. "How set on breakfast are you?"

"That depends on what I get instead." He takes my hand and lowers it down his stomach, but it doesn't go far because his shaft is pressed against it. "Wow. I get a treat every morning."

"Is that going to be an issue?"

"Hell no." I wrap my hands around his length, pumping it.

"Don't be a tease," he says. "You're going to get it." I keep squeezing and pumping. "That's it." He pushes me on my back and doesn't even test me to see if I'm wet because he knows my body. He spreads my legs, positions himself between me, and thrusts, filling me. And I know what I want after the storm from now on.

"Ahh. Parker."

CHAPTER 12

Protect Her

Rain

It's Friday. Molly, a girl I have several classes with, told me about a party near campus. If I want to go, my only option is to go with her. I don't want to bother Parker since he's with his study group. My friend Jade is a PK, also known as a preacher's kid. Although she wants to go out, she hasn't figured out how to explain that to her father. So, Molly and I go together and get a car service to drop us off.

The door is open when we arrive at the one-story Eichler-type house, so we walk in. The house has an open plan, and there are around fifty people already in attendance. We make our way through the crowd. Pop music is blaring, and people are chatting it up, trying to talk over the booming sound system. Molly and I say hello to a few people we recognize, and then she whisks me off to a section where people are dancing.

The music is bumping in the background, almost too loud for us to be partying in the suburbs of Silicon Valley near campus. Molly spins around, shaking her hips, and I stop dancing when she faces me.

"It's hot. I need some water or something." Even though I'm wearing ankle jeans and a crop top, I'm sweating. I go to the sideboard where mini water bottles are in a cooler on ice, open one, and take a swig. I turn and scan the room, noting others I recognize from class when I see Kevin. Shoot. He makes a beeline straight for me.

"Raven." He sounds so sure of himself.

"That would be me." My tone is nonchalant.

"I've seen you with that Page guy," he says over the music before stepping closer.

"His name is Parker Page. The clip in your tone leads me to believe you have an issue with him. You should take it up with him. Not me."

"I have nothing against him if you like that type of guy."

"I do. So, keep stepping," I say, waving him off, and I'm surprised when he walks away. It becomes obvious why he left when Molly returns from dancing.

"Was that Kevin?"

"*Was* is the operative word. Listen, Molly, I'm going to head out of here, and you should, too. This is not my crowd," I tell her.

"No, let's get some punch and dance some more. Forget Kevin. He's just jealous of Parker. Even as rich as these people are here—they can't compete with his family status." She pulls me over to the food and drinks.

"I can't drink this stuff. I haven't eaten dinner yet."

"Just have a sip, and we'll dance it off."

She hands me a cup, and I take a sip. It tastes like strawberry lemonade but ten times sweeter. I take another sip but then put it down before I get diabetes. Molly does the same, and we go dancing. They change the music and throw an old Montel Jordan song on: *This Is How We Do It*. When I dance, Molly tries mimicking my moves, but they look more like spasms than anything. By the time the song is over, I feel hot, sweatier than before, and slightly dizzy, so I stand near an open window close to the door. I take out my phone and text Parker.

Me: Parker, I don't feel good.

Parker: Rain, get in bed. I'll be there shortly.

Me: Not home.

I look up and watch Molly dancing with some guy until I feel even more lightheaded than before.

Parker: Babe, where are you?

I can barely read the screen, and my brain is fuzzy. Molly is still dancing. The music is loud. My head is throbbing. I return the text.

Me: With Mol.

Parker: Babe?

Me: ...

I can't seem to focus on the letters. If I can get outside, I can send a voice note. I scan the room. Molly is dancing with another person. My phone flashes again.

Parker: Hang tight—be there soon.

As I'm leaning against the wall, I hear a familiar voice beside me. "You and Molly looked good out there."

"What?" I snap, annoyed by the intrusion.

"You and Molly."

I turn toward the last person I want to talk to, Kevin, and I feel his breath touch my cheek as he talks. His scent is a mix of beer and something that smells of cheap hotel soap, and I feel the burn of bile pushing its way up my throat, making me want to hurl. It's enough to pull me out of the fog but not enough to walk away. The wall is the one thing holding me up.

"Seriously? I thought you got the hint the first time. Walk away, Kevin. I'm not interested."

"You're missing out. I'm a total catch. I got what you need," he says, wearing a smug smile like he's god's gift to women.

"Dead fish baking in the sun—noted. Now, get the hell away from me. I have a real man." I blurt out, not feeling like myself.

"So, what do you see in this Page, dude, anyways? I have more going on than him," he says, taking a piece of my hair and twirling it around his finger. On instinct, I slap his hand away, leaving a residual sting in my palm.

"Now here I am being all nice. You need a guy like me to teach you what a real man is." This time, he stands in front of me, and I use all the energy I can gather to push him back before he can cage me in.

"Get the fuck out of my face. You have no idea what you're doing," I scream.

"I know exactly what I'm doing. You're leaving with me," Kevin demands. He reaches for me, but he's snatched away before his hand makes contact.

"She said get the fuck out of her face."

Parker. Closing my eyes, I breathe a sigh of relief. I open my eyes and watch the scene unfold before me.

"The fuck, Page. You're going to regret this," Kevin says seconds before I hear a crunch. Blood sprays from Kevin's face. I hear another crack, then another, and then he's on the ground. Parker picks him up, holds him by the neck, and hits him again. This time, he throws him across the room toward some people, but they scatter, and he falls to the floor. I watch as Parker scans the crowd of partygoers.

His hand gestures back toward me. "If *this* woman ever says back the fuck up, or anything remotely resembling that—then back the fuck up, or you will end up like Kevin or worse."

He turns to me, scoops me in his arms, and carries me out. "I got you, babe." And that's it. Parker gently puts me in his car and takes me to his house. By the time we arrive, his doctor is there, and he looks me over, does some preliminary tests, and takes a sample of my blood.

"She'll be fine," the doctor assures. "She needs some food and water. And she may need one of these." He hands Parker Ibuprofen. Parker walks the doctor out. Then, he types something on his phone. He disappears into the bedroom briefly before returning to me.

"Hey, beautiful. You're going to be okay. Take this." He hands me the pills and some water, and I take them. "I'm going to bathe you, then we'll have dinner," he says. Parker picks me up and takes me to the bathroom. I begin undressing myself, but he takes over. Afterward, he removes all his clothes, and we get in the shower. He holds me close to his body and bathes us both, allowing the water to wash over us. It's not sexual but sensual, and I know he's holding me in fear that I can't manage myself. He dips his head and kisses my neck from behind me.

"You okay, babe?" I nod, realizing I haven't spoken a complete sentence since he entered the party. He helps me out of the shower, dries me off, and then we go into the bedroom. I sit on the edge of the bed while he lotions my legs and I lotion my arms. When we're done, I slip on one of his T-shirts. The doorbell rings. He helps me up. I sit in the kitchen while he collects our food at the door.

"Parker," I say, extending a hand to him when he enters the kitchen.

He puts the food on the counter, stands before me, and takes my hand. I look at his hand and see the swollen and torn skin from where his knuckles met Kevin's face.

"Thank you for finding me. I don't know what happened back there."

He cups my face with his free hand, dips his head, and kisses me. It's soft at first, then he parts my lips with his tongue, and we find ourselves hungry for each other. He pulls me to my feet so that I can feel what

I'm doing to him. He's hard and hungry but pulls back because he's Parker. He's thoughtful and knows I need nourishment first.

"Rain." My name comes out breathy. "Sit down," he says, helping me back to my seat. He grabs some dishes and plates our meal. He sets a plate in front of me and sits next to me. "Want me to feed you, babe?"

I laugh. "No, I'm good."

"So, Rain, we need to talk."

"Okay."

"First, if you're going to drink syrupy sweet stuff, you need to eat first. And never drink anything from a punch bowl, especially at a party, because, as you discovered, it could be spiked." Like the man I've come to know these past few years, he dives right into the topic—me.

"I realize that now, but I didn't drink enough to get drunk."

"Rain, the point is, you have no idea what was in that drink. And I would have taken you to that party if I'd known you wanted to go."

"It was a last-minute thing. I didn't know I was going. Besides, you had a study group. You know I'd never interfere with that."

"You should have told me. Nothing regarding you is an interference."

"Next time, I will. How'd you find me?" I take a bite of vegetable lasagna.

"That's the thing I want to talk about. I'd like us to share our location no matter where we go because I don't like not knowing where you are. If something were to happen, and I couldn't get to you—I'd be devastated."

"But you found me."

"Rain, babe." He holds out his hand, and I take it. "You're right. I can use my resources like I did tonight to find you, but I don't want to do that. Either we share each other's location via phone, or I can give you a GPS device. You choose."

"What? What in the world? Parker, this is crazy. I don't want to talk about this now."

"Rain, I'm not trying to upset you. You had a difficult night already, so we can table it for now, but at a minimum, you need to turn on your locator for me. Can you handle that?"

"Yes." My voice comes out small.

"And I'll share mine with you, but I'll always tell you where I'm going. Okay?"

"I understand. Is that how you found me? Through my phone?"

"Through yours and Molly's phone GPS. I called in a favor to gain access so that I could find you. But Rain, I don't like how it felt not knowing whether you were safe. I'm glad you sent me a note when you felt something was wrong. I'm glad you trust me to help you, but babe, in the future, we need to communicate before it gets to this. Had I been a few minutes later? God, Rain. I don't want to think what would have happened."

"You found me. Nothing happened."

"Still. I could have reached you sooner."

"I didn't want to bother you."

"Rain, I'm your man—you're not bothering me. I would have taken you to the party, no questions asked, if that's where you wanted to go. You only had to ask. Study groups can always be rescheduled."

"I was about to leave the party before I got sick. I didn't really want to go. I didn't want to be alone tonight."

"Oh, Rain. You could have just said something. You can tell me anything anytime, no judgment. Whatever is on your mind, say it, babe. Tell me you'll always be honest with me no matter what?"

"Okay, I promise to tell you whatever is on my mind, no matter what."

"No matter how hard you think it might be for me to hear. Tell me—like you did just now. It crushed me not knowing where you were or how you were. And I swear if Kevin had hurt you, he would not be walking out of that house on his own tonight. As it is, I can guarantee he will never return to Stanford, and the owners of that house and the people who threw that party will deal with a mountain of legal issues. It's not over for them, Rain. Those people facilitated what happened to you, and they'll pay for their role is this."

"Parker, what are you talking about?" I'm sure he can read the shock on my face. What the hell is this?

"That's how this works."

"I don't understand."

"Rain, if you let people walk on you, they'll continue using you as a doormat. In this case, they totally disrespected you. That doesn't fly with me, and those who disrespected you will pay the price for their actions or inaction, depending on what side of the fence they were on. Someone should have stepped in, but they didn't. Kevin tried to forcibly take you with him while others watched on the sidelines. No woman should be afraid for their safety. You deserve the highest level of respect. After today, people will understand that."

"And Molly?"

He huffs in annoyance. "Molly won't be inviting you to any more parties. I didn't even know you two were friends like that."

"We're not."

"Then that makes her fate easier to digest."

"You're serious."

"Rain, honey. This is me. Come here," he says, and I let go of his hand long enough to get off my stool and go to him. He lifts me onto his lap. "Rain, you're so beautiful." He brushes the hair over my shoulders and sweeps his thumb across my cheek. He kisses my forehead and continues. "Yes, I am serious. I don't know what you're used to, but I'll always be honest with you. I'll answer any question you ask. I will always protect you, and God help anyone who hurts or attempts to hurt you. You were in a vulnerable situation tonight, and several people took advantage of that. Some even disregarded it. I don't take what happened lightly. Can you understand where I'm coming from?"

"I understand."

"As long as you are in my life, I will cherish you even when you do crazy things—which you do sometimes. Because my girl is wild. I love you, Rain, and I'll do everything I can to make you happy. And if you asked me to make love to you every day—I would because that's how I feel about you. So yeah, anyone that led to you having the horrible experience you had tonight has a steep price to pay."

"This is a lot to take in." It's all new to me. His concern for me is overwhelming because, for the longest time, I've been looking out for myself, yet I'm grateful for Parker. Tonight could have ended a lot worse.

"Don't give it a second thought. It's over."

"You're too much."

"But hopefully not too much for you because after I get you fed and rested, I plan to make love to you and ensure your day ends the best way."

"I had a role to play in all this tonight."

"The only role you played was not telling me what you wanted. I'll never deny you anything. Ever. Just ask."

"I just want you."

"I'm yours," he says, then kisses me senselessly.

CHAPTER 13

The Way It Is

Rain

AFTER PARKER ENSURED I WAS WELL-FED, HE KEPT HIS PROMISE AND made love to me.

When I arrive back in class, it is noticeably quiet. I don't see Kevin. There are no texts from Molly. I notice a few students glancing my way, but when I catch their gaze, they look away. *Parker.*

I think back on what he told me about the party. Even my ex, Breck, pretended he didn't see me when I passed him outside, walking between buildings. Whatever happened was enough to get these overprivileged people in check. The strange thing is that they should always have been checked. Just because you have more than someone doesn't give you cart blanche to treat them like they are less than you. We all bleed red blood.

I'm about to get to my next class when a familiar voice calls my name.

"Rain, hey. You good?"

I turn just in time for Parker to grab my waist and pull me toward him. "Hey, Parker. You miss me already?"

"Always," Parker whisperers against my forehead.

"Are you walking me to class?"

"I guess I am," he says, leading me into the building. When we reach my classroom, he tucks my hair behind my shoulders like he always does and stares at me. The way he's looking, I know something is on his mind, but I'm not going to push him to tell me.

"I'm pretty sure I'm going to ace this class, but I don't want to get a mark against me for attendance," I tell him in my not-so-subtle attempt to get him to let me go. He knows what I mean. He dips his head and kisses me.

"Text me when you're ready to head home. I'll walk you," he says. He watches me from the door until I sit. When the last student arrives, and the door closes for the class to begin, I see Parker through the small door window as he walks away.

My phone buzzes. It's Parker.

Parker: Don't forget to text when you're ready.

Me: I will.

The class is business as usual. Occasionally, I notice someone sneaking a glance at me that is so brief I wonder if I'm imagining it. A few minutes before the end of class, I text Parker. He's waiting at the door and slips his arm around me when I exit into the hallway.

"How was class?"

"Good. No issues."

"We can go drop our stuff and go out for dinner or make something ourselves. Your choice. Then we can study."

"Let's order in."

"Okay, that's an option, too."

Parker takes me to his place and orders smothered shrimp over rice from my favorite Cajun restaurant to be delivered. Instead of sitting at his kitchen counter, we sit in the dining room, which he rarely uses. I figure it might be nice to have a more formal dinner like the ones I'm sure he's used to with his parents. Although the few times I was there, Mrs. Page allowed us to eat at the kitchen counter.

"What's on your mind, babe?" he asks. "I know something's there the way you've been watching me."

He's right. The whole classmate disappearing act was strange. "Lately, our talks have been heavy, so maybe after dinner we can sit and talk."

"We can do that. Are you okay?"

"I'm fine. It's just that hashing through things while we're eating is awkward. I don't want all my memories of our meals to be about issues—like when someone takes their partner to a restaurant to break up. You know these things get stuck in my head," I tell him, hoping he'll understand. I prefer to be in his arms of protection when we talk.

"I get it, babe."

I eat a few bites and then take a sip of my sparkling water. "Hey," I say mid-bite. "In the meantime, will you help me practice for my mock trial?" I look down. The smell of shrimp in herbs and Cajun seasonings is so good. At this point, I think I'm just eating because it tastes good. I load my fork with more food.

"Is the defense ready?" Parker's baritone voice booms across the kitchen, catching me off guard. I freeze before the fork reaches my mouth.

I turn to Parker. "What in the world?"

"Answer the question," he says in his mock trial voice.

"Yes, your honor. May I approach the bench?"

"The defense may approach the bench."

I stand next to Parker. He swivels his chair so I can stand between his legs. I rest my hands on his thighs and lean in so my face is close to his.

"Parker Page, Esquire. Don't scare me like that again. I wasn't ready."

He swallows a smile. "Judge Page."

"Judge Page, your honor." He leans closer and kisses me. It's soft and loving—all the things it should be. Everything it needs to be to keep me from chastising him. I deepen the kiss. He breaks it.

"Sorry, babe. I didn't mean to scare you." He smiles against my lips. "Are you going to tell me what our talk is about?"

"After dinner. We can resume practice later. I can already tell you're going to be a tough judge. I need to be ready."

I go back to my seat and eat the rest of my meal. He glances at me every few seconds like he's trying to figure me out. I imagine he's worried about what I'm going to say. To reassure him, I touch his knee. He smiles, picks my hand up, and kisses my fingers. We sit like that for a moment, then finish eating. When we're done, we clean up the kitchen and go to Parker's family room. He sits on an oversized lounge chair, and I sit astride him. He reaches up and rubs his thumbs along my cheeks.

"You're beautiful. I hope you know that."

I smile. "You won't let me forget."

"Kiss me, honey."

I dip my head and kiss my man, and Parker puts his thumb on my chin, making me open my mouth to receive his tongue, deepening the kiss. I get lost in him but break the kiss when I feel his body rise hard beneath me. "Parker." My breath comes out needy and rushed.

"I know, babe. You wanted to talk. I'll come inside you later." He lowers his hands and cradles my butt pulling me closer to him. "Okay, tell me. What's on your mind?"

"I didn't see Kevin or Molly around today."

"This is about the party."

"Yeah."

"Rain, babe. We talked about this."

"Parker, we didn't talk. You told me what to expect. Now, I want you to elaborate."

"What do you want to know?"

When he opens the door, I know he's being earnest. We promised to tell each other everything and be honest no matter how hard the truth is.

"I want to know what happened to Kevin."

"Kevin has been expelled. He can never come to campus again. He can never come around you again. Ever."

"Like physically?"

"Yes." He doesn't have to elaborate. I know what he means. Over the past month, I've told Kevin several times that his advances were unwanted.

"And Molly?"

"Transferred. And she agreed to stay away from you unless you contact her first."

"And the homeowners?"

"Facing several charges."

"Why?"

"Reckless behavior. Underaged drinking. A host of reasons. They endangered you. And Kevin had mal intent." As he rattles off the list, I sit in shock. A man who stupidly dared to push his boundaries with me now has a restraining order against him and has to start over again at another school. The number of people Kevin's actions have impacted is astounding. I search Parker's face, trying to comprehend what I'm hearing. Trying to come to terms with the power that being with someone like him wields. The status that by proxy passes to me. I close my eyes briefly.

"Are you telling me that this is my life with you? Consequences for those…"

"For those who dare to slight you, to put you in harm's way or try to harm you. God forbid anyone lays a hand on you, Rain."

"Parker." I lean back, but he pulls me closer.

"Don't pull away from me, Rain. I'm not the enemy."

"I don't think of you that way. I love you. It's just…it's a lot to take in." No one has ever stood up for me like Parker.

"Understandable. But I make no apologies. This is the way it is. You can forget what life was like before me. There are consequences for how people treat you. Can you handle that?"

"It doesn't sound like I have a choice."

"Rain, you're my woman. Most people don't know what that means, but this is how they learn. This is how they discover you are untouchable."

"This is wild."

"Is it really? What's so wild about it?"

"People's lives can be destroyed by something they've done to me."

"You think it's okay for them to scar you for life with some crazy shit they've done to you? To leave you with memories to relive over and over while they walk through life sipping champagne, disregarding the pain they've caused?"

"No, I don't."

"There are no free passes for them, only penalties. My life becomes yours."

"Parker, it's a lot. I'm not used to this."

"Rain, I understand it's a lot for you to take in. I need to make this clear to you. People may not know our names when we enter a room, but I can guarantee they will notice us. There will be times when we go to places, and it immediately becomes quiet. Sometimes, there may be hushed whispers and stares like you experienced today. That's because people notice something different about us—that there's a quiet power we wield. But you also need to know that anyone who messes with us will pay a price. I'll make sure of that. That's the way it is."

Parker has given me a lot to think about. When I met him, I didn't know who he was. But like he said, I noticed something different about him when he entered the room. Being one of the elites evokes confidence by embracing the cloak of power that comes with it. It's a world I don't yet understand.

I haven't felt part of anything since my father left. My mom was closed off, my dad wasn't around, and my sister had her friends. And in school, I was the weird kid, the "freak" in class who could recite the teacher verbatim. But I'm not the weird kid around Parker and his family. I'm the woman they've welcomed as his partner. By proxy, I'm an elite.

"Rain, are we done talking? Because I really need to be inside you."

I dip my head and press my lips to his. Parker stands, taking me with him, and carries me to bed.

CHAPTER 14

Happy Birthday to Me

Rain

The sun is barely up. Parker is still sleeping beside me. I went to his house after school yesterday because today is my birthday, and I wanted to wake up in his arms. His breaths are slow and deep, and I count them. One, two, three. My arm is stretched across his chest, rising with each breath he takes. I slide my hand down his body and caress his length, which grows in my hand.

"Parker," I whisper in his ears and kiss his cheek. "Fill me," I say. He opens his eyes, pushes me off him, and rolls me on my side so my back is to him. He lifts my leg back over his, then reaches over me and massages my sex until he's satisfied by how wet I am. Even with the soft touches, I'm ready to come, but he's not done. He positions himself between my legs from behind and pushes slowly into me, filling me with his body. Then he begins pumping slowly, in and out, in and out, and it's so wonderful that I can feel my body clench around him.

"Come for me, babe. Feel how hard I am in you," his voice is low, raspy. Reaching around, he holds my breast and squeezes. I push back against him, wanting more.

"Harder, deeper Parker," I call out. He pulls me close to him and angles me so my butt is slightly in the air. He pushes into me, and I come hard. He continues pumping harder, deeper until I come again, and I feel him chasing his release. Finding it, he fills me with his seed.

"God, Rain," he growls into my back before he collapses on me. I can still feel traces of the pulsing between my legs, milking his shaft until he pulls out. I turn toward him.

"Kiss me, Parker." He rolls partially over me and covers my mouth with his, and his kiss is so powerful and loving that even though he's not in me, I come again. He can feel my body responding. Lowering his hand, he inserts it into the mixture that's all ours and pulls the rest of my climax from me.

He breaks the kiss. "Woman, you have me so hard again, fuck Rain." He sighs. "I'm going to take you again, babe, and I need you to come one more time. I love you so much."

I don't even have a chance to respond. He nudges my leg open with his knee, positions himself between my legs, and in one thrust, I'm full. He's hungry. His kiss comes wet and sloppy on my face, and his body moves hard and fast in and out of me. The only sound in the room is the sucking noises from our kisses, clashing of our bodies, and moans.

"Now," he grunts, and my body responds in a violent wave of climax. He grunts again, and at that moment, I feel his warm release come in waves over and over again until he's empty, and I feel all his love sliding out of me. I'm full of everything Parker has to offer me. Full of him. Full of love.

"Happy birthday, babe," he whispers.

AFTER PARKER MADE LOVE TO ME MOST OF THE MORNING, WE FINALLY decided we were dirty enough to shower and get my birthday started.

Honestly, I would have preferred to stay in bed all day. Parker is that good in bed. He's big everywhere and strong, and I like how our bodies fit together. Ugh, I need to stop thinking about it because I still have to shower with this man.

"Parker," I say, following behind him to the bathroom.

"Yeah, babe." He turns on the shower and then looks at me.

"I think we should shower separately."

"Why's that?"

"Because I'm about to come, just thinking about stepping in there with you."

He shakes his head and smiles. "Rain, honey, it doesn't matter how often you come, as long as I provide the pleasure. Now get in there so I can make you come again," he commands. And it's so sensual that my sex clenches.

He steps in the shower and under the water, letting it wash over and down his body, and I watch as he washes all his muscles. I want to touch him, and I do. I grab his butt and squeeze. He doesn't flinch. He laughs.

"You want me to fuck you, babe."

"Clean me then you can." He turns around, puts soap on a cloth, and washes me everywhere, and when he reaches between my legs, his hand moves back and forth over my sex. Then he hangs the towel, replaces his hand between my legs, and plunges his fingers in me. My body responds immediately, and I come on his hands, pushing out his seed from earlier. He dips his head and kisses me and then lifts me until I'm straddling him. His hands are pressing firm against me, but I reach down and position his length to my entrance, and he pushes in, and oh my fucking god, I don't know what to do. It feels so good.

"I'm going to come again, Parker."

"Then come with me, babe." He pushes in and out.

Pumping into me, he feels so good, and I arch my back, calling out to him, "Oh, god, Parker." My voice echoes off the walls. I crave more as he continues, and I do exactly what he says: I come with my man.

Happy birthday to me.

We finally make it out of the shower and into some clothes.

"Rain, babe. I know it's your birthday, but I'd like to do more than just sex you up. Not that I'm complaining or anything. Sex with you is fantastic and one of my favorite things, but I'd like to take you out." He takes my hand and leads me through the house.

I follow Parker to the kitchen. "Do what you will today. I'm along for the birthday ride," I tell him and surprise him by jumping into his arms.

"Babe, what are you doing?" He laughs because what else can you do when your hands are full of your girlfriend?

I wrap my arms around his neck and tighten my legs around his waist. "I don't know. Whatever you tell me. Like I said, I'm just along for the ride." He shakes his head. "You didn't expect that, did you?"

"With you, babe, anything is possible." He kisses me, then sits me on the counter. "Get down now, babe. We need to get some breakfast in us."

I unlatch myself from Parker and make myself comfortable on the counter, watching him move around the kitchen. First, he makes us some coffee, sets a cup near me, and takes his cup to the stove while making us eggs and toast.

"Fruit?" He holds up a container of strawberries.

"Please," I tell him. He cuts up berries and puts them on the plate. He doesn't make two plates. He puts everything on one plate and then sets it next to me. He stands between my legs and gives me a hug.

"Hey, beautiful. Happy birthday."

"Thank you."

"How do you feel?"

"Great. Hungry. Do I get to eat some of that?" I look down at the plate beside me.

"Yes, but first: kiss me."

I lean into Parker and kiss him. It's slow and sensual, and he tastes like coffee, cream, and strawberry, and I suck all of it from him. I tighten my arm around his neck and pull myself to the counter's edge to get closer to him. He pushes his body into mine so I don't fall off. Our kiss gets superheated, and he reaches up my shirt and cups my breast. At that moment, all I want is my man. He breaks the kiss.

"Breakfast." He pants.

"Parker. That's not fair."

He smirks, and he's so sexy. He reaches beside me, gets a fork full of eggs, and holds it to my mouth.

"Eat first. Then I'll fill you again."

"Parker."

"Eat," he commands, and I open my mouth and accept the eggs. He scoops some up for himself and then gives me a strawberry. And we eat like that, with Parker standing between my legs, feeding both of us until the plate is clean. And when we're done, he takes me to the nearest room and fucks me senseless.

CHAPTER 15

Insatiable

Parker

I MADE PLANS TO TAKE RAIN OUT FOR HER BIRTHDAY TODAY, BUT SHE wasn't kidding when she said she wanted to stay in and have sex with me. I'm exhausted, but I'm happy. Anytime I get the opportunity to sink into my woman, I take it. However, right now, my baby is tired and lying naked in my arms while I'm propped on the chaise lounge. I pull the cozy knit blanket over her shoulders. She fell asleep before her favorite movie, *Wuthering Heights*, ended. She must have seen the movie a hundred times. This is the second time I've watched it with her. My girl cried when Heathcliff left during a storm, and Cathy got lost in the rain. I held her tight until she fell asleep. Then I turned the movie off.

I stroke her hair and listen to her soft breaths. Her body radiates heat, warming my soul. Usually, if she were resting like this, I would have some soft music playing. I don't because my girl hasn't slept since late last night. I lost count of the times I made her come today, and it's not even noon. She's insatiable, and so am I. I can feel my body respond just thinking about her. If she were awake, she would, too.

My life thus far has been good. The first two years of being around Rain on campus, watching her navigate campus life and other friendships as her friend were challenging. Many guys had their eyes on her. She even dated a few. They were jerks. I had to pretend to befriend them to understand their motives around her. Needless to say, none of them were up to any good. But I monitored what was happening, ensuring we were solid as Rain and I grew our friendship before finally asking her to be mine. Now she is, and I can't get enough of her. I don't know what it is about Rain, but she's my life force.

She stirs beneath me. I wonder what she wants to do now. Watch more classic movies? Eat cake? This is frustrating and fun at the same time. I have a little control over what we do, but Rain has the majority. This makes today hard because I wanted to do a bunch of things for her, but she had other plans: sex and more sex.

"Rain, honey. You up?"

She is. Rain crawls up my body, and I already know what she wants. Her eyelids are weighted because she's tired. She's horny. You can't have as many orgasms as she had today and not crave more. When she finally gets into the position she wants, she kisses me, and it's beautiful. Her breath is warm and naturally sweet. The scent of jasmine and honey clings to me. She cups my face, deepening the kiss, searching for my tongue, mingling it with hers. I lick and suck in my girl until she comes up, searching for air.

"Parker."

"I'm here, babe. Tell me what you want."

"This." She kisses me again. She lowers her hand between us and grabs my length. It's already rock hard—it has been since she laid on me. She begins stroking me.

"Rain, honey. Don't. Not unless you want to get fucked." She continues stroking; if she continues, it will be rough because I'm unleashed. "Rain," I growl, and it's wild and loud. "Get off me, Rain. Now."

Rain sits astride me and looks me in the eye. "No. Take me."

I stand, taking Rain with me. I carry her to my room and toss her on the bed. My girl is insane unleashing me like this. She knows I can't resist her.

"Get on your knees and bend over," I command. She turns away from me and gets into the position. I get on my knees on the bed behind and reach between her legs and stroke her sex, and oh my god, my woman is fucking drenched. I lick my lips because I need her. I widen her legs, put one hand on her back, and lower her down further to have complete access to her sex. I take my length in my hand, rub it along her slickness, and then push right in.

She gasps as I fill her full in one thrust. I grab her tight around the waist, and I pump in and out, and it's fast and hard, and my body is slapping against her hips into her sex, and she's moaning and calling my name. I pump even faster, harder, deeper. And she comes around my dick, coating it, making it even slicker, and I move even faster. It's hard. It's feral, and I feel the start of something building in my body.

"Come again, Rain," I growl. I pump in and out, in and out, and she comes around my dick again, and her walls clenching my body pulls my climax from me. "Babe." I pump, growl, and hold her until I empty everything, all of me that matters into her. "Rain."

"Parker."

I collapse on her back, roll to the side, and pull her over me.

"Was that what you wanted, babe?" She's breathless, speechless, and sweaty but nods against my body.

CHAPTER 16

Every Precious Moment

Rain

I'M GOING TO CELEBRATE MY BIRTHDAY ALL WEEKEND. I'VE NEVER had this much sex in my entire life. But this morning, I'm so sore, I can barely walk.

"Hey beautiful, are you ready?" Parker stands on the threshold between the bathroom and bedroom, which means the bathtub must be full.

"I'm ready." He walks over, lifts me off the bed, takes me to the bathroom, and lowers me into the tub. Then he gets in on the other side. We sit there looking at each other as we bathe.

"Babe, you're too much. You realize that we spent the entire weekend having sex. I'm sore but will take everything you offer." He laughs, and it's lovely and loud, and it bounces off the bathroom walls, and I laugh with him. Because my man, Parker Page, is fine; he gave me everything I needed and more yesterday.

"For the record, I'm sore, too, Parker. So, if we do anything today—go easy." He finds that even more funny.

"Don't worry, babe, I'll be gentle when I eat you tonight. Because you don't get a day in my presence without an orgasm. Now wash up so I can give you the present we didn't get to yesterday. And no, it's not sex-related."

"Can I have my cake for breakfast?" I lather my towel and wash my neck and chest.

"Anything you want."

"I have a question for you," I say. He reaches beneath the water and strokes my leg.

"Shoot."

"Have you thought about where you're doing your JD?"

"I plan to continue at Stanford. Why? What were you thinking?"

"I was debating either going to Berkeley or out of state."

"Are you looking for my opinion or something else?"

"Just wanted to know what your plans were."

"Stanford. What else do you want to know?"

"Do you care what school I go to?"

"Rain. What's the question behind your question? Do you think I'd object to you going somewhere else, or I'd leave you or something?"

"I don't know."

He tips his head to the side. "You know the answer."

"There's a possibility."

Parker grabs my ankles and pulls me close until I straddle him, with my chest pressed against his. The sudden movement causes water to slosh up the sides of the tub.

"Never going to happen. This…." He gestures his finger between us. "Is forever. You're all I want. All I'll ever need."

"Parker."

"Babe, go wherever you want. I support you. I can't believe you'd think otherwise. We made a promise to each other. I'm yours. Done."

"You can't mean that."

"I've never spoken a word I didn't mean. What we have is a

connection that I know will last forever. You feel it, too…it's why you cling to me the way you do. If you haven't noticed already, we gravitate to each other like magnets. We can't keep our hands off each other. When you walk into a room, my eyes instinctively find you. And you can't help but answer the call to come to me. So yes, Rain, I mean every word. Go where you want. Do what you want. Reach your goals. You'll always have me. If I have to take the jet every week to be near you—I will. Mark my words. One day, Raven Rain Nichols will be my wife. That ring on your finger is my commitment. So, did I answer your questions?"

He holds my gaze and caresses my cheek, waiting patiently for a response. This man always gives me his full attention.

"Yes. Thank you."

"Are we done talking? I want to get out of this tub and give you your birthday gift."

I hug him around his neck and press my head to his. I feel him grow thick beneath me. I lift my body, align the tip of his dick to my entrance and ease down, and he fills me.

"Rain, oh, god, you feel so good," he says, and I ride him.

PARKER AND I FINALLY WASH UP, PUT ON SOME CLOTHES, AND MAKE IT to the kitchen. He got me a red velvet cake, just like I asked for, and he plates me a piece. I sit on the counter like yesterday and let him feed me. He eats fruit while I drink coffee and have cake.

"How's it?"

"Good. I might have two pieces."

"Hey, it's your cake. Eat up. You want a strawberry?"

I shake my head. "You want to eat icing off me?"

He laughs. "Maybe later. I have a gift for you. Let's finish up so we can get to it."

I devour my piece of cake while Parker eats his fruit. When we're done, I help him clean the kitchen. Afterward, we go to his study. He walks to his desk and sits in his chair. I follow him and sit on his lap. He opens a drawer and pulls out a square gift wrapped in black paper with a white bow.

"Happy birthday, babe." He hands me the gift. I pull one end of the white ribbon, and it comes off. I flip the gift upside down, slip my finger beneath the wrapping, and peel back the layers, revealing a green box. I open the box. Inside is a gold Rolex watch.

"Parker. This is too much. What are you doing?"

"This is a reminder that time is precious, which is how I feel about every moment with you. I cherish every second with you."

I hug Parker, dip my head, and kiss him briefly. "Thank you. It's beautiful."

"It's already set. All you need to do is put it on."

I slip it on my wrist and click the claps together. "It fits perfectly. This is such an elaborate gift." I grab his wrist. "It matches yours."

"That's the idea. But mine is slightly different than yours."

"I don't understand what yours would have that mine doesn't."

"GPS."

CHAPTER 17

Track Her

Parker

I WASN'T EXPECTING TO HAVE THIS CONVERSATION WITH RAIN ON HER birthday, but here we are.

"GPS? What are you talking about?"

"A tracker. Everyone in my family wears one."

She pulls back. "Parker Page, what are you saying? What for? Why do you need to be located?"

I laugh because the question sounds funny on the surface.

"No one is looking for me, babe. But if they were. This..." I flip my wrist so she can see my watch. "This will generate a signal to locate me no matter where I am. It's a precaution. And there are a lot of other legal ramifications for me wearing it, too, that I can't go into. I'll add my code to your phone, and you can track me, too."

"I don't need to track you, Parker."

"Doesn't matter. You're my girl."

She touches my watch, unsnaps it, slips it off my wrist, and examines it. "But you take it off when we shower."

"I don't have to, and neither do you. Our watches are waterproof. I only take it off to shower out of habit and before bed."

"Parker, this feels extreme." She hands me back my watch, gets off my lap, and sits on the couch opposite my desk. I put my watch on.

"I understand, honey, but it's necessary. My family is important. So are you."

"Not *that* important."

"We're a team, Rain." I stand, walk around my desk, and sit on the front, leaning forward to talk to her. "This is part of that. It's not a big deal."

"Parker. I don't know what to think about this. Should I be afraid? Is someone coming to look for me? Is this like in the movies where someone will try to kidnap me?"

"No, Rain. You have nothing to fear, ever. I'm not asking you to wear a tracker, but you need to know I wear one. That's it." I need to calm her down; she's beginning to spiral, and I'm the cause. This is supposed to be a celebration. I sit next to her on the couch and then pull her onto my lap so she's facing me. "Rain."

"Parker."

"Honey. I hear your concerns. This is nothing to stress over. I promise. You trust me?"

"Yeah."

"Do you love me?"

"Yes."

"Kiss me like you love me." Rain dips her head and kisses me, using her tongue to part my lips. She deepens the kiss, and I take over, licking into her like she's giving me life because she is. Rain is everything I've ever wanted. Everything I've ever needed. I can't see my life without her in it.

I reach my hand beneath her shirt and caress her bare breasts. They fit perfectly in my hands, like they were made for me. I break the kiss, lift her shirt, and put my mouth around one of her breasts.

"Oh, Parker." My name comes out rushed and sultry, and I know she's no longer thinking about our conversation.

I suck the other breast, and Rain strips her shirt over her head, providing me unobstructed access to her body. I flip her on her back on the couch and lick and suck her, alternating between her mouth and breasts. She is so soft, warm, and mine. I can't get enough of her.

"Make love to me, Parker," she pleads. I reach between us and into her pants, sliding my fingers between her folds. She is so ready for me. I stand and slide her pants and underwear off, then I take my pants off, freeing my raging cock. I drop one of her legs off the couch, lower myself, and sink my manhood into my girl. I pump in and out and immediately feel her body respond, sucking me in like she's been waiting for me forever. Her body clenches around my length, and I quicken my pace because I can't hold back this time, and I'll come with my girl.

"Rain, together," I growl, pushing in and out with powerful, steady thrusts until we both come hard, calling to one another.

CHAPTER 18

Fear of the Unknown

Rain

PARKER AND I HAVE SEEN AND TALKED TO EACH OTHER EVERY WEEK since our silent discussion in class in our first year of college. And since the day he asked me to be his woman, the best way to describe us has been inseparable. When he asked me to move into his off-campus home, which turned out to be an Eichler-like house in Atherton, I initially felt hesitant, but our attraction drew me to him.

I've never lived with anyone other than my family. When my dad left, it left the three of us. After that day, so much shifted in our family dynamics. My sister was in sixth grade then, and I was, as usual, head-deep in studying.

Now I'm watching Parker make coffee while I pick at the avocado toast I made.

"What are you staring at?" He doesn't have to turn around to know I'm watching him. He can feel my stare.

"Watching the finest man alive about to fill me with caffeine." When the steam stops, he's done. He turns around, cup in hand, and brings it to me. I look up at him, and he dips his head and gives me a sloppy, mouth-watering kiss. I can tell it's not enough for him when he puts his arm around my back and pulls me to the end of the barstool until my body is flush with his.

"It's good that it's the weekend, so I can fill you with more than caffeine."

"It wasn't a challenge, but I'll accept it." My hands instinctively reach for him, wanting to feel proof of his desire. And when I do, I'm not disappointed.

"Rain, babe. Your coffee is going to get cold."

"Will you heat it back up for me?"

"If that's what you want."

"That's what I want." Parker scoops me up from the chair. I wrap my legs around him while he carries me to the nearest guest room. He lays me down and hovers over me, arms on either side of my head. He dips his head and licks my lips.

"Babe."

"Parker."

"You know I'll give you anything you want." He kisses me again.

"I know, Parker."

"Tell me what you want."

"For you to make sweet love to me. To have your body consume mine. For you to find your release in me. And then, when we can't take it anymore, you can heat up my coffee."

I watch as Parker's eyes go darker. He gets off the bed, removes his sweatpants, and returns to me. He lifts my t-shirt over my head and tosses it across the room. He kisses one breast, sucks, and then switches to the other. He lowers his other hand between us, between my folds, and slides two fingers in me, bringing them in and over my clit, massaging me, making me wetter.

"I need you in me."

He kisses me. "I'll give it all to you, Rain," he whispers. He nudges my leg with his knee, reaches between us, and guides his thick length slowly into me, then pulls out slightly, lubricating himself as he goes until I'm full of him. Slowly, he pumps in and out of me, and I lift my hips to capture each push. I squeeze my walls around him as he goes in and out, and we continue like that until I give into the feeling and begin to fall into the rhythm that I know will take us over the cliff. Parker feels it, too.

"That's it, Rain, feel what I do to you." He continues his pace and covers my lips with his. That's all it takes to send my body over the edge. I want to cry out as he pumps his tongue in me, matching the rhythm of our bodies. He feels so good. It's too much. I feel like I'm floating amongst the stars. He lifts his head and watches me fall.

"Parker. Ahh."

"That's it, Rain. I'm here. Come for me." And I do. And before I completely come down from my high, he increases his pumps, and I know he's chasing his own release, and I know I'll follow...again.

"Come again, Rain. Come with me." We climax together, saying sweet nothings, loving until he collapses on me.

"Rain. I love you."

When we're done, he pulls me over him. We're still connected because he's so hard and thick. I feel his seed sliding out of me onto his body. He holds me like that until he softens and slides out of me. Then he rolls me on my back and kisses me senselessly.

"Hey, you're too much," I tell him, pushing him off me.

He gets up, goes into the restroom, and returns with a warm towel to clean our release from between my legs. He leaves briefly to get rid of the towel, then slides back in bed with me. He pulls me to his side.

"How do you feel?"

"Cherished, because you make me feel that way."

"Because you are, Rain. You are everything to me. I exist to be with you."

I sit up in bed and Parker does the same. Sometimes, when he says things like that, it scares me. Parker is rich and powerful. His family is part of a quiet elite group that runs this city. He doesn't need anything. Everything is at his fingertips, and for him to say I'm everything to him is incomprehensible. He watches me watching him, confused.

"That frightens you." He's not confused; he can read me. He knows me, which makes me more afraid. "Rain, babe. It's okay. Tell me why you're afraid." He pulls me onto his lap so I'm straddling him. "Talk to me. Why are you afraid?"

"Because I don't know what this is. Why do you want me? Why…?"

"Why what, babe?"

"Why me? I'm not from your world, Parker. We would never have met if we had never had a class together. I wouldn't be here in your arms."

"Maybe. Maybe you wouldn't be here right now, but that doesn't mean you would never be in my arms because the gravitational pull between us feels like forever, like it's been there my whole life. Like all these years I've been waiting for *you*. I know we would have met at some point, now or in the future, and we'd be locked like we are in each other's arms. I've never wanted anything, Rain. You're right about that part. I never wanted anything, that is, until I met you. And right now, I have you, and I'm happy. You're all I need. I believe that what we have between us will last forever. So, don't be afraid of me, Rain. Just let me give you everything you need. Let me make love to you. Let me hold you. Let me make coffee. Let me protect you. Let me be your everything. Let me be your life force. Because I'll never do anything to make you afraid of me."

He pulls me into him, and just when I think he will kiss me, he doesn't. His lips hover, his breath mingles with mine in the air, warm with the scent of sex and sweat rising between us.

"Show me you're not afraid of me," he says. I know what he wants—for me to close the distance, take what he's offering, take what's rightfully mine, to give myself to him freely without fear.

I lean forward and lick his lips like he does mine. Then I taste him, press my lips to his, and open my mouth to welcome him. He licks into me, and that's all it takes. At this moment, with a symbolic kiss, I give myself to Parker. I'm his.

CHAPTER 19

Object of His Desire

Rain

I DON'T KNOW WHAT TO EXPECT. THIS WILL BE THE FIRST BIG DINNER with Parker's family—an introduction to the secret San Francisco society that only those in it know about. These are the uber-rich people who protect their own. The people you don't hear about unless they want you to.

"Parker, are you sure I look okay?" I stand before the mirror in the middle of his walk-in closet, which is the size of a small apartment. He comes up behind me, wraps his arms around my waist, and rests his chin on my head. I'm wearing a black midi-length strapless dress with crystals descending the side seams. Parker loves sparkles on me, so he picked out the dress, and I had a seamstress add the adornments.

"I've never seen anything more beautiful. I can't wait to unwrap you—you're the best birthday gift ever." He turns me in his arms and stares at me, reading my face and caressing my lip with his thumb. "I'm glad you haven't put your lipstick on," he says right before covering my mouth with his, giving me a knee-weakening kiss.

I break the kiss. "Parker. We have to go soon." He pulls me closer, and I feel his need to be in me.

"I know, babe. It's hard to focus when you're around. Hold on. I have something for you."

Parker opens the top dresser drawer and removes a flat, square box. He turns to me and opens it, revealing a spectacular diamond necklace.

"This is for you," he says, taking it out of the box and unfastening the clasp. "Turn around, babe." Holding my breath, I turn and face the mirror again, and Parker puts it on my neck. I touch the diamonds that are cool against my skin. My man is so generous.

"Parker. These are beautiful. Thank you," I say, rubbing my fingers along each diamond.

I never had anything this beautiful or extravagant before. When I was younger, my schoolmates would tell me about their parents passing down expensive family jewelry to them. That wasn't my experience. When my dad left, so did my connection to his side of the family. And my mom, well, sometimes I wonder if she even likes me. If I wanted something, I saved to get it for myself.

His hands snake around my waist. "Rain. Look at me." I look up. "This piece is the second in the collection that I plan to give you. The promise ring was the first. Real diamonds take a long time to create and are forged under extreme circumstances. It's nature's most unique and precious gift. Long after everyone is gone, they will remain. That's how I feel about our love—it's something precious that will last forever. Rain, I've been waiting for you my whole life, and one day in class, I finally found you. And now that I have found you, I'll never let you go. I know this is the start of us, so on my birthday, I want to celebrate us—our love. Let the diamonds you wear symbolize the ties that bind us forever. I love you."

I swallow my tears because I'll go into the ugly cry if I don't. "Parker."

"Rain, I can't wait for the day when you're ready to wear my ring."

He tips his head to the side and stands there, holding me, observing me. I watch him watching me, and he turns me in his arms and crashes his lips to mine. I deepen the kiss, giving him everything he needs from me. This time, I don't break the kiss. I let Parker enjoy the moment because I do, too. Then he breaks the kiss, panting against my lips.

"God, babe, you're so addicting. I want you so bad." He gives me a chaste kiss, then steps back, adjusts himself, and smiles at me, trying to bring his heat down. The desire in my man's eyes reflects he's two seconds away from taking me to bed. "We're not staying all night. These parties have less to do with me and more with my mom and friends."

Parker told me before that half the people who come to his birthday party are there to honor the family, and there's no way better to do that than to celebrate their only child. Because I'm Parker's girlfriend, I've become part of their circle and one of the people expected to stand alongside him and his parents.

"So, what do I need to know about these people?"

"I'll introduce you to everyone by name. You don't have to remember anything tonight. They'll be watching how we interact as a family unit. So just be normal, like you are whenever you're with my parents. It'll be fine. I promise."

"You realize it's a given that I will remember everybody."

"Sorry, babe. You're right."

"When you introduce them, it might help to give me more information than just their names. And what if they ask me questions?"

"Be yourself. You'll be fine. The biggest thing we need to do is follow Mom's protocols and make sure we're available for the toast, cake, and my thank you speech. Then we can exit when it's time."

"That sounds doable."

"It'll be a piece of cake."

It doesn't take long to reach Parker's parents' house. Because it is his birthday, we are required to be there before the guests arrive. Once inside the house, we go into the library to stay out of the way of the staff going between rooms making final touches for the party. Parker's mom and dad join us.

"Raven, darling, you look amazing." I don't know what I thought Mrs. Page would do when both of us were in full dress, but hugging me wasn't on the list. Surprisingly, she does, and I can tell by the pressure that it's genuine.

"Thank Mrs. Page. You look amazing, too. Thank you for inviting me."

"Darling, you're always welcome here. You've made my baby so happy."

Parker clears his throat. "Uhm, I'm right here, Mom. Stop fussing over Rain."

"It's ok, Parker. I like your mom."

"See, son. Raven, the guests will be here soon. This will be your first time meeting them, so I'll—."

"I'll introduce her, Mom."

"Honey, let me handle this. I'm sure you told her it's all formalities. Raven can follow my lead."

"I did," he acknowledges.

"Raven, I have a better plan. I know this might be nerve-racking your first time, but I assure you, it'll be fine." I watch the dynamic between Parker and his mom before jumping in.

"Mrs. Page?"

"Yes, darling?"

"Parker may not have explained, but I have perfect recall." Her eyes shift between me and Parker before landing on me again.

"Perfect. That makes my plan even better. I was going to suggest that when I introduce you to someone, I give a little background on the person. Like Mary Blane, her political reach knows no limits."

"Mom." Parker rolls his eyes.

"Parker, honey, it's okay. Raven and I've got this."

That's all she needs to say. Once the guests arrive, I get insight into the inner San Francisco circle. I never knew any of these people existed despite living here all my life. Each time I attend something with Parker, I meet someone new.

"Raven, this is Mrs. and Mr. Corinth. Their generosity to hospitals in the community is unmatched, and their affinity for the finest wines is responsible for the collection at the top of the Wade building on California Street."

"Nice to meet you."

Now I know why Mrs. Page has such a fine collection of wine. Whoever provides for them provides for her. I'm beginning to see how this works. This is how a massive hospital dedicated to providing free access to the underprivileged gets funded by people like these. At events like this, maintaining these connections is how the elites continue to thrive. Access to the best of the best that not even the one percent know about. It's why I've met the person who invested in and controls access to the most expensive bottle of alcohol that the one-percenters consume. Why I've met the chairman of a significant investment advisory firm with over a trillion in assets. Holding major stock or investment in various tangible goods is more valuable than the ability to buy because the person with access has the key to a door. A door they only open for a ridiculous payday they don't need. The people I'm being introduced to don't need anything.

Mrs. Page slips her arm in mine and walks me to another guest. "Mrs. and Mr. Kane, I'd like you to meet Raven, my son's partner."

"Raven, it's so lovely to meet you." Mr. Kane greets me. "You look familiar."

"Mr. Kane is astute in law."

Maybe his money funded my scholarships, I rationalize, because I've never seen him before today.

"I've only worked as an intern so far. You may be thinking of someone else," I tell him.

"Possibly. I rarely forget a face. Perhaps I'm thinking of your father."

I'm unsure how to respond without airing my personal business. "Maybe," I say.

"Well, if you need anything, I'm happy to help. I have connections in several top firms."

"Thank you. I'll keep that in mind." I talk with him and his wife for a minute, and then Mrs. Page and I head in another direction.

"Rain."

Parker scoops me away from his mom and takes me back into the library, where we started the night. He once told me his mom's library was his favorite room in the house because there was so much knowledge, and it was the most peaceful room in the house. Once we're alone, he pulls me into his arms.

"You okay?"

"Yeah, I was just caught off guard by Mr. Kane's question. Maybe it's a case of 'we all look alike.'"

"Don't. He's not like that—none of us are. If he says you look familiar, there's a legitimate reason. He's a brilliant man."

"If you say so. Anyway. Why'd you pull me in here?"

"To check in on you. And…I've been watching you all night, dying to do this." He dips his head and captures my lips with his, pushing in with his tongue and mingling it with mine, and I feel the texture of his tongue juxtaposed with the smoothness of the walls of his mouth. He tastes smoky and sweet, like whatever whiskey he just had. His kiss is so deep I imagine him buried deep inside my body.

"Parker." My whisper against his lips elicits a seductive smile from him, and I feel every promise it offers up. Passion, protection, everything that is Parker.

"Rain, I need you."

"Your mom is going to kill us if we leave now. We haven't had cake." He puts his forehead to mine.

"You're right. Let's go do this, then I'll do you."

We return to the crowd, and a tall, handsome, dark-haired man with green eyes approaches. *Josh.* I've seen him on video call several times, but nothing could prepare me for seeing this stunning man in person. He's dark and mysterious, and I can't take my eyes off him.

"I guess I owe the birthday boy congrats on another year around the sun. And, of course," he locks eyes with me, "I finally get to see this gorgeous woman in the flesh. Raven, it's a pleasure to finally meet you in person." Josh takes my hand, bringing it to his lips, and kisses it.

"Josh Blumberg, it's good to meet you. Parker tells me you live on a plane." He smiles at me, and wow, he's beautiful. The symmetry of his face is perfection. He might be the same height as Parker, but I can't tell because of the thick dark brown curly waves at the top of his head that are slightly gelled to control them. He and Parker both have natural waves, except Parker's are dirty blond. Josh's hair is almost the color of dark chocolate with a hint of blackberry.

"Yeah, when I'm not in class, I work with my dad."

"Man, are you just getting here?" Parker jumps in.

"Dude, don't hassle me. I flew in for this and, of course, to meet Raven. I need to head back to Dallas tonight. I'm working on something with Dad."

"Tell him I said hi."

"Sure thing. Happy birthday, man."

"I'm glad you were able to make it. Parker tells me you're like a brother to him."

"I wish it hadn't taken this long for me to get time with you two. When I return, we should all go to dinner. If you don't know it by now, Raven, you're the love of this guy's life."

"Josh," Parker warns.

"The woman needs to know."

"She knows, but thanks for the PSA." Parker pulls me into him. I nod in confirmation.

"So, where's the cake?" Josh asks.

"You and your sweet tooth. You do remember this is my birthday, right?" Parker teases.

"But I'm the cake lover," Josh counters.

"You don't look like a cake lover." The words slip out before I realize. "I mean, you seem like you watch what you eat."

Josh winks at me. "Thank you. I do, and I work out a lot. I really only get to indulge twice a year. My birthday and this guy's."

"That's because my mom is your supplier in both instances."

"You talk like she's his dealer," I say.

"He acts like she is," Parker adds.

Josh looks at me. "She knows where to get the best cake."

A server comes through with a tray of champagne. Josh grabs one, hands it to me, then gets one for him and Parker. He lifts his glass.

"Cheers," he says. Everyone toasts in unison.

"So, Josh, if you're serious about cake, I think I have a solution."

"Oh, he's serious. This is a real thing. Can't you tell he's anxiously waiting?"

"I'm also a picky eater—so it has to taste a certain way, and the texture has to be perfect."

"For everything?" I ask.

"Just cake."

"Okay. I have a solution. Do you and your dad have an executive assistant?"

"Yeah. She arranges all my travel."

I hand him my phone. "Put her information here." Josh enters the information into my phone. "Cate" is her name. "Got it. You can thank me later."

Parker pulls me into him and kisses my forehead. "What are you up to?"

"I'm helping your best friend. He's working hard, attending school, and even being here on your birthday. All he wants is cake," I say, earning me a smile from Josh.

"If you find my mom, I'm sure she'll break out the cake, knowing you're ready for it, man."

I smile at the two fine men arguing over cake. "There she is." I tip my head in Mrs. Page's direction.

Parker flags his mom over. "Mom, Josh is ready for cake."

Parker's mom wraps her arm around Josh's. "I saw you when you came in. You're just in time for dessert."

"Josh thinks it's his birthday."

"Play nice. You know Parker gets the first piece. And you're never too old for me to put you in a time-out." Parker barks out a laugh when she says that. Josh shakes his head, then looks at me with a "see what I have to go through?" look. It's broody and sexy as hell, and I have no idea how this man is still single.

While we're standing there, Parker's dad, Preston, comes to get his wife, and she gathers the guests so they can celebrate Parker, and he can cut his cake. Parker gives me the first piece, but I feed him from my plate, and Josh gets the next piece. We all raise a glass and toast my man.

The night's formalities have been by far the easiest thing to deal with. The secret society of people that Parker has introduced me to is now etched like an inscription in my mind. A permanent rolodex of people that run the one percent. The hardest part of the night was not giving in to Parker's desires. It's his birthday. In a house full of people honoring his life, family, and legacy, he only asked for one thing. Me.

Back at his Atherton home, Parker tails me like a wolf on the hunt from room to room. A fine as fuck six-foot-four wolf.

"Babe, I know you like that dress, so I'm asking nicely for you to please take it off."

"You'll have to unzip me to get to your gift. Then I can take it off. So set aside that 'you've got five seconds before I pounce you' look for a moment. And don't rip it."

"I'll buy you another one."

I turn around to look at him. "Parker Page, what did I say?"

"Don't rip it." As his reward, I throw my arms around his neck, get on tiptoes, and kiss him. I try to deepen it, but he pulls back. "Babe, don't be a tease. Get out of the dress. Unless you don't want me to worship your body."

Well, when he puts it like that, my sex clenches, and I'm sure it's dripping.

"You're so damn hot. I could never resist you." He turns me around, spanks my butt, then holds his hands there a second feeling me up. "Uhm, you can unzip me anytime now." He unzips me and kisses the bare skin as he exposes it. The dress pools around my feet on the floor. Parker smooths his hands down my neck, over my shoulders, down my back, over my butt. He wraps his hands around my waist and pulls my back to his front. I feel his desire pressed against me. He wraps one arm around my breast, the other sliding between my folds. Parker's mouth is sucking and licking on my neck.

"Babe, you feel so good. So slick. So warm." He squeezes my breast, pinching and pulling with one hand while stroking in and out of my sex with the other.

"Parker. I'm going to…" The words escape me as my body contracts around his hand, as he continues moving his fingers, pulling my orgasm from me until my legs buckle. He's holding me so close. I turn my head to capture his lips, and he's all fire and passion. He turns me to face him. His hand drops to my butt, and he lifts me so my body conforms to his. He deepens the kiss, and I writhe, wanting him in me.

"I love the sounds you make when you come." He carries me to the bed and then gently lays me down. Parker pulls me to the edge and then kneels in front of me. "Now I'm going to have my dessert," he says before pushing me to the bed and lifting my leg over his shoulder. He covers my mound with his mouth and eats me. And when I come, he licks it up like it was dessert.

"You taste like lust and honey."

"Parker."

"It's true, babe. No gift will ever compare to having you on my birthday. You are all I've ever wanted. The object of my desire."

When he says that, tears stream down my face.

"Rain, don't cry." He pulls me up the bed toward the headboard. He hovers over me and places kisses all over my face. He wipes my tears with his thumbs. Then he kisses me on the lips, and I feel his knee nudge my leg aside, and without breaking the kiss, he pushes in me inch by inch until I'm full. It's good. My body immediately responds as he moves in and out in a slow, steady rhythm. He breaks the kiss and watches me as he moves. "I can feel your body squeezing me. Come for me, baby." He pushes in hard and deep, my walls contract, and I fall apart, pulsing around him.

"Ahh, Parker." My breathing hitches in time with my body's natural waves.

"That's it, babe." He pushes harder, faster, milking the last of my orgasm, and as he pushes in and out faster and faster, I feel another breaking through. "You feel amazing. This time, come with me," he tells me, and I do, and we fall into a kaleidoscope of growling, calling each other.

When Parker said he wanted to worship my body for his birthday, he did that and more. Now that I've had Parker, I know no one will ever compare. I don't keep track of the number of orgasms he's pulled out of me. At one point, we were such a mess that we had to get in the shower, where he took me twice before changing the sheets and going at it again. I crave him as much as he craves me, and I doubt I would ever want anyone more than him…ever.

Now it's morning, and I can't get back to sleep as usual. My head is reeling with things that have nothing to do with my man. Parker made me promise to wake him up to get through this. I'm sure he needs sleep, but I know he'll be upset if I don't wake him.

I touch his lip with my finger, then gently replace my finger with my lip, dusting his lips with a kiss. His arms tighten around me, and he pulls me into his chest.

"Babe." His eyes are closed. His voice is gruff. "Is that what you want? Kisses? Take what you want," he tells me.

I kiss him, and he deepens the kiss, swallowing my groans. Then, in a smooth move, he rolls me on my back and looks into my eyes.

"Tell me what you feel."

"I felt a little overwhelmed and lost in thoughts before I kissed you."

"You want to talk about it?" I shake my head. I'm okay as long as I'm with him.

He dips his head and presses his lips to mine. The kiss is soft, almost chaste.

"What about when you heard my voice?"

"It pulled me out of my thoughts. It's like cutting a cord. I could see the other end attached to memories slipping into a void."

"And?"

"And when I kissed you, the other half brought me to you, and I felt light as a feather."

"Now, what do you feel?"

"Now…I just want you in me."

PART 3

"Love is a combination of care, commitment, knowledge, responsibility, respect and trust."

— bell hooks, Communion: The Female Search for Love

CHAPTER 20

Rules of Order

Rain

Seven Years Ago

I'm finding my grounding at Berkeley. The vibe in the East Bay versus the Peninsula is entirely different. My classmates are more chill than I experienced at Stanford and obviously more diverse. Many students here went to school in San Francisco and decided to study close to home like me. It's all good, but being away from Parker is the hardest part.

It's the weekend, and I had to cram most of my studying yesterday after class because I need to attend a fundraiser event for the mayor at the Page's this weekend. Usually, I would have spent Friday at Parker's place in Atherton and ridden in with him today, but he was required to attend a meeting with attorneys and some other folks at his parent's house, which is not uncommon for his family. He wanted me to go with him early and dress there, but I didn't want to. I needed extra time to finish my school project, which is how I spent most of my Saturday morning. I'm putting on the touches before my ride gets here—my ride being Josh Blumberg.

Parker was adamant that I have an escort. I told him that sending a driver was sufficient, but he informed me that it was important to be formally escorted and that I could not show up alone. Apparently, this is a thing. I get it. There are protocols that I need to follow when participating in elite events. Since I'm always with Parker, I didn't realize I needed to be escorted.

My doorbell rings, and I know who it is. I open the door to the second most handsome man in the world.

"Hey, Josh. You look handsome as always."

He's wearing a charcoal grey suit that's almost black and his signature white shirt.

"Hello, beautiful. May I?" He's always so polite.

"Yes," I tell him. He opens his arms to me, and I hug him.

I've come to realize that Josh is a hugger. He's not like that with everyone, though—mainly the Pages, his family, and me. Just those he lets into his inner circle. He's a hard worker, dedicated to his family business, and a deep thinker who gives a great deal of his time back to the community when he's not working or attending college. Next year, he'll finish university with his master's ahead of us since he's not in the legal space.

He releases me. "Is this the coat you're wearing?" He takes my long black dress coat from the hook near the door.

"Yeah." I turn and slip my arms in.

"We may have some traffic heading into the city, but we'll be on time. Ready?"

"Ready."

I hold Josh's arm, and he leads me to the car awaiting us. The driver is holding my door open. Josh helps me in, then goes around the car to get in.

"So, Josh, you're done with your studies next year. Are you excited?"

He blows out a breath. "I'm not sure excited is the word. More relieved than anything."

"It takes a little off your plate, right? I swear I've never seen anyone work as hard as you."

"Thanks for noticing. It does free up my schedule, but that'll likely be filled as I go full-time at the firm."

"You don't really have to work. Neither does your dad, yet he built a multibillion-dollar consulting firm. You work like your life depends on it, and you spend as much time as I do in the community. I don't know how you manage it all. Then you have time to escort me. It's impressive. Whatever woman ends up with you has to be special." He laughs tentatively, and I can tell he's a little embarrassed, if that's possible for someone with his power.

"Well, when you put it like that…do you have a clone?"

Now it's my turn to laugh. "No, but I'll certainly be on the lookout for the perfect person for you. I promise."

"Thanks, but to answer your questions, I like working. It gives me a sense of purpose, and what I do in the community is equally important. I aim to build a private school in every major city's underrepresented community. My schools will be privately funded, and our teachers will have the best curriculum to prepare students for college."

"See, this is what I'm talking about. Who are you?" He barks out a laugh.

"My father's son. Although I'm trying to keep up with Parker."

"Yeah, I see your point. Except Parker's not on a plane every week."

"That's the consulting business for you. Hey, I want to thank you for solving my sweet tooth dilemma." He smiles so wide I can't help but return it.

"I'm glad it worked out. I can't believe you never thought of it. So, what's the arrangement your assistant made for you?"

"Cupcake delivery at home once a month only if I'm here a full week. Our flight crew added the vendor to their catering list, and if I'm out of the country longer than three weeks, the staff where I'm staying have the recipe."

"Wow. You really do like cake."

"A specific kind. So, thank you. You have no idea how happy I am. It's the small things." He holds his hand up to me, and I give him five. "I think I'll start referring to you as my fixer. Next up on the agenda to find me a woman."

I smile at the thought of being Josh's fixer. "I think I might have someone in mind. Hmm. Let me work on it. Like I said, the woman needs to be special."

"Let me know if there's ever anything I can do for you."

For the remainder of the ride, Josh and I discuss how classes are going for me, and he reinforces my decision on the companies I'm considering. Then, he briefs me on what to expect at tonight's function with the mayor.

When we arrive, we go through the standard protocol of being greeted. I hand off my coat, we walk a little further, and we get champagne. We don't immediately see Parker, so Josh introduces me to members of society I haven't previously met.

"Raven, have you met the mayor before?"

"No, why?"

"Okay, she's here. You need to be formally introduced by the family."

"Why?"

"Because, technically, you're considered part of the Page family."

"So, if this were a Blumberg function, you would introduce me."

"That's right. I see Mrs. Page. Let's say hi. She'll know exactly where Parker is."

The more time I spend with this group, the more I learn how bad our manners are in normal society. The respect I receive amongst this group is unheard of. Since the Pages are hosting this event, it puts them in the highest order for the night, and my status equates with theirs because I've been brought into their fold. Wow. It's like *Roberts's Rules of Order* but at a higher level.

When we reach Janis, she hugs me, then Josh. Even that has an order: family first, women before men, then other elites.

"Raven, you look lovely. Preston and Parker are done with their business. He's just in the other room."

"Thanks, I'll go find him."

"Let me introduce you to the mayor first." She takes Josh and me past a few people to a lovely mocha-colored woman wearing a red dress. Several people are speaking with her, but they step away when Janis approaches.

"Mayor Snead, I'd like you to meet Raven Nichols, my son's partner."

"Raven. I've heard so much about you. I hope you're enjoying Berkeley."

"Mayor, it's an honor to meet you. Berkeley is good. I'm learning a lot."

"My colleagues tell me you have your hand in the arts helping our students in the community. Thank you for being so committed to the children."

"It's the least I can do." She smiles and then turns to Josh.

"Josh Blumberg. I'm surprised to see you. How are your parents?"

"Lovely to see you again. My family's good."

We stand there a few moments before Josh leads me away. He introduces me to a few more people before we spot Parker. He's standing talking to a few people, and a woman with long blond hair puts her arm around his waist.

"Parker, come on. It's me you're talking to," she says. He steps aside slightly, but the woman doesn't let him go. He doesn't see me.

Josh must see the same thing because he stops in his tracks and grabs my arm. He turns and stands in front of me.

"Look at me." He surprises me with his clipped tone. I've never heard him issue a command, let alone one to me. He's standing so close that I have to look up. Holding my gaze, I get lost in his eyes. He's so beautiful yet commanding that it's hard to focus. "It's not what you think. That's Tina. She's one of us. We grew up with her. He has no interest in her. However, you need to remember two things: you're the love of his life, and I'll always be honest with you. Let me handle her. Nod if you understand." I nod and bite my lip because I trust Josh. "Good. I got this."

CHAPTER 21

The Only One for Me

Parker

As the days with Rain pass, I fall deeper in love with her. I didn't think loving a woman this much was possible. Before we started dating, I wished Rain could spend the summer vacations with my family and me. Since we've started dating, she's been able to spend the past three summers with us, and it's been wonderful. We timed our trips to accommodate her schedule. She had a three-week break between the time school ended and her summer work schedule began. So, we spent two weeks traveling with my parents and a week alone just loving each other. Everyone she meets loves her just as much as I do. Even my mom has abandoned trying to set me up with other women.

Although this is our first year going to separate schools, Rain and I have found our rhythm. Our schedules are packed between school, dating, community obligations, family, and society events. My family obligations are increasing, so I spent much of my day with my father and our attorneys today. It's also why I'm having Josh escort Rain to the party for Mayor Snead tonight.

After the meeting, guests arrive, and I work my way around the two rooms, talking to people. I greet the mayor, and she tries to get me to come work for the city when I complete my JD. I let her know that's not the path I plan to take.

I chat it up with a few more people, and then I see Tina with a few of her friends heading my way. She's the last person I want to see because she's constantly trying to rekindle something from high school that never was.

"Parker, look at you looking so handsome. I'm surprised your twin, Josh, isn't with you," she says. When we were younger, people used to call Josh my dark-haired twin, although I don't think we look anything alike.

"You do know we're out of high school, and he has a life of his own."

She grabs my arm and tries to hug me. "Parker, come on. It's me you're talking to." I step aside, but she doesn't get the hint, so I remove her hands from me.

I scan the room and see Josh turning around. "If you're looking to reminisce, there's Josh." I lift my chin to him. Then I see Rain. She's wearing a strange look, a mix of confusion and something else. Ignoring Tina, I move past her and go to Rain.

"Rain, honey. You look stunning." I snake my arm around her. She stiffens. I look at Josh, and his eyes shift to Tina. I get it. I dip my head and catch Rain's gaze. She starts to look away, but I don't let her. "Honey, look at me." She does. I whisper, "I love you." Then I kiss her, and she relaxes, and that's all I need.

"Josh, we were just talking about you." Tina's voice pulls me out of the moment.

"Tina, you're always talking about someone. What did I do now?"

"Back in high school—."

"Let me stop you before you take a trip down memory lane. Those days are gone. It's time to move on. Grow up. Now, what did you need with me?"

"Well, who is this?" She directs her attention to Rain.

"Rain, this is Tina Bahler. We dated for exactly four months in high school," I disclose.

Before I can go on, Josh pipes in. "And they were like oil and water. Thank God that's done and buried."

"Tina, this is Rain, the woman who captured my heart." I pull Rain closer.

"Tina. Nice to meet you. Were you the oil or the water?" Rain asks. Josh and I can't help but laugh. Josh winks at Rain.

"Tina, have you spoken with Mrs. Page yet?" Josh inquires.

"Not yet. What's your point?"

"So, in addition to not growing up, you forgot your manners?" Tina rolls her eyes at Josh. Then, without another word, she leaves.

"Sorry, Raven. Sometimes, she needs to be reminded of things," Josh says. "Listen, you two, there's a few more people I need to catch up with. I'll check in with you later. May I?" He looks down at Rain, waiting for her. She nods. Josh hugs her, then whispers something, and he leaves.

"Rain, come with me."

I take Rain to my favorite room, the library. It's quiet and off-limits for this set of guests. I close the door behind us, lean on the desk, and bring Rain to stand between my legs. I stare at her, admiring her beauty. When her eyes meet mine, I smile.

"Hey."

"Hey."

"You okay to talk?" She nods. "With words?" She gives me a small smile.

"Yes."

"Are you upset with me, Rain?"

"I didn't know what was happening when I initially saw Tina hugging you."

"What did you think was happening?"

"Flirting. Interest. I'm not sure."

"What did I do to cause you to doubt my feelings for you?" She looks down then back at me. I know in her mind she's replayed the entire scene.

"Nothing."

"But still there was doubt. I saw it in your eyes the second you entered the room. I tried to reassure you."

"You did, but the initial sting was hard to let go."

"Rain, you're my woman. You're wearing my ring. There's nothing between Tina and me. Even back in high school, I realized it was a mistake. I have no interest in her. She's here because she's an elite. As you can see, Josh and I tolerate her."

"It took a second, but I got it watching her."

"But you didn't answer my question. Are you upset with me?"

"No."

"It stung when you pulled away from me."

"I was caught in the moment."

"I realize that, but it stung all the same. I'm the man who loves you. I trust you. I want you to feel you can trust me. Without that, this will fail. I know you've experienced things in your past that taint your perception, but you can always trust me. Just like I trust Josh with my life—he's the only person besides my family that I trust with you. What can I do to gain your trust? What can I say to help you understand how much you mean to me?"

"I understand."

"Do you Rain? The look on your face broke my soul. I didn't want you to go the rest of the night rethinking us. Not knowing if I'd done something wrong. All I've done is cherish you. You're the only one for me. I love you."

"This is what I needed, a moment to get it out of my system—to hear the words you just spoke."

"Then show me you know that I'm your man."

Rain wraps her arms around me and kisses me. It's gentle at first, and I open my mouth and receive her tongue. I lick into her and pull her closer, deepening the kiss, and I kiss her until she pulls back breathlessly.

"Can you feel me?" she nods. "You're all I've ever wanted, Rain."

"I know."

I rub my thumb along her cheek. This woman has no idea how precious she is to me. "You good with Josh?"

"Of course. He's doing what I suspect you wanted…looking out for me."

"He always will."

CHAPTER 22

Tender Loving Care

Rain

I'M HEADING OUT OF THE GROCERY STORE WITH A FEW ITEMS FOR this weekend when a call comes through from Josh. In the five years I've known Parker, Josh has only called a few times. It's usually time-sensitive regarding an event we need to attend or about the arts curriculum in the private schools. I've been helping him, recommending professors I've worked with in the community. But hooking him up is hard because he's always so busy. So, I have no idea why Parker's best friend is calling me, but it must be important.

"Hi, Josh. Tell me you're not on the prowl for women this weekend. A man like you should have a line out the door."

"No. But thanks, Rae. Listen, I need you to get over here ASAP. Parker's not well."

"What? Where are you? What do you mean not well? Is he hurt?"

"I'm at Parker's. He has a bad cold; he's coughing but won't take anything."

"I talked to him this morning. He seemed fine."

"He's hiding it from you." Oh, my goodness. What is Parker doing?

"Okay, I'm on my way."

My head is reeling knowing Parker is ill and didn't tell me. He's always cared for me when I get sick. I don't understand why he didn't tell me. I pull up to his house and rush in. Parker is lying on the couch. He looks terrible, slumped sideways with an arm over his forehead. I go to his side. He covers his mouth and coughs. It sounds like a dry cough. Good, no congestion. Josh stands in the corner, watching me.

"Parker, honey, how are you feeling?" He tries to talk but starts coughing. "Oh my god, why didn't you tell me?"

He needs hydration. I can make him tea and soup, and give him honey to get rid of that cough.

"Have you eaten anything?" He shakes his head. "Have you tried?" He shakes his head.

"Josh, what did you try to give him?"

"Food."

"Like what kind of food?"

"Soup, but he won't eat it."

"Wait. Do you even know how to cook?"

"No, but—."

"Oh my god, Josh. What the heck?"

"It's canned soup."

"Did you give him any medicine?"

"He won't take it. You know he likes natural remedy stuff." He's right. Parker is conscious about what he puts in his body. I think he only drinks wine because I like it.

"Do me a favor. Strip all the things off Parker's bed. Put all the dirty things away, wash your hands, and then go home. You don't want to get whatever this is."

"I've already been exposed. I've been here two days."

"What the heck, Josh? Oh my god. I wish you'd called me earlier. Get rid of the dirty stuff, and I'll take it from here. I'll call you if I need you. I promise."

Josh disappears, and I go to the kitchen, put on the kettle, and make tea. I take an extra step, crushing Tylenol in it. I set it on the side table near Parker, and then I get a warm wet rag to wash his face. I need him to feel some semblance of care. Not just Josh looking at him and asking him questions. After I wash his face, I hug him and whisper in his ear.

"Hey, Parker. I want to help you get better, but you have to cooperate. Can you do that?" I feel him nod against my neck. "Good. I'm going to try and lift you, but you'll need to help me." He coughs. "It's okay. You don't have to say anything. Just move in the direction I pull."

I pull him, and together, we manage to get him in an upright position. I leave the room briefly to refresh my towel, then return and run it across his face and push his hair back. He's so beautiful even when he is sick.

"Try and drink some of this. It's tea, and I spiked it with Tylenol. Sorry, not sorry." My joke earns me a slow smile, and I know my man will be okay.

He tries his best to drink without coughing. But I have something else to solve that.

"Listen. If you can drink that, I'll take you to the shower and bathe you. Can you handle that?" I get a fast, smile-filled nod. I prop myself on the couch and kneel beside Parker to help him drink his tea. Josh enters the room.

"All done. I put fresh sheets on the bed. How did you get him to do that?"

"You mean drink tea with medicine? I asked." He shakes his head. If he wasn't so damn sexy and sweet, I'd curse him for calling me a day late. But I realize he was doing his best with Parker.

"That's why I called you. You have some superpower over this man I don't understand."

"You said you're done. You can go now. I promise. I got this. Parker will call when he's able."

Josh walks over to me and says, "May I?" I nod, and he bends down and hugs me so tightly. He's probably the only man who can get this close to me when Parker's around. He lifts his chin to Parker.

"You're in good hands, man. Call me," he says, letting himself out. I know Josh is relieved I'm here. He's right. I'm the only one that Parker lets handle him.

I help Parker finish up his tea. I take the cup into the kitchen, go to the bathroom, and turn on the shower. I position the water so it sprays on the marble bench, warming it. Returning to Parker, I help him up.

"Honey, we're going to take a shower. Then I have to get rid of that cough." His eyes question me, but he works with me to guide him off the couch and to the bathroom.

I strip off all my clothes in the bathroom because I know he won't get in that shower unless I do. After removing my clothes, I put on my shower cap and help Parker remove his clothes. He sits on the bench where the water is spraying and sighs. I know the steam is exactly what he needs, but he's still coughing. I lather a washcloth with his favorite liquid soap and wash him with slow, gentle strokes. Then I shampoo his hair. I help him stand to rinse the soap off. I run my fingers across his back down to his butt, then stand before him and rinse down his neck, shoulder, chest, and arms. I reach between us to his rock-hard length and massage it because I need to confirm he is okay, that he will be fine. Not really, but he feels good in my hand. When he's clean, I dry him and myself off, take him naked to bed, and prop up a pillow so he can sit up for a bit to ease the cough. By now, the Tylenol should have kicked in to reduce his pain and eliminate his fever.

I grab a robe and leave the bedroom, knowing Parker is watching. He always does. I go to the kitchen, retrieve a jar of honey from the cupboard, and then return to the bedroom and remove the robe.

"Babe," he calls to me and coughs. "What are you doing?" He's struggling to talk without coughing.

"I'm getting rid of that cough so you can talk to me," I tell him.

Then, with wide eyes, he watches as I get on the bed, straddling him naked. I remove the lid from the jar, insert my fingers, and then spread honey all over my breasts, first one, then the other. I lean in and hold a breast to Parker's mouth. He opens his mouth and sucks and licks my breast, which feels fantastic. My sex clenches, and I know I will come from this alone. When Parker is done with one breast, he repeats the action on the other. I add more honey to my breast and repeat the process until I know my man has what he needs. Then I rise again, pull the sheet back, position his steel at my entrance, and fill myself with him. Slowly, I move, sinking down on him and pulling back in a steady rhythm. I reapply honey to keep his cough at bay, and he sucks until I feel my walls clench around him.

"Ahh...babe. I love you. Come for me," he says. The sound of his voice is beautiful because he's not coughing.

I lean back, place one hand behind me, and rock into my man. He reaches out to hold me, and I ride him until I climax around him.

"Parker." I push through my climax as Parker thrusts his hips forward, driving into me and increasing the pace. "Fill me, Parker. Show me that I'm yours. Claim me."

"Rain," my name comes out in a growl. "Rain. Fuck." He calls again.

I know he's chasing his release, and I feel my walls clench around him again. He takes control pumping in and out and sucking my breast until we come together, calling to each other in love.

~

After Parker and I made love, he fell asleep, and I was happy to see him get some rest. His cough subsided, but he wanted more of me when he woke, and I gave myself freely. This time, he felt strong enough to climb on top of me. We made love twice more before I put him into the shower.

Now I'm making him soup.

"You're going to eat this," I tell him. "And if you're good, you can have me again."

When I bring his meal, he's sitting in a lounge chair in the family room, wrapped in a blanket. He pulls me into his lap.

"Feed me, babe." He opens his mouth. I lift the spoon, and he sips the soup. We sit that way until the bowl is empty. I feel satisfied to see him eating and looking much better than he did when I arrived.

"I think all you needed was sex."

"I did, but I also needed everything else you gave me. Thank you. I couldn't pull myself out of it earlier. Poor Josh."

"Josh didn't know what he was doing."

"He tried. I suppose I just wanted you and your body." He pulls me into him and hugs me. "And your breast, oh my god, babe, that honey did the trick. Can I do that again before we go to bed?"

"Yeah, Parker. I'll soak my breasts in honey so you can suck them." I roll my eyes.

"That's my girl," he says, squeezing my boobs.

"Let me put this away before you get all handsy and mouthy with me again." I put the dish away and return with water. This time, when I sit, I straddle my man.

"Babe, are you sitting like that because you want to talk about something?"

"I do. Why?"

"Because honestly, babe, I still don't feel that well and just want to suck your boobs, make love all night, and do it all over again." He lifts my shirt, latches his mouth onto one of my breasts, and starts sucking. Parker is insatiable.

"Well, I'm going to say what I have to say anyway," I tell him. He continues sucking and reaches his hand between us into my sex and rubs. I try to concentrate on what I have to say. "Parker. I just wanted to remind you…ahhh. That feels good. Let me know when you don't feel well. I'll always take care of you." I don't get to say anything else. With his hand between my legs, Parker makes me come. He pulls his fingers out and sucks them dry. That's the only time he breaks from sucking my breasts. Then he flips me on my back, nudges my legs open, frees his shaft from his boxers, and pushes into me. And we make love on the lounger. It's good and loving, and my boobs are sore from all the attention.

"I love you so much, Rain."

"I love you too, Parker."

PART 4

"Love recognizes no barriers. It jumps hurdles, leaps fences, penetrates walls to arrive at its destination full of hope."

— Maya Angelou

CHAPTER 23

The Days with Rain

Parker

Five Years Ago

IT'S BEEN FIVE YEARS SINCE I CEMENTED MY CONNECTION TO THE woman who has become half of me by making her my girlfriend. The days with Rain make me feel alive, and I feel loved.

Rain and I plan to spend some time at the Transamerica building, where we had our first date. Not being at the same school as Rain has been brutal, but we're in our final year and will soon start our careers. Although my parents wanted me to take over their foundation, they seemed excited about me working with the law firm once I get my degree and pass the bar.

Although Rain said she'd be okay to drive to my place, I insisted on picking her up. She looks lovely in a slip dress topped with a sweater and boots. I dip my head and capture her lips when I enter her apartment. Kissing her after not seeing her in weeks is like spring after months of rain. Refreshing and new.

"Rain. You're so beautiful, babe. When you're in my arms, I can't think of anything else. I feel whole with you."

"Thank you. You're the best boyfriend. I missed you."

"I mean it, babe, you're everything to me." I push her curls over her shoulder and hold her face in my hands. Her eyes are smiling as they trace my face. We have a habit of reading each other's expressions even after all these years. And right now, Rain looks uncertain about something. She's smiling, but it doesn't quite reach her eyes.

"I know, Parker. You show me all the time. You're my world, too. Now, what have you planned for today? I know you're up to something."

"Babe, how are you feeling?"

"I'm fine. Do I look different than this morning on video?"

I pull her to me, hold her, and allow the scent of jasmine and honey to embrace me. Something is wrong with my girl, and I need her to talk to me. Leaning my chin on her head, I put all my energy into holding her so she knows I'm here for her.

"Babe, you're stunning. There's a world of women that can never compete with your beauty. But to answer your question, we're going to your favorite spot today."

My response seems to both settle and satisfy Rain. She grabs her purse, and we head to the car. Once inside, we head to the city.

"I think you're more sentimental than me," she tells me. We're standing at the base outside the pyramid-shaped building.

"I'm sure you're right. But in my defense, I'm only that way with you," I say, leading her to the small park. It's the weekend, and there aren't many people in the downtown high-rise areas. I sit on the bench and bring Rain to my lap, wrapping one arm around her waist. With my other hand, I reach into my pocket and pull something out for her. "Rain, I got you something," I say, handing the box to her.

"What are you doing?"

"Giving my girl a gift."

"You always give me things."

"Well, this is not an orgasm." She nudges me with her shoulder.

"That's not what I meant. You're generous. Always buying me things. You have me spoiled."

"I appreciate you for being my world. This is part of my promise to you. A celebration of us. Open it." I nod to the box in her hand.

Rain opens the round box and reveals a diamond bracelet.

"Parker, this is…wow…this is beautiful. Help me," she says, holding out her wrist. I take the bracelet, open the clasp, and close it around her wrist.

"It pales in comparison to you." Rain dips her head and kisses me, and she's warm and sweet, and mine. I break the kiss before we go too far.

"I remember you told me diamonds last forever, as will our love—that one day, the final piece of this collection will be on my finger."

"That's right, Rain. I love you."

"I love you too. Can we sit awhile?"

"Of course, babe."

We do. We sit, and Rain talks about her family and her attempts to build stronger relationships with them. I offer to help, but she still insists she can handle it alone, and I need to respect that. She tells me about her classes, the teachers, and the most demanding projects. We talk about my classes, and I catch her up on the latest with my family. She holds me around my neck during our conversation, weaving her fingers in and out of my hair. It's one of her favorite things to do; she can't help it, but it makes me hard, and I really want to take my woman home and make love to her.

"Rain, babe, are you ready to go eat?" I whisper into her neck, and she strokes my head.

"You booked us at the Italian place?"

"Yeah, your favorite. I figured you wouldn't mind lunch there."

"Can we order it to go?"

I untangle myself from Rain to see her face. She fakes a smile to mask whatever is happening inside her head. After seven years with Rain, I know her well enough to know something's bothering her. "Honey. What's going on? Is it your family?"

"I don't know. I feel blah."

"Give me a second." I pull out my phone and message our family concierge to have them handle getting our meal. "Okay, Rain. Our lunch will be brought to us. I'm taking you back home with me." I escort her back to the car. She knows I won't press her to talk if she doesn't want to.

The thirty-mile drive back to Atherton is uneventful. Rain rests her head on the headrest while I hold her hand. Traffic is light heading down the freeway this time of day, so we arrive home in record time.

"You want me to carry you in? You look relaxed."

"Don't be ridiculous. I can walk." And she does.

"Lunch should be here soon." I pour us both a glass of sparkling water. Rain makes herself comfortable in the living room, and I sit next to her and pull her on my lap. "Kiss me, babe." My request is answered with a passionate kiss. I know she loves kissing and everything we do that's affectionate—the touching, making out, the loving. We have a hard time not being together in the way that couples are.

She stands and positions herself to face me, then sits back down, straddling me. When we first started dating, and she would sit this way, I thought she was positioning herself for me. I quickly learned Rain likes to look at me and take me in. She wants to face me while exploring my body. It is strange because I know she has every inch of my body etched like glass in her memory, but she still studies me like she missed something. Our morning routine to help her quiet her mind involves her purposefully tracing my features with her eyes or fingers, depending on whether we're within reach of each other. She's doing that now—calming herself.

"Make love to me, Parker." It's a request I'll never deny her. I'd fly around the globe to get to her and answer the call to make love.

"Before lunch or after lunch?"

"Now."

I text the concierge that we'll be indisposed and to let herself in to make the delivery. Then I stand, bringing Rain in my arms, and carry her to bed, where we make love until she's spent.

CHAPTER 24

The Parent Trap

Rain

I WAS UNDER THE WEATHER WHEN PARKER CAME TO PICK ME UP THE other day. He's so wonderful. He tried everything in his power to make me feel more like myself. I was content to be with him and make love all day. I think the constant drag of being separated, the stress of school, and the strain of my family situation are getting to me. I'm in my final year of law school and need to buckle down and focus, but it's all weighing heavily, and I feel like I'm drowning.

Adding to my pressure, Mrs. Page has been discussing plans for our future, like birthdays, family trips, charity events, awards dinners, and so on. And I'm convinced she's trying to prime me to be her daughter-in-law. Initially, I thought she'd be one of those women who thinks women should cater to the needs of men. Her actions do not reflect that, and she's okay with the fact that I will be an attorney. Thrilled, actually. Lately, her requests for me to attend functions with her have been more frequent. She means well. However, her need to host events that involve Parker and me showing up as a couple, albeit lovely, seems more self-serving. She wants us married. That freaks me out because I'm nowhere near ready for that. I'm too young. I have a life and a career to forge.

On the other side of the Bay, there's my mom. Ever since my father left, my mom has been acting strange. She's like a clam when it comes to discussing my dad or Bill. Strangely, my dad's side of the bed wasn't even cold before she started dating Bill. By then, I was nine. That's a long time to call someone your boyfriend. I have no idea what the story is there. I can think of several reasons why they aren't married. Either one or both are legally married to someone else or are not committed to each other as they pretend. I don't know whether my mom and dad ever divorced. My gut tells me Bill had something to do with my parents' breakup. Maybe Dad was cheating, and she decided to give him a taste of his own medicine. Or perhaps Bill was a rebound fuck that turned into something more. Whatever the situation, she's been an absentee mom, like when I asked her to take me to and from baseball practice or debate competitions. She never attended. Most times I took public transportation to get there. When I was trying to decide on colleges, I did that alone. Thank goodness my academic achievements allowed me to obtain a scholarship to pay for college. I doubt I would have received financial support from her. My mom is her usual non-committal self. She thinks she can attend my graduation if Bill, her software developer boyfriend, is in town. Whatever.

My sister, Robin, takes after my mom and is still determining if she can break away from Seattle to attend my graduation. Sometimes, I wish I had a typical family. Not like the Pages, but like an average family without a trillion dollars. A family that does things together without drama. People that at least act like they love each other.

The good news is I have Parker in my life. I'm not sure what happened the other night, but I felt awful, yet Parker was so good at taking care of me. He's always that way—someone I can count on.

"Rain. How are you doing today? You have me worried. You didn't look so good yesterday."

"I'm fine, Parker."

"Are you sure, honey? Let's schedule an appointment to get you checked out. Or I can have Dr. Wilton come by to see you."

"Parker, we don't need to do all that. I'll be fine. We only have a short time together before we head into our final quarter. Let's make the most of it," I tell Parker so we can get on with our day.

"Rain, if anything happened to you, I don't know what I'd do."

"What can I do to satisfy you?"

Parker walks over and sits next to me on the couch. He pulls me onto his lap so that I'm sitting astride. He wraps his arms around my waist and pulls me into him. He hugs me like I might disappear if he lets go. Dipping my head into his neck, I inhale his essence and embrace the moment, allowing him to fill himself with whatever he's seeking from our clinging bodies. He places his hands on my head and strokes down my hair. His hands roam over my shoulders and back until he reaches my hips. He cradles my butt and pulls me closer to him. Our bodies are so close that I feel our hearts working to synchronize themselves. When they finally sync, Parker touches my face, pulling it to his, and kisses me deeply. I'm lost in the magnitude of the kiss, and I can feel forever in his arms. His love is so consuming that I can't breathe.

Parker breaks the kiss. His breath is labored, and for the first time in five years, I see unshed tears in his eyes. The depth of his feelings for me is overwhelming. I'm unsure if I can handle the depth of his love.

"Parker. I'm fine."

"I hear you, babe. I can't lose you. Please get checked out for me."

"Okay. Monday. I promise."

I feel Parker's chest rise and fall with a sigh of relief. The level of attachment he has for me is scary at times. I've never had anyone love me like he does. At least I haven't felt love like this since before my father left. There was a time when I felt my father would do anything for me until he didn't. Until he didn't turn around when I called his name. That simple fact haunts my dreams. I realized a few years ago that I'd recall that memory when I tried to make deeper connections with friends. It stopped me in my tracks to know that someone else could have the power to do that to me. It's the reason I don't have many friends. I never want to feel that again. In order to not feel that, I can't give unconditionally ever again.

"Now, are we going to stay in all day or go out?" I ask.

"Your choice."

"We should go out for dinner. I ruined it yesterday."

"Rain, babe, don't say that. You didn't ruin anything. We had a change of plans and spent a nice evening together. Let's do this. Dinner for two coming up."

Parker was true to his word. We strolled around the downtown area and did some shopping before dinner. After dinner, Parker took me to my apartment and made love to me twice. He left early this morning for his commute. And like I promised, I made an appointment to see the doctor following class.

CHAPTER 25

Best Laid Plans

Parker

EVEN THOUGH I TRY TO EXPRESS MY FEELINGS TO RAIN, SHE HAS NO idea how deep they run. Since the day I met her, I couldn't imagine living another minute without her. After five years of dating, that's only grown stronger and deeper, and I can't wait to make her my wife because I know that Rain is the only woman for me. One day, she will be mine. And now, because she's been under the weather, I need to check in on her before I head to my next class. I text her.

Me: Babe, checking in. How are you feeling?

Rain: Great. Heading to class. My doctor's appointment is after class.

Me: OK, keep me posted. You are my everything.

Rain: I will.

My day is filled with the typical pressures of learning in an academic environment where everyone is brilliant. I'm happy to have already secured a job at one of the firms for which I'd previously interned. They're major players in the entertainment and media space with global offices. I would like to start my own firm, but I want to learn the inner workings before venturing out on my own. I know my family has the resources for me to do whatever I want, but I plan to prove I can master this on my own. Speaking of which, I owe my mom a call.

"Parker, honey. I'm glad you're thinking about your mom."

"You asked me to call."

"I did. We need to discuss graduation plans. I'm planning to host a party for you. And, of course, I want to ensure Raven is there."

"She might have something happening with her own family."

"Honey, I'm sure we can work around that. I'll be hosting it at the house. Please email me the list of people you want to invite. When do you start your new job?"

"In January. I have some time off after I take the bar."

"Will you be traveling? I want to make sure I know what events you can attend. Your father and I would like to spend some time with you before you head off into your career. Also, what about Raven? When are you two settling down?"

"Mom, which question do you want me to answer first?"

"I'm sorry, son. This is such an exciting time for you."

"I realize that. I appreciate your interest."

"Okay, so let's start with graduation and your list. Can you send that this week?"

"Sure, Mom. I'll send that by tomorrow. As for Rain's plans, I'll have to discuss it with her and get back to you."

"Things are okay between you two, right?"

"Yes. I don't want to presume anything regarding her plans."

"That's understandable."

I hear the deflation in her voice. My mom wants Rain to attend the graduation party and all her events. I love that Mom has taken a liking to Rain, but at times, she's pushing for this relationship to move forward faster than I'm ready. However, I know with certainty that I'll ask Rain to marry me one day. I need to wait for the right time. To allow Rain the opportunity to explore our relationship fully beyond the pressure of learning, exams, and stolen moments between quarters. To get stability in our lives to see if we can sustain a new normal where we both work to sustain…us.

"Mom, I appreciate everything you're doing. I promise to answer all your questions."

"I love you, Parker."

"I love you too, Mom."

CHAPTER 26

The Results Are In

Rain

It's been almost a week since I last saw Parker, but we talk via video every morning and sometimes in the evening. He told me his mom is hosting a graduation party for him. I informed him I was planning to have dinner with my mom, although I don't know whether it's even something she'll agree to. I know in her own way she loves me. However, I think she has other issues preventing her from fully being the mom she should be. I always sense that she's avoiding me, that something lies beneath the surface she's not revealing.

Regardless of what she has going on, I'll press the issue about doing something for graduation. It's not like I will ever graduate with a JD again. I think the first step is to call my sister.

"Hi Rae, what's going on? Did I miss something?"

"Not this time, but I am calling to let you know I'll be graduating on the sixteenth of June if you want to watch me walk across the stage."

"Yeah, I'll be in Houston for a conference, but I can see if someone can fill in for me."

"Don't rearrange your schedule. I'll see if any other student's parents are videoing. I'll get a copy and put it online."

"Sorry, you know, life gets in the way sometimes."

"Sure. How are things with you? Are you glad you made the move?

You've been there long enough to be settled."

"It feels good. Things are great. I met a guy."

"That sounds promising."

"Yeah, he's good to me."

"Well, I hope to meet him one day. Listen, I don't want to hold you up. I'll let you go."

"Okay. Let's catch up in a few weeks."

"Sure," I tell her, knowing that if I don't initiate the call, it won't happen. The same seems true for my relationship with my mom. I have to initiate. I have only bad examples of parenting. If it weren't for Janis and Preston, I wouldn't know what caring for a child looks like. They treat me as if I'm part of the family when I'm around them. Most times, I don't feel worthy because I'm not theirs. It's not their responsibility to care for me the way they do. Ugh. I need to focus and not get lost in thought.

My phone rings. I recognize the doctor's number and pick it up. During my initial appointment, she performed a basic exam and gave me a referral for lab work. I did that earlier this week.

"Hi, this is Raven."

"Hi, Raven. This is Dr. Nars. Is now a good time to talk?"

"Yes. Now is good."

"I'd like to go over your test results. You mentioned that you were having anxiety as a result of a flood of memories, and that was making you feel more ill than in previous bouts. Your blood pressure readings are normal. I'm emailing you some techniques to help you refocus and keep your brain from spiraling."

"That's good to know. But I felt so ill, not just black-out ill."

"About that. Raven, the test results show that you're pregnant."

My mind registers her words in slow motion. "I'm what?"

"You are pregnant."

"I thought I was late because of stress from school and not eating right."

"Sometimes that can be the case, but that's not your situation. Let's talk about the next steps," she says, reviewing a list of things I need to consider.

My brain hears her words but is thinking about my life, my upcoming career as an attorney, and all the things that will be impacted by the news I just received. Parker.

Oh my god, what will Parker think? That I trapped him. That I'm trying to get his money. He's not like that, but we're both about to begin our careers. I don't know how to be a parent. I don't want to be the distant mom that my mom was when I was young. I don't want a husband who walks out on me and leaves me to fend for myself.

"Raven? So, what do you think?"

"Uh, I'm sorry. Can you repeat the question?"

"Did you want to schedule time to come in?"

"Uh, sure."

CHAPTER 27

Come Inside Me

Parker

It's been a few weeks since I've been with Rain. Since we both are coming down to the wire in our final semester, I'm trying to give her breathing room and not dominate her life. She's been feeling super stressed lately, but the doctor provided her with techniques that we practice together when she tells me she's having an attack. She mentioned on the call yesterday they seem to be coming more frequently. She is a bit more standoffish than normal. I don't know what that's about, but she agreed to spend the weekend with me to have time together. I compromised and let her drive here after she wouldn't let me pick her up or send a car for her. She is so stubborn sometimes that it makes me want her even more.

When she arrives, she rings the bell instead of using her key, which is odd.

"Babe, did you lose your key?" I wrap my arms around her and bring her into the house.

"No, just didn't want to barge in," she says, but I have no idea why. Nothing of mine is off-limits to her.

I help her out of her sweater, put her things away, and then head to the kitchen. When she's settled at the counter, I plate our meal.

"You always have my favorite."

"Why wouldn't I?"

"It's either pasta or sardines. I don't know why, but…."

"I know…if you were on an island and could only have one meal, it would be one of those."

"Yeah. It's a toss-up."

"You want something to drink?"

"Sparkling water. No wine with your pasta."

"No."

I get us both sparkling water and sit next to her. I want to skip the part where I catch up and talk, but I don't. It's good to have her here with me. I crave these moments with her and want to have her with me all the time. Thoughts of Rain consume me so much that sometimes I think I can't breathe until I hear from her.

"Rain, babe…I'm forewarning you that I really need you tonight. Being away from you is hard. I miss you."

"I miss you too, Parker. I know it's been hard the past year and a half with us being in separate schools. But we'll pull through this. We have to. On the other side of this is a new life for us. One where we swap the pressures of school for the reality of work and building our careers, our lives."

"That's right, Rain. We'll be starting a new chapter in our lives. I'm excited about the future. How are you feeling about your classes?"

"Good. It's a lot to remember, but my brain seems to hold everything. The worst part is holding information on past events unrelated to me. Sometimes it's triggering."

"What's triggering them?"

"Watching the news, hearing people talk about similar events. Stuff like that. But then I use the exercises, and it forces me to focus."

"It seems to help when you call me and we talk through it."

"Yeah, you've helped me through some of the worst episodes."

"I'm here for you, babe. Are you done with that?" I stand and take her empty plate. "Did you want anything else? Dessert?"

"No. Just for you to come inside me."

"I thought you'd never ask." I take our plates and put them in the dishwasher. Rain grabs a towel, wipes the counter, and puts the leftover food in the refrigerator. When she's done, I grab two water bottles and place them on the counter.

"Come here," I tell her, and when she's close enough, I grab her by the waist and pull her to me. "You're my world." I dip my head and kiss her, taking my time to savor everything that is her. My body craves her like a life-saving drug. Her hands move up my chest, which signals me to break the kiss so she can breathe. It's crazy how we know each other so well.

"I'll hold these," she says, picking up the bottles. "And you can carry me to bed. How about that?"

"I'd say you have yourself a deal."

I lift Rain so she's straddling my waist and carry her to the bedroom. Once there, I gently sit her on the bed, take the bottles, and put them on the nightstand.

"Let me unwrap you, babe," I ask her, and she stands before me. I lift her shirt over her head and toss it on the chair. Next, I unzip her jeans and slide them over her hips and down her legs. I kneel at her feet and help her step out of the pant legs one by one. Reaching up, I pull her silk underwear down. She steps out of them. Still kneeling, I bring her body close to my face, kissing her thigh and her sex. I stand, kissing my way up her body. I reach behind her and unhook her bra. I lower my mouth to her chest and caress her nipples with my tongue and alternate sucking each. Finally, I make my way up her neck, inhaling her essence. Her breaths come hard and hurried.

"Kiss me, Parker."

She knows I'm slowly working my way to her mouth, but my girl wants what she wants, so I cover her mouth with mine and part her lips with my tongue, and the sensation of tasting her is like…Heaven on earth. I pull her body so that it molds with the hard truth between us. I reach between her legs to test her readiness, and my girl's body is crying me a river.

"Rain, I'm going to slide in so easy," I say, gently guiding her to the bed and laying her down. I nudge her leg open with my knee and position my straining shaft to where her body is calling me. I push, basking in the first feel of her slickness as I glide in. I pull out and push in again, deeper, harder, in and out over and over until I can feel Rain's body contract around me. I keep a steady rhythm in and out until Rain comes on me, calling my name.

"Oh, god, Parker." She looks so beautiful when she comes. Her eyes flutter closed, her cheeks turn a shade darker, her mouth falls open, and I want to see her come again. I continue moving in and out of her body until I feel the beginnings of my release brewing.

"Babe," I grunt in her ear. "One more time," I say, feeling her walls contract around my length. And it's all I need to find my release as she comes hard around me, and I pump every drop of me into her.

"Rain. I love you."

Our breaths are labored, rushed. I collapse on her and then roll over, bringing her with me. And we lay like that with me holding the only woman I want in my arms.

CHAPTER 28

Soulmate

Rain

I HAVEN'T TOLD PARKER ABOUT THE BABY YET. MAINLY BECAUSE I don't know what I want to do. If there is one person's baby I'd have, it would be Parker's. Like it or not, he's my soulmate—the one person who feels like the other half of me. I don't know what this means for my future. I doubt he'd suggest that I raise it alone, and Parker's too much of a family guy to want to get rid of it. I don't know what this means for us. Will it change how he feels about me? I don't know. The only way to find out is when I tell him, which I plan to do this weekend.

CHAPTER 29

Be My Wife

Parker

THE LAST TIME I SAW RAIN, I KNEW ONE THING FOR SURE. I WANT HER to be my wife. I want to spend the rest of my life with Rain and wake up every day with her in my arms. I don't want to wait until we're much older, more established, or any other excuse people come up with to stay apart and delay a future together. I want Rain for life.

Knowing how she is about imprinting information, I need to ease into this with her and discuss the next steps in our relationship. The last thing I want to do is scare her away by surprising her with something she's not ready to do. Getting her input is essential. The way that she reacted to me giving her a promise ring is an indication of how she'll handle me asking her to marry me. I plan to talk with her this weekend.

CHAPTER 30

Something's Wrong

Rain

Tomorrow is Friday, and I get to see Parker. I don't have class since we took our test this morning. We plan to meet early. I'm nervous about the news but committed to doing this. I thought about it, and no matter what happens, I'll get through this. This baby and I will get through this. I power walk across the campus so I can make my way home. Parker hates it when I walk back home. He doesn't like that some areas of Berkeley are more volatile than others, but I'm in a good location, so I don't worry about that. If he had it his way, he'd have a driver take me to and from school, which is unnecessary. Besides, the sun is shining. It's a beautiful day, perfect for walking.

On my way, I stop at the store to get more sardines. I don't have cravings, so I follow the doctor's orders, do my normal stuff, and avoid the foods we discussed. I also grab some rice cakes for Parker. I don't know why he likes them so much. He tries to eat them as a healthier alternative to satisfy his craving for plain potato chips. It's not the same, but maybe it's about the crunch. I grab two bags and head home.

I'm about a block from home when my phone rings. It's Parker. My hands are full. I can't see him on video.

"Hey, Parker. I just grabbed you some treats."

"Oh yeah, what did you get me? Don't say sardines."

"No. Rice cakes."

"They'll be the best ones I ever ate because you bought them for me," he says, causing me to smile.

"Did you call to see what I was up to? You know I'll see you tomorrow," I tell him, then I almost fall, tripping over the uneven pavement.

"Yeah, I was calling to..."

"Shoot."

"Babe, what's going on?"

"Lost my balance."

"What? Did you fall?"

"Almost. I'm okay but just a little off balance. Parker, let me call you back when I get in the house. That weirded me out a little."

"I was calling to say I'm on my way. I'm almost there. I'll see you soon."

"Okay," I tell him, rushing him off the phone. I head upstairs. Now that I think about it, I don't feel so good. I don't know if I want to throw up or what. I make quick work of putting the snacks and my school stuff away. I feel like I have gas, and I have to poop. I'm headed to the bathroom when I hear the door. It's Parker, and I go to him.

"Wow, Parker. That was fast. I didn't expect to see you until tomorrow."

"Babe, what's happening?" he asks when he sees me holding my stomach.

"I don't feel so good," I tell him, and then I feel liquid coming down my legs, soaking through my clothes.

"Rain. You're menstruating." When he says that, I break out into tears. He holds me.

"No, Parker. Something's wrong. I'm pregnant," I say before everything turns black.

CHAPTER 31

My Beautiful Rain

Parker

PREGNANT. MY BEAUTIFUL RAIN, THE LOVE OF MY LIFE, IS PREGNANT with my child—evidence of our love. The feeling of bliss knowing Rain is having our baby is brief because she collapses in my arms.

"Call Dr. Wilton," I bark the command into my phone. When I reach Dr. Wilton, I tell him that Rain has fainted in my arms and that she appears to be hemorrhaging. I ask him to meet us at the local hospital. My mind is moving at warp speed. I collect Rain in my arms, take her to my car, and rush to the emergency room.

When we arrive, the staff is waiting for Rain. Everyone moves efficiently, but my mind is reeling, and it feels like things are moving in slow motion. My heart stops when the doctor confirms my worst suspicion.

"I'm sorry, Mr. Page. Miss Nichols experienced a spontaneous abortion."

The room is spinning. I place my hand on the wall to keep my balance. I can't breathe. Oh my god. Rain. Our baby.

Helpless, I watch as the medical team takes all the necessary vitals and prepares her for a procedure. They brief me on everything before they put her under. Then they wheel my beautiful woman away. I'm told the procedure will not be lengthy. However, I can't stop pacing, and I have the urge to go to Rain and hold her hand through the process. A kaleidoscope of emotions washes over me, and I'm unable to distinguish what I feel: scared, confused, grieving, hurt.

Finally, the love of my life is out of surgery and is moved into the recovery room. I sit beside Rain, holding her hand and waiting for her to wake. I've never experienced this before. I don't know how to do this or what to think. How do I hide the pain I feel? What do I say when she wakes up? Rain is my heart, my life. My everything.

It takes Rain a while to get her bearings and figure out that she's in the hospital. The doctor is aware of her memory situation, so I asked that we have this conversation together with her so I know everything she hears because, on the reverse side of this, I need to help her through it. The doctor looks at all her readings, and she's stable now.

"Parker." My name is the first and only word that escapes her lips. "Did I faint?"

"You did, honey. I'm here."

"I wanted to tell you…."

"You don't need to say anything. I love you, Rain."

The doctor moves closer to the bed, we lock eyes, and I nod.

"Ms. Nichols. I want to cover a few things with you. Is that okay?" She looks at me, I nod, and she continues looking at me when she responds.

"Yes."

Dr. Wilton explains the D&C procedure she underwent. Rain listens but doesn't say a word. Understandably, she's devastated. We both are. Wrapping my arms around her, I hold her tight as we process our loss. Her breathing is uneven, her shoulders shake, and hot tears stream down her face onto me.

"Give us some time," I tell the doctor.

When the doctor leaves, I continue holding Rain and don't leave her side. As she cries, I finally allow my emotions to take over and tears to fall from my eyes. They fall for Rain, for our baby, for our pain. I love her so much that my heart hurts seeing her this way. Deep down, I know we will get through this. Somehow.

I pull her tighter, and we sit like that until we're all cried out. The next day, when she's discharged, I take my beautiful Rain home.

CHAPTER 32

A Part of Us

Parker

Yesterday, I brought Rain home from the hospital. Naturally, she's shocked by what transpired in the past twenty-four hours. I'm also trying to wrap my head around everything. Since the day I met Rain, I felt an immediate connection to her. As time passed, our bond grew stronger, which developed into passion and, ultimately, love. I love Rain. She's the only woman I gave my seed to because I knew she was the one I wanted to build a life with. Now, my heart is hurting for her, for us, for our baby, for the only two things I've ever desired.

"Rain. Don't try and get up, babe. What are you trying to get?"

"I'm just going to take a shower."

"I got you, babe. Give me a minute to get the temperature right." I tell her. I go to the shower and turn it on. I ensure all her products are accessible before returning to the bed to collect her.

Putting my knee on the bed, I bend and slide my hand underneath Rain. I pick her up and take her to the shower. I set her feet on the floor, help her out of her things, strip my clothes off, and shower with her. Looking down at Rain, I watch as she places a hand over her stomach, and my heart breaks. I put my hand over hers. Tears roll down her cheeks, and I pull her into me and hug her tight as water washes over us. I wonder what she thinks about the life we created. There are so many things to talk about, but it's not the right time.

"Rain, I got you. We'll get through this." Somehow.

"I was going to tell you."

"I know."

"It was too late. I wasn't strong enough."

"Honey, you are everything you need to be—loved. I'm here," I say, not knowing what to tell her.

We didn't get to discuss what happened when she first learned she was pregnant. There was no discussion on why she didn't tell me right away. Rain likes to be physically near me when we talk, but I wish I had known about our child sooner. I would have never left her side. Maybe I could have done something different to help her...perhaps the doctor could have seen this coming. Now I know what Rain feels like when her mind is spinning out of control. I need to stop and be strong for her.

I continue holding her as the warmth of the water streams down our bodies. Breathe. I lift her head from my chest, grab a washcloth, soap it up, and begin bathing my woman because I know she likes it. My hands wash down her neck, shoulders, and breasts and reach her stomach. I use soft, gentle sweeps of my hand. I reach between her legs, and she hesitates for a second.

I dip my head to kiss her lightly. "I got you, babe. It's okay." She nods, and I wash her there, turn her around, and wash her back. When I'm done, I rinse her off and clean myself, and then I stand there and hug her for a minute.

"I think I'm clean now." She lets out a hint of a laugh, and I know my girl is fighting her way back to me.

I hold my hand out to her and step out of the shower. I dry us and put her in a robe before giving her some space to do whatever she needs to. When she comes out, I hold my hand to her, and she sits on my knee and puts her arm around my neck.

"You smell lovely. Do you need me to lotion you, babe?"

"No, I did it already."

I rub my hand up and down her back, and Rain hugs me tighter. "Do you want to stay in the bedroom, babe, or come with me?"

"I'll hang with you. I don't feel any pain, Parker."

I stand, bringing her to her feet. "Okay, just tell me what you need." She takes my hand. I walk with her to the family room, and she sits on the couch.

"Since we got up a little later than usual...maybe some brunch."

I dip my head and kiss her. "I'm on it."

I go to the kitchen and make something for us. Since my house is open plan, I watch from where I am. She's reading something on her phone. She glances my way every few moments, and I wink at her. This is hard; we're both hurting in our own ways, and I want to hold her, but I also don't want to smother her. When I'm done preparing our meal, I bring it out to her.

"Do you want to sit there or at the table?"

"Here is fine." I position a plate on the side table near Rain so she can reach her meal. Then, I sit on a lounge chair opposite the couch.

"You want to talk?" I ask.

"Parker, I honestly don't know what to say. I don't know what this means. Maybe it was a sign."

"I don't understand what you mean by sign."

"Like, I wasn't ready."

"Oh honey, don't say that. We don't know why this happened. We can't read anything into it. You should know that having a child with you is the greatest gift; one day, it will be our time. I love you so much. But now, we need time to remember the life we created together. And you need time to heal." When I say we created life, I can barely breathe, so I stand and excuse myself.

I go into the restroom and wash my face. *Our child is gone.* Rain is okay, which gives me peace, but I struggle to get past losing a part of me—a part of us. I put my hand on the wall to balance myself, take a deep breath, and blow air in my cheeks. *I can do this.* I must, for both of us. I go into the room, but I sit near Rain this time.

"Babe."

"Yeah, Parker."

"Can I hold you?"

"Of course, handsome." She opens her arms to me.

"I love you so much, Rain. You need to know that my world revolves around you. You also need to know that our children will be my world. I'm so sorry you had to go through this." I bury my head in her neck to hide the grief I feel. I feel her hand slide through my hair, knowing she knows how much I love her.

"This is so hard."

"I know, babe. We'll get through it…together."

AFTER RAIN HAD BRUNCH, SHE FELT EMOTIONALLY EXHAUSTED AND wanted to rest. I carried her to bed, tucked her in, slid in beside her, and she fell asleep on my chest. She's been like this for a while, so I gently slide out of bed without waking her. She needs rest, and I need to talk to my mom and let her know what's happening.

My mom picks on the first ring. "Mom...."

"Honey, you don't sound like yourself. What's wrong?" I can see her worried look over video.

"I just brought Rain back from the hospital."

"What? You didn't tell me. I would have come to see her. How is she? What's wrong? What can I do?"

"She had a miscarriage," I say, hearing her gasp on the line. "She's resting, but oh god, Mom—."

"Oh, Parker. I'm so sorry for you both. Oh, honey. What can I do?"

"Mom, we were going to have a baby. I love her so much—what do I tell her? How can I help her?"

"Tell her how much you love her. Be there for her. Honey, she'll be okay. You'll be okay."

"But what does this mean, Mom? Will Rain be able to have a child again in the future?"

"Yes, honey. Give her time. Were you two planning this?"

"No, I didn't know until something went wrong. She was planning to tell me. Oh my god, Mom, my baby."

"Parker, you'll have another. Right now, just focus on helping her heal. Then, when you two are really ready, you can work on building a family—but give it some time," she assures me.

"I understand."

"I promise you: you'll get through it. Your father and I did."

"What?"

"Honey, years before you were born, I also had a miscarriage. Your father and I were devastated at the time. It's not easy knowing a part of you was there, and then it's gone. For the longest time, I was scared to try again, but your dad helped me overcome that fear. His unconditional love and devotion helped me see we can get through anything as long as we're together. Then we had you, and we realized that we have to let life happen the way it needs to in order to get to perfect. That's what our life is with you—perfect, and despite the pain and loss, I wouldn't change a thing. I love you that much, son."

I sit with this new revelation of how our lives parallel. I could have had an older sibling. It's the one thing I've wished for, and it's why Josh and I are so close—we're like brothers.

"Mom, I love you."

"I know, honey. I know."

CHAPTER 33

My Other Half

Rain

IT'S BEEN THREE WEEKS SINCE I LOST MY BABY, OUR BABY. I ONLY missed a few days of school. Parker felt I was going back too soon, but there was no reason for me to hang around at his house. My doctor cleared me, so I returned home to my side of the bay. I've seen Parker almost weekly but haven't been intimate with him. I haven't felt like it—I keep thinking about what happened. My mind wanders to the fact that we created a life. That's a big deal. My only saving grace about that day is that I passed out, and in doing so, I have no memories of what happened. Parker told me I fainted in his arms. I don't recall that moment, either. But somehow, my child imprinted on me, and I know there was another life in me, and now it's not. I can't get past that fact. I never will.

I love Parker. He's my other half. Somehow, I need to find my way back to him. Parker and I are trying to prepare for finals, graduation, and everything we need to do to establish ourselves as working adults. I secured a job with the law firm where I did my internship. The people are great, and I'm excited for the future.

I've been thinking about our recent loss and how having a child would have changed my life. Would I have been able to join the firm this coming January? I would have been showing by then, and shortly after that, I would have had to take time away from work to give birth. That wasn't how I saw my life going. I want to build a career. To explore the world, live my life, and gain some experience before trying to raise a family. Then, when I am ready, I want to impart what I've learned and experienced to my child. I'm not ready. Parker wants a family; he wants me, but I'm not ready to become more than we are. I need to find myself, grow, and breathe. I need air.

My phone ringing brings me out of the state I'm in. I look at my watch. Oh my god, I lost twenty minutes.

"Parker?" His beautiful face appears when I accept the video call.

"Rain. This is the third time I called. Are you okay, babe?"

"Yeah," I lie.

He's reading my face, searching for signs. "Babe. What happened? How long were you gone?"

"Parker, I'm fine."

"I'm coming over there."

"No."

"Babe, please don't tell me no."

"Okay, Parker, I won't tell you, no, but I will ask you not to come. I'm okay. I'll see you next week."

"Babe."

"Next week. I promise." *I promise I'll find my way back to you.*

CHAPTER 34

I Love You

Parker

RAIN IS ON HER WAY OVER, AND I CAN'T WAIT TO SEE MY WOMAN. To hold her, to tell her how much I love her. She's been struggling the past few weeks, and so have I. It's been hard trying to keep it going at school, knowing we're both moving into this new phase of our lives, the stress of exams, and the pressure of parents. We both have to study and sit for the bar soon. It's a lot, and I know we'll pull through it. We have to. This is how we grow.

The doorbell rings, and it's Rain. I don't know why she doesn't use her key. Sometimes she's strange like that, but she's my kind of strange, and I love her.

"Babe." I bend to kiss her, and I'm surprised when she deepens the kiss, and I take it all in.

"Parker, are we going to stand in the doorway all night?"

I laugh because it's the first time she's said something lighthearted in a while. "No, babe, come in. Let me get you some wine. Dinner is already done. I hope you're okay eating this early."

"It's fine. Stop treating me like I'm new."

"Then kiss me again, babe." She gets on her toes and kisses me, and I let her take the lead because she needs to show me what she wants. She knows what I want…her. Going without being inside the love of my life is torture.

Rain deepens the kiss, and our tongues mingle. She's soft and sweet, and I love everything about her. She consumes me, and the world stops for a moment.

We stand, kissing, until she comes up for air. "Parker." She pants, then steps back. She holds my gaze, and I see something in her eyes, like pleading but also a bit of pain, and I don't know what to do with that knowledge. She surprises me by jumping into my arms.

"Take me," she says, crushing her lips to mine, and somehow, with my lips still on her, I find my way to the bedroom.

I gently lay her on the bed and kiss her while freeing her from her pants. I break our kiss to pull her shirt over her head, exposing her bare breasts and wrapping my mouth around one, then the other, sucking, licking, and biting. I want my girl so bad I can almost taste her come.

"Parker, I need you in me right now," she commands. I remove all my clothes and kneel over her, dip my head, and kiss her. I slide my hand between her legs and through her slick folds. She's so ready. I spread her legs, position myself, push in slowly, and ease out, coating myself in her juices. Rain feels so amazing. I begin pumping in and out of my woman, creating a rhythm for us, guiding our bodies to move as one.

"Ahh, Parker. It's so good." Her voice is uneven and breathless, and I dip my head and swallow her moans with a kiss that is wet, messy, and full of the passion I feel for her. Full of the love I feel, full of us. "I'm going to come, Parker. Come with me." I pump, allowing the release that's been building in me to overcome me, and my girl's body clenches around me, pulling my release from me, and we come together, calling to each other. It's all the things life should be, like when all the stars align, and you find your special someone. She's mine.

"Rain. I love you."

"I love you too, Parker. Always."

CHAPTER 35

There Is No Me Without You

Rain

FRIDAY, WHEN I CAME OVER TO PARKER'S, I DIDN'T KNOW WHAT WOULD happen. It was the first time we made love since.... Since.... Well, it's been a while. Having my body full of him was beautiful. I feel that whenever he's around and when he's in me, I can't focus on anything else. But I need to focus. I need to get my life together. The trauma of losing my father and now of losing my child is something I'm struggling to move past. The look on Parker's face when I looked at him with confusion was too much to bear. I don't want Parker to be weighed down with my mess. He needs to thrive and be a whole man without me. I'm so fucking broken. I don't know whether it was the right thing to have gone through with the pregnancy. I have nothing to offer a child at this moment. I barely made it out of my own childhood unscathed. I still bear the scars which reveal themselves every morning. I can't do this.

It's Sunday morning. Parker and I have spent a lovely few days together. But they were only pleasant because I've been hiding. Hiding what I feel, masking the pain, hiding grief, hiding the hate I feel for whoever up there took a life from me. I loathe that I love Parker so profoundly that I'm forced to let go of everything good we've built.

I need to get in the shower before he wakes. Usually, I shower with Parker, but I know if we take one together, soon he'll be inside me, and

I won't be able to go through with what I need to do.

I quickly shower, and by the time I'm dressed, Parker is standing at the door.

"Babe. You okay?" He's searching my eyes, looking for me. But he won't find me because I'm channeling all the grief and pain I've experienced to get through this.

"I have to go, Parker."

"This early? Babe, let me take you where you need to go. Are you okay?"

"Parker, no. It's over."

"What are you talking about, Rain?"

He grabs me by the waist, and I try to break free, but I can't. I must do this. I have to do this. I have to save him from me.

"Us, Parker. You have to let me go."

"Rain." The look of shock on his face is unbearable. "No, what are you saying? We'll get through this. Whatever it is, we can get through it together, babe—you and me. There's nothing we can't solve or do. Together."

"Parker, I can't do this. You need to let me go. I'm begging you."

"What are you asking me, Rain? You're the love of my life. The day I kissed you was the day you breathed life into me. You are my air, the source of my being. You're everything to me. I want you by my side always."

"Parker. I'm doing this because I love you. You need to let me go. I need to find myself. To be me without you. I need to figure out who I am. I can't do that like this. I need to be whole before I can be with someone else. Right now, I'm the spoiled fruit that ruins the whole bowl. We can't build a future like that. I'm sorry. Let me go. Please, let me go."

"Rain. Please don't do this. Let's work it through together. We'll figure it out. We'll get whatever help we need. Just don't walk away. Stay with me, Rain."

"No." I pull away from him, find my purse, and head to the door with Parker on my heels.

"Babe. Don't go." I only stop because he asked. "Rain, look at me." Turning, I look at him. "You, Rain, are the one true love of my life. I don't plan to live a life without you in it. Honey, I hear you saying you need time to fix yourself. I believe we can work through this together. We are, like it or not, connected, Rain. There is no me without you. There is only us."

"I know, Parker, but you must let me do this. Please let me fix me. Maybe our love will bring me back to you when it's time, when I'm ready, when I'm whole—when my head is not a mess. I promise to try and find my way back. To us…to love. But now, you need to let me go, Parker. Please."

He walks over to me, hugs me, and presses his lips to mine. I can feel his body shaking with fear I caused, and I feel the bile rising in my throat. I need to get out of here. Closing my eyes, I call upon all the demons in my head to help me rip out my heart and walk through the door. I feel myself slipping away. I'm in my family's living room. It's dark, and I can barely see the silhouette of my dad as he walks out the door, and I follow him.

CHAPTER 36

Hell on Earth

Parker

HELL ON EARTH, DROWNING IN A FLAMING POOL OF GASOLINE. THAT'S exactly how I feel now and every second since Rain walked out the door and out of my life. I only have myself to blame. I promised her I would never deny her anything. Never in my life would I expect the love of my life to ask me to leave. To give her time—to end us. She asked me to let her find herself, and I only let her walk out the door because my baby asked me to give her time to heal. Every moment until then, I'll be waiting for her to return to me, return to our love, to be whole one day.

The day Rain left, I texted her so she knew I was always available, no matter what.

Me: My love for you is eternal. I'll never be far from you. When you're ready, I'll be there. I love you forever.

That was two days ago. Since then, things that seemed so easy have escaped me—eating, sleeping, and focusing on anything is like trudging through waist-deep mud wearing weights. I tried holding back the tears so I could remain strong for both of us. Still, they fell.

Even now staring at the blue sweater in my hand she left behind, water welling in my eyes distorts my vision, causing the colors to blur, blending with my jeans. It's hard to be my usual self when all I want to do is burn this house down. Inside, my world has ended. Outside, the world still turns. Finals are coming, and after that, graduation. Having lost the two loves of my life in a matter of weeks is devastating. There will be no celebrating for me. My heart is shattered into a million tiny pieces, and I feel like I'm dying. I need to breathe, to pull myself together. I need help. *Fuck.* I wipe the tears from my eyes and pull out my phone.

I call Josh. "Hey, man. What's up?" he says when he answers.

"Josh, I need a favor."

"Anything. Name it." That's Josh—the one friend I can trust with my life. All the rest are great, but Josh is the brother my parents never gave me. He's lived my life, both of us being only children of elites. If it wasn't for him in my life growing up, I wouldn't know what being a somewhat normal kid was.

"I need you to keep watch on Rain."

"You've never been far away from her. Talk to me, man."

"I need to get away for a couple of days. We've both been through a lot, and I need eyes on her. If you notice she needs help with anything, don't hesitate to step in."

"Does she know?"

"That I'm leaving? No."

"She needs to know I'm there for her. You okay if I reach out with my normal family stuff as a guise?"

"Sure—that's your in. Just don't ask her about me."

"Where will you be?"

"Helicopter flight away, down the coast, trying to get my head together."

"That bad?"

"Worse."

"I got you both. Let's talk when you return."

CHAPTER 37

Casualty of Love

Rain

I CAN'T GET OUT OF BED. FOR THE PAST THREE DAYS, I'VE LAID HERE AS dark memories cloud my head. I walked away from the love of my life—Parker, the one man who, if I asked, would give me the world. Our connection is so strong I can barely breathe when thinking of him. But that's the issue. I'm getting lost in him. I'm so tied to every fiber of him that I can't find myself. What do I have to offer anyone if I can't help myself?

I blame you, Dad. Where the hell are you? Why did you do this to me? The day you left, you created a monster in my head that I used as a weapon to slay my love. I used it to cut out my heart with a dull blade. You shattered my life, leaving me broken. Splayed like a shattered mirror on the floor. In turn, I'm left crawling on bloody hands and knees through the sharp pieces of my life in the dark. The two men I loved most are no longer in my life—casualties of, I don't know what, of love? I'm living a shell of a life that my father left behind when he walked out the door. A casualty of love that Parker provided me so unconditionally. I'm a casualty of the monsters in my head that I can't forget.

One day, I hope to find my way back to love, to life… to me. That's it—I need to fix me. If I can do that, I can have my man back. I can have love.

CHAPTER 38

I Used to Be Yours

Parker

THE SOUND OF HAPPINESS IN THE VOICES SURROUNDING ME AS PEOPLE greet each other, cheer, and laugh grips me like a vice, and I need to leave. Being here is bittersweet. But I wouldn't have missed watching my girl graduate for the world. Standing, I straighten my tie and scan the crowd. It's not like she will see or even expect me to be here.

When they called her name, I held my breath and watched as she stood. Rain...my love. I used to be yours. I used to be the love of your life, the first voice you heard in the morning, the last at night. You told me once I was your everything.

I kept my eyes fixed on her as she approached the stage. When she reached the center, I smiled, so proud of her. She's intelligent and beautiful, and she deserves this moment. When a camera flash caused a glint of light to highlight the sparkle on her ear, I held my breath. She was wearing the diamond earrings I sent as a graduation gift. It's the third part of a four-piece collection I have for her. When I gave Rain a diamond necklace on my birthday, it was with a promise that it was the first of many pieces to come and that the final piece would be her wedding ring. So, I didn't think she'd accept the earrings. I thought she wanted to erase all memories of me. Now, I know that's not the case. Rain is still mine.

She was beautiful walking across the stage in her cap and gown, poised in heels, head high. However, the luster that usually sparkles in her eyes wasn't there, and I know she's hurting. I'm hurting. But still, I watched breathlessly as she received her diploma. And I hoped she could feel my presence. Feel my love.

Goodbye, Rain. I say, leaving the building. *I'm glad you remember that I used to be yours.*

Over the past few weeks, it's been hard not seeing her, not calling her. I've spent my days looking through the hundreds of pictures we took over our seven years together as friends, lovers, and now here as… this. What is this? A breakup, a separation, a miss? She promised to find her way back. She can't disregard that. *Can she?* I love her.

Today is filled with pomp and circumstance. I blow through my cheeks, nerves getting the best of me as I head to my car, not wanting to upset her with an accidental meeting. I need to head to my own celebratory dinner with my parents. I asked them not to go through with having a big party like they had planned because I couldn't see myself talking to a lot of people. The only thing I want right now is Rain.

As I arrive at my parents' house, I take a deep breath and settle myself. This has been hard for all of us. We all love Rain.

"Parker, how are you, darling?"

"That's a loaded question, Mom."

"Honey, let him get his bearings," my dad says.

"It's okay, Dad. I'll get through this."

"Were you able to see her today?"

"Yeah, Mom. She was beautiful. She was wearing my gift to her."

"Ah, honey," my mom says.

My dad puts his hand on my shoulder. "Son, it will be okay."

"I know, Dad. Let's eat."

"I can't wait to see the pictures," my mom says.

Prior to our breakup, she asked if she could arrange for a photographer and videographer to document the moment for Rain as a gift. Rain agreed. At the time, Rain was unsure whether anyone from her family would attend. I don't tell Mom the vendor has already sent me a close-up of Rain receiving her diploma. My mom loves her so much. This is heartbreaking for all of us.

We sit in silence until I can get my emotions under control. Eventually, we discuss the bar exam, and I talk about the law firm I settled on working at. My head isn't entirely in the conversation because I watched my woman walk down the aisle today—except it wasn't with me. One day, it will be.

PART 5

Every new beginning derives from a former beginning's end. That's the way with love. And so, we begin again.

— Rita A. Gordon

CHAPTER 39

When London Calls

Rain

Four Years Ago

It's bleak outside. The clouds are grey and water rolls down the window pane. It rains a lot here in London. Even over five thousand miles, I can't get away from my former life. The constant rain reminds me of him. The love of my life. The man who calls me…Rain.

"Rain. I love the sound of that. It reminds me how essential it is to all life. Can I call you Rain?"

With those words, Parker sealed our fate.

I'm not used to this, but I need to adjust because this is where I live now. I've taken a job with Saola Technology as an associate attorney. I've been in London for a few days, and I expect each day to get easier, but they don't. But I will try to be the woman I need to be without Parker. He's been my emotional rock in more ways than I had expected one man to be. I fell hard and fast for him, but in doing so, I was masking a deep wound that reopened when my baby died. Oh god, Parker, this is so hard. One day, I need to apologize to him for how I ended things.

At the time, I didn't know how to tell the person I loved that I had to walk away and breathe on my own. Time to heal is what I need. Time to discover the woman I'm supposed to be. To walk into all the walls, fall on my face, place my hand in the fire, feel the heat and pain, and bear the scars on my own without someone saving me.

It has been over six months, and I miss him, but I feel his love daily. My sleep terrors still haunt me like the ghosts of Christmas past, but I push through them. I wake in a sweat, confused and scared, then I grab my phone and listen to the message Parker left. He has left a message every day since I walked out his door. It's slightly different every day, but it always starts the same.

"Rain, I love you. I hope hearing my voice helps you get through the day knowing you are loved. Knowing that every breath I take reminds me that you are my life force. And I want to be that for you. I love you so much. Have a good day, babe. I'm waiting for you."

I'm getting my bearings around London and preparing for the week ahead at my new job. I'm excited and scared at the same time. But I'll get through it because this is my new life. I look down at my phone and remember I need to let my family know I'm here. It's morning in San Francisco. I owe my mom a call first.

Although we're not close, I update her on my life and whereabouts. This is my attempt to keep whatever ties I have to my family.

When I call, she answers right away.

"Hey, Mom, it's Rain."

"Rain. Are you in London?"

"Yes, I made it the other day. I'm getting settled and start work on Monday."

"I still don't know why you had to start in London instead of here."

"I told you. Learning about my company's international business is good experience for me, especially if I want to be an international attorney. How are you?"

"I'm good. I talked to your sister the other day. She said to say hi if I spoke with you."

"She could have called."

"Now, don't start." She's right; I need to focus on myself, not my dysfunctional family. Part of pulling myself together is working through my family issues, too. One day, I'll find out why Dad really left, and maybe I can rid myself of the memories that haunt me like a persistent ghost.

"You're right. I just called to let you know I'm here."

"Do you have everything you need?"

"Yeah, I'm good. Listen, Mom, I need to go. I have to make dinner before it gets late. Call me next week if you have time." I end the call.

I know she won't call me. She never does.

CHAPTER 40

A New Year

Parker

IT'S A NEW YEAR—THIS YEAR WAS THE FIRST IN SEVEN YEARS I HAVEN'T celebrated with Rain. I hope it will be my last without her. I'm getting my woman back.

I promised my girl she'd never want anything, and I'd always protect her. Even though she didn't know, I drove to her place every day to check on her. She turned off her tracker the day she left, but that won't stop me from watching out for her. When she decided to start her career with her firm in London versus San Francisco, I did the same to be near her. Which is why I just stepped off a plane heading to my house in London. As soon as I get in my chauffeur-driven car, my phone rings.

"Josh. You couldn't wait, could you?"

"No, man. I wanted to check in on you and see how it's going."

"Just landed. Heading home now."

"And Rain?"

"I'm sure she's home, but she doesn't know I'm here."

"But you received a text from her."

"It's not what you think. She's struggling with something—It wasn't anything she wanted me to respond to, but it's a start." I was happy to receive her simple text message.

Rain: I'm counting.

In one of my daily voicemail messages, I told Rain to pretend I was there sleeping while she counted out each breath I took before she decided to wake me. She used to love to watch me sleep. I know my girl well enough to know she's been listening to my voicemails to help get her through her mornings. Once she told me the sound of my voice was the only thing to pull her out of negative space, I made sure she never went a morning without hearing me call her name and telling her how much I love her.

"Man. I'm sorry about all of this. Make sure you give Rain the space she needs to do whatever she's trying to do. I know you love her and mean well, but take your time with this. Let me know if there is anything I can do for you. It sounds like the text is the beginning of something new."

"I sure hope so, man." I sigh. It's heavy and long, and all I can do to keep from crying like a baby.

"I'll let you go. Just wanted to make sure you're okay."

"Thanks for looking out, man."

The drive home is wet and slow. As the rain washes over everything, I think about what tomorrow brings. Hope for a clean slate—another chance to glance at my girl so I can breathe. Breathe…do I even know what that's like anymore? Rain is my air. She's everything. Well, at least I'm in the same city, so when she's ready—I'll be here…waiting.

CHAPTER 41

Begin Again

Parker

It's early. I look out the window following my shower and am pleased to find a clear day in March. It's not that I don't like the rain. Some of my best memories are rainy days, staying in and cuddling with my woman…Rain.

My life is different now. I get up early to record a message for Rain, send it straight to her voicemail so it doesn't wake her, and then I get ready for work. In my walk-in closet, I grab my watch and put it on. Six o'clock. Rain should be up now. God, I miss holding her. It's been almost a year—a little over ten months ago, we lost our baby. Then, shortly after that, the love of my life walked out with a promise that she'd try to find her way back. The only things keeping me sane are therapy and the hope of Rain returning to me. Being here in London near to her gives me hope for a better future. The fact she initiated a text message with me gives me faith in our connection. I'm about to take the next step. I text her.

Me: Babe, are you listening to my voicemails?

Rain: Yes.

Me: Are they helpful?

Rain: Yes.

Me: Do you want me to continue sending them?

Rain: No.

Me: No?

Rain: No.

Me: Would you prefer a video?

Rain: No.

Me: You want me to call instead?

Rain: Yes.

Me: Now?

Rain: Please.

I close my eyes and say a silent prayer to the divine. Opening them, a sense of relief washes over me. I video call Rain. She answers immediately. When I see her face…wow. It's like seeing an angel for the first time. It's too much; it's hard to breathe. I exhale.

"Rain. You look beautiful. How are you?"

"Parker. I'm fine. I…I've missed you."

I can hear the weight in her sigh as if she's been holding her breath for a while, and I feel the same.

"I miss you too. Tell me, really, how are you?"

"I'm good, Parker, really, I am. The mornings are still hard to get through, even with the voicemails, but they help."

"I can start calling you in the morning if that helps you get through it. Let me know if that's what you want. I promise I won't bother you with anything else. It'll allow you the time you need to clear your head. If you want to talk about anything, I'll be available to listen or to bounce ideas off." I don't tell her I'm in town and can be there whenever she needs me.

She looks at me with a mix of fear and confusion that makes me worried, but I need to find what's comfortable for her. I don't want Rain to be afraid of me. I know she's not, but she is scared of something, and if it takes a lifetime to figure it out and solve it—I will. I already lost the most important part of her. I won't lose her again. There's no way I can survive without Rain in my life. I'll take this little bit she's offering if it's all she can spare.

"Parker. Hold on. Just give me a minute," she tells me.

I watch her beautiful brown eyes as they scan my face. Her eyes sweep across my head, starting with my hair. They dart from one side of my face to the other, and I smile because she's mapping my cheekbones. I know that because the times she did this in person, she would touch my face and trace the curve of my jaw with her fingers. Then she would outline my lips like she's tracing them now with her eyes. I hold my smile, hoping it will give her the comfort she needs. Hoping it will push the traumatic memories back into the darkness and away from her consciousness. I watch her chest rise and fall and her breath steady, knowing she's okay. Knowing somehow, I've helped her. She has to be okay. I'd die in order to give her life. I love her that much. Rain.

"Thank you, Parker." She exhales.

"It's okay. Do you want me to call you in the morning?" I hold my breath, waiting for her response. She blinks.

"Yes."

How can one word provide you with the air you need to take your next breath when you're in the middle of the sea drowning? It must be the same for a man asking a woman to marry him, the anticipation of her response. I felt this way when I first asked Rain to be my woman. She has to know that it was meant to be forever. With one word she solidified it doesn't matter that she asked me to leave, or she told me we couldn't be together. What matters now is that she answered my call, that we are still connected, and she's still mine. With one word, my life can begin again.

"Okay, Rain. I'll call you in the morning. Did you want to talk about anything else?"

"No. But thanks again, Parker. Bye."

She hangs up, and although she doesn't hear me, I say, "Bye, Rain. I love you."

CHAPTER 42

Saola

Rain

My steps feel lighter heading into the office this morning. I think Andrew Adler, my boss, can sense something different about me. He always briefs me on my assignment for the day, talks through my previous work, and provides feedback to help me with this new career. He's an excellent manager who takes my job seriously. I've heard these good old boys' networks make it difficult for women to survive or succeed in the workforce. That hasn't been my experience at Saola.

The Adler brothers, Alexandros, Aaron, and Andrew are fantastic. Andrew is the youngest of the three; his oldest brother, Alex, founded Saola Technology. Alex likes rare things, so he named the company after the rarest mammal. When I told Andrew about my recall ability, he felt that having me shadow him would provide better training. The things he and his brother do to ensure my success are unheard of. Now I see why one of Janis's friends recommended I consider them when interviewing for an internship in my second year of grad school. They hired this incredible Chief Operations Officer named June Ross, another phenomenal African American woman. She suggested I meet with her biweekly to learn her side of the business, hoping that when I'm up to speed, I can work with her to open a local office.

"Raven, you seem different today. Anything going on?" Andrew inquires.

"No, things are good. I was thinking about my experience working here."

"Are you glad you started in our London office?"

"Oh, absolutely."

"At some point, we'll want to ensure you return to the States and work with the team there. A year here will give you a compulsory understanding of this part of our organization and provide you with the necessary knowledge of our clientele. But our bigger client base is in the San Francisco Bay Area."

"So, you suggest I finish a year here and then move back to the Bay Area?"

"Yes. It would be good for your career."

"What do your brothers think?"

"They agree. Aaron and I spent some time debriefing Alex. He's on board. You have a brilliant legal mind. June will return to the States soon, and I know she'll benefit from having you on her team. The deals she'll be working on are much more complex as California has some of the most restrictive real estate development laws, and we're opening a larger space there."

"I'm intrigued," I tell him, and I am.

However, I don't know how returning to the states will impact my relationship with Parker. When we're together we're inseparable. I don't know if I can handle being so near to him again. I haven't seen him face to face since I left. That was over ten months ago. Yesterday was the first time I saw his face live. It felt good seeing him again. It was almost like he was here. Even now, it is as if our connection is so strong that I can feel him nearby. But that's not possible. He's working in his new job, and I know his brilliance shines through. He will make a partner at his law firm faster than most people his age. I sigh because thinking of him gives me a sense of peace I didn't realize I needed. This morning was the first time I felt the weight of guilt leave my chest. I didn't know if he'd accept me back into his life after the way I left him.

I knew he was happy to see me again by the relief on his face. I'm glad I said yes. However, underneath it all, the sting of death, the destruction of life, and the demolition of our dream still lie hidden. And I don't know how to resolve that. How do I resolve being in his life and disassociate the pain I caused and which he endured because of me? I can never do that to him again—cause so much grief and pain; the best way to solve that is never to be that person again. He has to find his person, a whole person. That's not me. I come with too much baggage. I don't know if I can ever fix this…fix me.

I agree with Andrew about going to San Francisco in the new year to continue to build my career with Saola Technologies. Later in the day, I shadow Andrew, and we go to a client site to discuss implementing Saola's security software at their company. In addition to being good at what they do, the Adler brothers are very charismatic and beautiful to look at, so when Andrew walks into these client meetings, he has everyone's attention. During the meeting, I observe as our senior counsel points out the required disclosures related to an implementation. I recognize some of the issues and conditions from my school training. The others are specific to the technology industry, and some stipulations are particular to the company and its offerings. I listen to all the questions and objections; my brain soaks up every detail like a sponge.

My brain flashes to a contract clause the client misstated, which I correct. "The contract states you need a forty-five-day review period. Not ninety. It's noted on page five, section IV, J, line two."

"I stand corrected. Thank you, Ms. Nichols," the client says. Andrew nods and smiles.

The meeting goes smoothly, and afterward, Andrew and I go to lunch at a local British cuisine restaurant serving fish and chips.

"Great catch back there. You don't miss a thing, do you?"

"Unfortunately, no."

"Raven, it sounds like you have reservations about your ability to recall facts. That's usually the norm for attorneys. They can consume a lot of information and recite almost everything they've read. Which means most have some level of photographic memory. You happen to have a more advanced condition. Don't be down about how it plays out at work. It's to your advantage. Leverage your ability. It will take you far. Be the best, and don't hold back. People who are lesser skilled than you won't hesitate to do whatever they can to overtake you."

"You're right, Andrew. I appreciate the feedback. This does play to my advantage. It's just on the personal side that it's more of a disadvantage."

"I understand. You don't have to elaborate. I want to ensure you know you have the upper hand over the rest of us in this game. Take it by the reins and lead in the direction you want your future to go. I commit that my brothers and I will ensure that as long as you're with us, we'll help guide you."

I smile, and he nods. We finish our meal and head back to the office. The day is a mix of work and learning; by the end of the day, my brain has reached its capacity for both. When I get home, I strip out of my clothes, shower, put on my loungewear, and make myself a snack. If I were in California, I would either be at Parker's place or on video with him, or we'd be summoned to his mom's house for dinner or an event. I miss those days. I miss my friendship with Parker. That's it. We can be friends. I reach for my phone, and before I realize what I'm doing, I video call Parker.

"Rain?"

CHAPTER 43

Small Victories

Parker

To say today that I won a small victory is an understatement. Seeing Rain on video this morning after ten months that felt more like ten years was unexpected. Having Rain tell me she wants me to call her every morning is priceless. My heart is full, and I feel I am floating even when negotiating a multi-million-dollar media deal for my client. The company could not convince us to back down from our requests. I had a retort for everything. In the end, they signed. My client got everything they asked for, plus some extra cash.

Following the meeting, I head back to the office. I have several video conferences since most of my clients are based in the United States. I try to conduct the United States side of the business later in the day since that's the best time to catch them in their morning time zone. By the end of the day, I'm emotionally drained. The anticipation of talking with Rain in the morning is overwhelming.

It doesn't take me long to get home since I live near the office and can walk. That's one advantage of being a Page: the endless supply of money and privilege. The things that even the people I work with don't know about. The fact that I never have to work a day in my life, yet I put my best foot forward daily, would be unfathomable to most people if they knew the truth. That was the easy thing about being with Rain. She understood me. The need to be the best no matter what, no matter who you are. The satisfaction of accomplishing and mastering something is a rush that money can't replace. Rain…I want my woman back.

At home, I take off my jacket and pour myself sparkling water. Rain got me into drinking this stuff. I think I'm addicted. Well, not really. I'm addicted to the idea of her and anything that reminds me of life with her. The scent of jasmine and honey is what I crave most besides the warmth of her body near me and the caress of her lips on mine. *Rain, can you hear me, babe?* I speak her name into the air. I take a big gulp of water and set the glass on the counter. My phone vibrates in my pocket. I usually keep it on silent while I'm at work. I slide it out. I can't breathe. It's Rain on video.

"Rain?"

"Hey, Parker. How was your day?"

"Good. I closed a big deal," I say, trying to remain calm.

"Always being brilliant. Your company is lucky to have you."

"Thanks, Rain. How was your day?" I keep the conversation light. I won't press her for anything beyond what I know she wants to give.

"Good. I'm learning a lot, and the owners have full faith in me and are doing everything to ensure my success."

"You are a smart woman. You'll succeed at anything you do. Did you get a chance to eat?"

"Yes, I had lunch after a client meeting with my boss and a snack when I got home."

"How are you feeling in general?"

"Like health-wise?"

"Whatever you want to share."

"I feel good. I still struggle with bad memories."

I want her to elaborate, but I don't want to press her and certainly don't want to trigger any memories she can't handle, especially if I'm not physically there to hold her. Although she doesn't know I'm here in London, I hope in her heart she never feels I'm far from her.

"You know you can talk to me. Tell me anything you want or nothing at all. What do you think about my hair? It's a little shorter than I used to wear it."

"I like it. It suits you. Makes you look even more distinguished and fits with your brilliance."

"Why do you call me brilliant?"

"Because law comes to you with ease. It's like you breathe law and were born to be an attorney. And the way you cite cases like you've lived through them versus me, I'm citing from memory. It's not the same."

"Ah, that makes sense. I do love law, but you already know that."

"Yeah. I know. But I say what I say because you are brilliant."

"Can you tell me about how London is treating you?"

"I don't like all the rain. Just because that's my name doesn't mean I want to spend so much time in it."

"Understandable. Does that feel strange to you?"

"What?"

"So much rain surrounding a beautiful woman named Rain."

"Parker."

"I'm serious. Is it that strange?"

"Only when I think about it. Most times, I try to think about other things."

"Like?"

"Like how green the trees are because of it. How happy the grass is. When I think of rain, I can't help but think about what you told me."

"What's that?"

"You said that rain is essential to all life. So I think about that and how appreciative I'll be for the sunny days in California."

"Do you want to go back to California?"

"Eventually, I'll have to if I want to further my career."

"I suppose."

"I think I'll complete a year here."

"Then back or somewhere else?"

"Back to California." Her voice trails off, and I feel her slipping into her mind. I catch her before she falls.

"Rain. What did you have for a snack tonight?"

"Guess."

"Really?"

"Yeah. Guess. Be your brilliant self."

"Well, a snack for you involves crackers, cheese, and, if you're lucky, sardines."

"Like I said. Be all brilliant, and you nailed it. Am I that predictable?"

"No, babe. You're not."

I know she's not because I would have seen her leaving me if she were. But I didn't see that coming. I would have realized that she could disassociate herself from a man she said she felt her only tie to. I would have known the look of despair in her eyes wasn't because she lost our child. It was because she was seconds away from telling me goodbye. From walking out the door to give herself time to heal. From being her without me. No, there is absolutely nothing predictable about her.

"You're being sweet. We promised—."

"Yes, I recall our promise. And I am telling you the truth. You're not predictable. You're many things, but that's not one of them. So, how were the sardines? Did you go spicy, Mediterranean, tomato, or olive oil?"

"Mediterranean because it has extra spice."

"You should have a little more nourishment than that. Do you have any fruit? Maybe have some of that before you turn in tonight."

"You're right. I'll make a fruit salad before it gets late."

I smile and wait for her to say something else, but she doesn't.

"Did you bring work home with you?"

"No. But I should make that salad and clean up before heading to bed. You'll call in the morning?"

"Absolutely. I'll see you in the morning. Sleep well, babe."

"Good night, Parker."

"Night."

I hang up, and my heart is pounding to break free from the walls of my chest. These brief moments with Rain are precious, and I feel bits of my heart that were previously ripped away being slotted back in place like a puzzle, one piece at a time. It so happens that this puzzle has a thousand tiny pieces, and she slotted in three today.

CHAPTER 44

Seize the Day

Rain

EVEN BEFORE MY ALARM GOES OFF, I'M UP AND WIDE AWAKE. USUALLY, when I get up this early, my memories are fast on my heels, chasing me beneath a cloud of darkness. Oddly enough, that's not the case. Instead, I envision Parker's face, his smile, and the way his lip curls up on one side when I stare at him in my attempt to free my mind. He intentionally distracts me and pulls me further into focusing on him, which works. I can see him now. It feels like he's nearby. My phone rings, and I know it can only be...Parker.

"Good morning, Rain," he says. He stares, reading my face, searching for me.

"Hi, Parker. I'm here." I smile so he knows I'm focused and see him, and for a moment, the nightmares are held at bay.

"You're wide awake. How long have you been up?"

I sigh. "About ten minutes. Maybe more. Not long."

"Are you okay?"

"I think I must have been anticipating your call. My sleep terrors didn't come this morning."

"Rain, that's great."

"Yeah. I guess it is. But now I feel like I'm wasting your time. You should be resting."

"About that. Would it be okay if I called you after work to talk about that? Shoot. You may have plans. I don't mean to intrude."

"I don't understand. Don't you have meetings? It'll be around ten thirty in the morning where you are, or are you not in the States?"

"No, babe, not at the moment."

"Okay…uhm. Yeah, I don't have plans this evening. I'm picking up something to eat and should be home around six-thirty tonight. I'd say that could be inconvenient for you, but I'll wait until you tell me where you are."

"Don't worry about the time zones. Wherever you are, I will always have time for you," he says in a cryptic way, making me wonder what Parker is up to.

"Okay," I say, dragging out the syllables. "I'll talk to you when I get back home."

"Rain, have a great day at work. Call me if you need me."

"Bye, Parker," I say, ending the call.

I take my usual time getting ready for work. I look out the window. It's not raining today, but I always carry an umbrella, even though complimentary ones are available at work. I head to the office but stop for coffee near the building. I see this guy staring at me like I'm dessert. I saw him here the other day. I look away and see Alex, my company's founder, standing in line, and I stand next to him.

"Good morning, Mr. Adler. You could have asked our coordinator to get your coffee this morning."

"Good morning, Ms. Nichols. You're right, but sometimes I do normal things like grab my coffee. So, how do you like Saola?"

"Would you believe me if I say I love it?"

"Yes."

"I love it. Working for your brother, Andrew...he's great."

We move up in line until Alex is next. He prompts me to order, then gives his order and pays for our drinks. We step to the side and wait as the shop continues to bring in a flood of people looking to get their morning fix.

"I thought people were mostly tea drinkers here," I say.

"There's quite a few of us coffee drinkers. Depends on what you need to get you going. In your case, I see that comes in the form of a triple shot."

"Yes, but it's the only time I'll drink anything with caffeine. Otherwise, you might find I'm a jittery mess later in the day."

"Fortunately for you, I've only seen you on top of your game. Which reminds me—."

"Cappuccino for Adler. Triple latte for Nichols." The barista's voice booms across the shop as she calls out our orders. Alex grabs the drinks and hands me mine. We head to the door. Alex opens it, and I step out.

"As I said in the coffee shop, my brother told me about your recent client meeting. He's very impressed with your work. We talked about you supporting the work June is doing in the States. She has a client she's working with, and Aaron, Andrew, and I agree you'd be the perfect addition to her team."

"He mentioned that to me yesterday. I was stunned initially, but it's growing on me. I knew I was doing good work, but sometimes doubt creeps in."

"Raven, we will always be upfront with you. While you think you're doing just okay. We know better. Your work is on par with associates that have been here for years. My brother doesn't hand out compliments without merit. Trust us. You are on a fast track. Stay the course."

We reach the building and take the elevator to our floor. Before I head to my office, Alex turns to me.

"I meant what I said. You are on the right path. Seize the day."

"Thank you," I say and go to my office.

Wow, I feel like I'm on information overload, having received good feedback from Alex and Andrew within two days. On top of all that, I saw my beautiful Parker. I genuinely hope he's getting along fine. Not a day goes by that I don't feel the pang of guilt wrenched in my gut when I think about how I walked away. I won't say I should not have done it. I needed to for my sanity and for his sake. But I could have handled it better. Having seen him on video, I know that the thread, the tie between us, is still there. We are inseparable, and I need to get a grasp onto that. To accept that we can still be an us without a sexual relationship. Maybe we can be friends. That's the hardest part. Rebuilding. Perhaps that's what I need to work on: rebuilding my life and our friendship, starting from scratch to have something stronger and better.

I spend my day shadowing Andrew with his clients. He could have easily pawned me off on a less senior executive with the company, but Andrew seems to have a vested interest in my success, and I will take any opportunity he gives me. I trust him and Alex. If they feel I'm on a good trajectory, I will seize the opportunity, as his brother said. Focus on my career and not let anything get in the way. Now, if I could just get my head together.

CHAPTER 45

Anticipation

Parker

Seeing Rain every morning gives me hope. Hope for a future as a couple, that we can move past the pain and be together. I hope that one day, despite our loss, we will have a family.

The day Rain said she was pregnant was the best and worst day of my life. We created a life together. Our connection produced life through love that binds us forever. That thought brings me to my knees. Consequently, I also learned that losing our child was the most devastating thing besides her walking away from me. Nothing can prepare you for that. I think Rain blames herself, but it's not her fault. A higher power or something else caused our loss. One thing I know for sure is that one day, Raven Rain Nichols, Esquire will be my wife. We will build a life filled with love and happiness and have our family. No matter how long it takes. Rain will find her way back to our love.

My phone rings, and it's my friend Josh. He's been my rock through this ordeal.

"Josh. What's happening? You should be at work, man."

"I am. That doesn't mean I'm tied to a desk. How's London?" Josh works with his dad. He started working for him before we graduated college. He's always been very driven. Rain used to say his focus on work was a good thing because his broody, sexy looks could get him into a lot of trouble with women. She also said he was my dark-haired twin. I laugh when I think about it.

"It's good. Work has been challenging but good."

"And your girl? How is she doing?"

"She's good. I finally got to chat with her live."

"That's huge. Have you told her where you are?"

"No. Not yet. I'm planning to this evening."

"I hope it works out. I really like Rain. She's a good person and great for you. How's your mom handling all this?"

"You know. She feels like she lost a daughter. I told her we have to give Rain the time she needs to figure things out."

"You have the patience of a saint, man."

"I'm not so sure. This might take a while. Rain's as stubborn as I am. We'll see."

"Well, I'm in your corner. I just called to let you know we're having a big event for the private school we're opening."

"You need a donation?"

"No, man. Your dad helped me build it."

"What do you need from me?"

"Just be present for the celebration. Check your email later today. I'm having my EA send you something."

"Okay, I'm in as long as I can make the date work."

"I'd love to see Rain there. Should I reach out, or do you want to handle that?"

"Let me handle it."

"Okay. I appreciate it."

I hang up. I need to think about how to broach both topics with

Rain. If there hadn't been any break between us, I would have Josh manage the invitation with her himself. But the situation is different now, and his cold call could trigger Rain. I need to protect her from emotionally taxing issues related to our past. I know she may not want my help, but I can't have her going through these things alone. That's my job. Protect my girl—at all costs.

As challenging as work was today, it was over before I knew it. Anticipating my conversation with Rain was the one thing running through my mind. Now it's that time. I sit in my study, which I know looks nothing like any room she's seen me in. I wipe my hands on my slacks to remove the sweat. Calling Rain makes me nervous. There's only been a few times in my life that I've been anxious. I come from an influential family. Rubbing shoulders with some of the most powerful people on the planet is my life. They don't make me nervous, but anticipating a call with Rain does.

When it comes to Rain, I hang off her every word. Yeah, the few times I've been nervous were all with her. Asking her to be my girlfriend. Our first kiss, our first date, the first time we made love. All our important firsts made me nervous as hell because I was living those moments with my soulmate. A woman who imprints all the firsts and makes them a part of her forever. Knowing I'm about to say something that will imprint on her…telling her I've been here in London with her all along, has me drenched in sweat.

The phone rings, and she immediately picks up.

"Parker. Hey." The sound of her voice is soothing. I want to leap through the screen and hold her. But I can't. She's mine but not mine at the same time.

"How are you, Rain?"

"I'm good. I'm just on the way home. Can I call you when I get there?"

"Of course. Call me when you're ready," I tell her. She looks like she is about to head up a street before she hangs up.

I get up from my office, go into the kitchen, and get myself sparkling water and fruit.

My phone rings, and I snatch it from the counter.

"Honey. Did the phone even ring?" I close my eyes and shake my head at the sound of my mom's voice. This woman.

"Mom, I thought you were someone else. How are you?"

"Missing my son."

"I know, Mom. Where's Dad?"

"He's getting dressed. I just wanted to hear your voice."

"I talk with you every week. You just want me home."

"I do. Where's Raven?"

"Just so happens I'm waiting for her call."

"Oh, honey. Let me get off the line. Keep me posted on how it's going. I love you."

"Love you too, Mom," I say and hang up.

My phone rings again. This time, I check the caller ID before I make an assumption. It's my buddy AJ.

"AJ, what can I do for you?"

"I hope you're still in town, mate."

"I am."

"Good. Get to my office as fast as you can."

CHAPTER 46

This Is Real

Parker

It only takes a few minutes for me to reach the office building. I text AJ as I enter, letting him know I'm on my way up, then head straight to his office. His executive assistant greets me.

"Hi, Mr. Page. Let me get Mr. Adler for you." She opens the door, and AJ comes out and closes it behind him.

"AJ. What's up, man?"

He claps my hand and pats my back. "It's Raven. She was returning to the office to grab something and fainted. You're still listed as her emergency contact. She wouldn't let me call the doctor. Per safety protocol, I can't release her alone in her condition, but you can take her with you."

"Oh my god, is she okay?"

"She's shaken. I happened to be passing at the time, caught her, and brought her here. I gave her some water, and my assistant brought her some fruit. You can go in." He places a hand on my shoulder as I turn toward the door. "She doesn't know you're here."

"Okay. I got this. Thanks for everything. Give me a minute." I blow out a breath as I stand at the threshold.

"Take all the time you need."

I open the door and see Rain leaning back on the couch with her eyes closed and arm over her forehead like she's blocking out the sun, although there is none. She's still not feeling well. I've seen this before when she's not eating right and over-exerting herself. I need to let her know I'm here and pray she's not pissed about it. Okay, I can do this. I walk to her and then kneel at her side.

"Rain." When I call her name, she doesn't immediately respond. Tears roll down her cheeks. She squeezes her eyes shut even tighter. "Rain, babe. I'm here. Open your eyes."

She lowers her arm, swipes a tear, and shakes her head. At that moment, I realize Rain thinks she has slipped into a dissociative state. I touch her hand. "Rain. Please, open your eyes. It's Parker. Honey, I'm here with you at Saola. Open your eyes."

She places her other hand on my hand, and her eyes pop open and lock with mine. They widen, and she blinks in disbelief, then her eyebrows furrow.

"I'm here, Rain. This is real. I'm in London."

CHAPTER 47

Holding Back the Tears

Rain

I DON'T UNDERSTAND WHAT'S HAPPENING. I CAN'T BELIEVE I PASSED out in front of my CEO. What the hell. Oh. My. God. Did he carry me here? Thank god he left. I close my eyes and try to piece together what happened. I felt lightheaded and hungry, and I don't know, anticipating talking with Parker…I was just in a rush. I remember at the house party in college, I felt like this. Kevin wouldn't leave me alone. Then there was that time I was at home by myself. I thought I went into a trance, but I rolled off the couch. I remember walking toward Parker the day our baby died. It all went black. God, I'm stuck in my mind.

"Rain." I hear my name. I can't hold back the tears because it's Parker's voice, but it's not real. He's not here. He's likely at work or something. But he keeps calling me, and I don't want to answer. I don't want to fall further into the void. I can't let Alex see me like this. I need to pull my shit together. Like we practiced, I think about Parker's voice and let that pull me out of the fog. That's it. I can hear him just like he's here with me.

"I'm here, Rain. This is real. I'm in London."

"It can't be." I open my eyes. God, I see his beautiful face. It seems so real. I can feel his hand on mine.

"Rain, babe. I'm really here. You fainted, hon." I hear him say, and I touch his hand and squeeze it.

"Parker?"

"Yes."

"You're really here? In London?"

"Yes, Rain." He laces his fingers in mine and kisses them. "I'm here. I've come to take you home."

"But I don't understand." He rises and sits beside me, and although I try to pull away, he doesn't let go of my hand. It's really Parker.

"AJ called me. I'm your emergency contact. He said you wouldn't let him call a doctor. I'll take you home."

"How are you here? Who is AJ?"

"AJ is Alexandros. He said you can leave with a medical professional or me. And I'm here because I love you. We can talk about the rest at home. Are you okay to walk, or would you like me to carry you?"

At this point, I don't know what to think. Parker is in London, meaning he was here when we talked earlier. I'm happy to see him but pissed at the same time. I need to live my life and figure it out on my own. Here he is saving me again.

"Uhm, I can walk." I stand, and so does Parker. My body sways, but his strong arms balance me. "Give me a second," I tell him, and he loosens his grip.

I start walking toward the door with my arm locked in his. He opens the door. Alex is sitting at the edge of his assistant's desk, talking on his cell.

"Yeah, mate. I gotta go," he says, ending the call and directing his attention to me. "Raven. How are you feeling?"

"Better. I appreciate your help. I apologize for the commotion."

“Raven. You needed help. It was all I could do.”

“You good, mate?” He extends a hand to Parker and pulls him into a shoulder bump.

“Yeah. Thanks for taking care of Rain.”

“She’s family. We got her,” he assures me. Parker helps me to the elevator. We ride down in silence, his hand holding mine. And all the while, I’m holding back the tears.

CHAPTER 48

A Promise

Parker

THE ELEVATOR RIDE IS INTENSE. RAIN IS STILL IN SHOCK AT SEEING me here in London. Holding her hand, I'm trying hard not to pull her into me and hug her. I'm happy she's okay but torn that she had to find out this way.

She is staring straight ahead. I look down at her and shake her hand a little so she knows it's the man she loves standing next to her. The elevator dings, alerting us we've reached the ground floor. I lead her out the elevator across the lobby and out the door to my car parked in front of the building. I open the door, but before I help her, I turn her toward me and brush the curls from her shoulders.

"Rain." I dip my head to catch her gaze. She finally looks at me. "I know it's a shock seeing me, but it's what I was going to tell you today."

"I can't do this here, Parker. Take me home." She releases my hand and gets in the car.

The drive home is just as quiet as the elevator ride, except I don't get to hold her hand. Thank goodness we both live close to her office building. When we arrive at her flat, I help her out of the car and walk her to the front door.

"May I come in?"

She takes a deep breath and nods. I follow her inside. Her home is beautiful. As expected, she decorated her space with modern aesthetics, which we both love. She takes her things into another room, and I wait until she returns. When she steps back into the living room that opens into her kitchen, she stares at me. Tears well in her eyes.

"Rain. You need to eat. Let me order something."

I need her to come out of this state of confusion. I know it's a lot to take in because I feel the same way. Even though Rain's no longer my girl, I pray she'll still honor our agreement. I hold out my hand, and she walks over and places hers in mine. I pull her to me and wrap my arms around her. I inhale her essence. It's been so long. I feel her body shaking against me, and her breathing is erratic as she tries to catch her breath. I let her cry like that for a few moments until her breathing comes under control. I walk her over to the kitchen barstool, and she sits. I roam the house, find facial tissue, and clean her face. I laugh when she pushes my hand away.

"Thank you," I tell her.

"For what?"

"Not kicking me out. I love you so much, Rain."

"This doesn't mean anything. What are you doing here?"

"Looking out for someone who means the world to me. Making sure you got home safe. Ensuring you're okay." I go to the fridge, get sparkling water, and rifle through the cupboards to get glasses and pour us both a drink. I hand a glass to Rain. I pull my phone out.

"What are you doing?"

"Ordering you dinner. I'll wait for it to come, then I'll leave."

She shakes her head. "I still don't understand why you're here in London." Her tone is not accusatory. It's a legitimate question. For all she knows, I should be in San Francisco.

"I work here."

"You're joking, right?"

"Rain, you know I don't joke with you. We made a promise to each other that I have never broken and never will."

"I remember."

"Tell me."

"We would keep each other informed of our whereabouts. Regardless of the discussion's difficulty, we would always tell each other everything. Lastly, we would never deny each other *anything*."

"And whatever we told each other would be the truth," I add. "So, no, Rain. I'm not joking."

I lean against the counter with my legs crossed, drinking water and watching Rain watch me. She is reacquainting herself with my face. It's a thing she does to avoid getting lost in her head. Then, as if she's thought of something, she pulls out her phone and opens it to my contact. Her eyes widen, and I know what she sees. My location shows I'm at her house. I never lied to her that day when I told her she would always be able to find me. She never had to guess how close I am to her. She covers her mouth. The doorbell rings, and I retrieve the order. I return to the kitchen, get a plate and fork, then plate her meal and set it before her.

"Bon appétit, Rain. I love you. Have a good evening." I bend, kiss her on the forehead, and leave.

CHAPTER 49

I'm Not Talking to You

Rain

Friday

ANDREW SUGGESTED I WORK FROM HOME TODAY. THANK GOD. I STILL can't believe I passed out at work. Not to mention, my head is reeling, discovering Parker is in London. Aargh. What the hell is Parker thinking?

When he video called me this morning, I didn't answer. I'm pissed at him, but I'm not a total monster. He did come and help me, so I texted him my response.

Me: Thanks for calling, but I'm not talking to you.

Parker: Why?

Me: ...

"Parker fucking Page, you can't just show back up in my life," I scream at the walls as I fling my phone across the room. Ugh. Why, Parker? Why?

~

Saturday

It's a good thing it's Saturday. I have time to go shopping. I need a new phone case after throwing my phone. At least the screen didn't break. I swipe my phone screen to see Parker's message.

Parker: Good morning, Rain. I love you and hope you have a good day.

Me: Thanks for the message.

Parker: You want me to video call you?

Me: Honestly, I can't handle this right now.

Parker: Okay. I understand.

~

Sunday

Parker: Good morning, Rain. Remember our promise to tell the hard truth? I knew you'd be angry at me for coming to London. I came anyway. I'd rather have your anger than your absence. I never stopped loving you.

I swipe a tear from my eye. He's an idiot if he thinks he's getting a response. Shoot.

~

Monday

Parker: Good morning, Rain. I love you. Remember our promise to keep each other informed of our whereabouts? There was only one time I wasn't near to you. When you left me, I was so broken I couldn't breathe. I flew down the coast to our property in Carmel. I sat in a chair on the deck and stared out across the water for three days. I wanted to drink my sorrows away, but even then, I couldn't bring myself to drink. My only thought was I needed to stay alert. What if Rain needs me? I made sure Josh was available to you the entire time I was gone. He said he could tell you'd been crying when he dropped by to check in. The break was hard for both of us to stomach. See, the truth is, when you walked away from our love, you walked away from us all. Me, Josh, Mom, Dad. We all love you. Our lives feel like they're on hold, waiting for you. Oh, and I was only there three days because, after one day being away from you, I felt like I was dying—that's how strong our connection is. There is no me without you.

Tuesday

Parker: Good morning, Rain. I love you. Remember our promise never to deny each other anything? Will you talk to me? Is that asking too much?

Me: Call me after work.

CHAPTER 50

Open Your Eyes

Rain

Seeing Parker last week was overwhelming. Getting his text messages was even worse. It's hard not to respond to him. He says he never stopped loving me. I never stopped loving him. I don't know how to navigate this thing with Parker. I don't think I've slept a whole night since I found out he was here. Now he wants to talk. I close my eyes and wait. I'm so tired.

I'm floating in a sea of blackness; my body is numb, and I feel hollow inside. It's cold, and I feel warm pressure on my hand. There's a ringing in my ears, a subtle siren signaling me to wake. I hear my name. "Rain." The darkness becomes grey, and slowly, light filters in. "I'm here." When I open my eyes, there's a bright light, and the walls are bare. "Babe." I'm in a hospital room. It's Parker. I see his face. "Rain, babe. I'm here. Can you see me?"

"I can see you, Parker," I say, but I don't think he hears me.

"Tell me what you feel?" I feel the warmth of his breath beside my ear. "Tell me what you smell." I smell a woodsy scent. Parker, can he hear me? Am I saying words or thinking them? "Can you feel this?" I feel my hand being squeezed.

"Yes. I can feel your hand on mine." I hear him expel a breath. It's Parker expressing a sound I'm too familiar with…relief. He can breathe a sigh of relief that I'm back from the damn abyss I fell into. Sitting still, I try to concentrate on what I feel, smell, and hear, practicing the ritual he taught me.

"Rain. I'm here. Focus on me." I do, and my eyes shift from the corner of the room where the window meets the wall to Parker in a black suit and red tie. I smile to myself because it's such a wonderful dream. "Rain. I'm here. I love you. You're safe." I feel myself being pulled into him. Then he leans back and looks into my eyes. "Take your time, babe. Then tell me everything you see."

I force myself to sit straight and look at him. He's here in my London flat. "The walls are grey. There's a painting behind you of Ocean Beach. You're wearing my favorite suit and tie." I reach up and touch his head. "Your hair is a little neater than yesterday." He laughs.

"That's right, beautiful. You're back." I look around.

"How long was I gone? Wait, how did you get in? No, oh my god, don't tell me. I can't handle this right now."

"I'm sure you know."

"No, I don't. Tell me how you got in. Tell me it's not what I think."

"I own this building. Well, that's partially true. I bought it for you. You own it, too. I bought it the day you told the landlord you wanted to let the space."

I shake my head because this man is insane. "The hell, Parker. See, this is the issue.... You can't keep doing these...things."

"What things?"

"I don't even know what to say to you, Parker. We're not together. We haven't been since—."

"You don't have to remind me. I relive that moment every day. It's a day I'll never forget. My worst nightmare."

"You're right—I'm sorry. I didn't mean.... We've been through a lot. Don't let that be the defining memory of us."

Parker rubs his thumb across my cheek. "Then Rain, babe, give me something else to replace it," he pleads.

I close my eyes and cry. It's ugly, uncontrollable, and unnecessary, but still, I do it. I cry because I can't give this man the forever he wants. Not right now. I'll break him, or he'll break me. I try to cover my face with my hands, but Parker grabs my wrist and brings me to him. He sits me on his lap and holds me. And I sit there crying, snot sliding out of my nose down my face, covering me and him in slime. My breaths are short and rough. I hiccup, and I cry until I'm all cried out. I cry for Parker. I cry for our baby. I cry for me. I cry for my father. I cry for my mother. And I cry for the life I should be living with my soulmate. But I'm not. I'm fucking broken. When I'm done crying, my face is sore. Parker sits me on the couch, goes to the restroom, gets a warm wash rag, returns, and cleans my face. Then he goes to my kitchen and brings us both some water.

I take a sip. "Thank you, Parker. But I'm still mad at you."

"It's okay, babe. Tell me. Why are you mad at me?"

"For following me here. For buying this. For taking over my life." He laughs, which confuses me. "Why are you laughing?"

"I'm going to preface this by saying we promised always to tell the truth no matter how hard it is to hear."

"I know. I've told you the truth."

"I'm laughing because you think I've taken over your life when it's you, Rain. You have completely consumed my life. You are the air that I breathe. You are the reason I wake up every day because there is a chance of being near you. Because one day, there is a chance of being us again, and I am not talking about this." He waves his hands between us. "Where we know each other and have a connection. I am talking about a forever kind of us. I know you're prepared to banish me, but I'll pull that one card you can't refuse, no matter what. Because we promised never to deny each other anything. So, when you told me to walk away—that you were leaving, that we were no longer a couple. I accepted that."

"What is it, Parker? What card are you pulling? What do you want?"

"Rain, don't ever ask me never to see you again. Don't ever banish me from your life. And don't ever ask me to stop being your friend or to stop loving you. Because I won't go. I will always love you."

I reach out my hand to Parker, and he takes it and pulls me up to where he's standing. I embrace him. It's the best I can do for causing him so much pain. I hold him tight, willing him to feel our connection is still there. Showing him that no matter what, our lives are intertwined.

"I'm sorry, Parker."

"You said that before, babe. I believe you. I won't press for more. At least not now."

I look up at him. "Friends?"

"I've always been your friend, even before there was an us, and I will be long afterward. Even now...." He hesitates to say the words because he wants more. "I'm your friend."

CHAPTER 51

The Start of Us

Parker

The love of my life is in my arms again, not as a lover or wife, but as my friend. Rain promised she'd never ask me to leave her, and I never have, never will. I also won't stop loving her, needing her, breathing her. I will be here for every heartbreak, every setback, every laugh, every celebration, everything, including the day Rain wakes up and returns to me. Because that's what she promised…to one day come back. I can only hope she meant it.

"Rain, have you eaten dinner?" I brush the hair from her face and slide it over her shoulders. Her eyes are red and puffy from crying, but she's smiling at me. She is beautiful. I desperately want to dip my head and kiss her lips, but I don't dare take what she hasn't given me.

"No. Not yet."

"Will you have dinner with me? We can go out or order in, or I can cook." She pulls away from me and covers her mouth with her hand, contemplating my question.

"I'm a freaking mess. You have me in here crying like I've been drinking and watching Heathcliff wander out in the snow looking for his lost love, Cathy."

"It's not that bad, babe."

"You're my friend. You have to say that."

"I say it because you are beautiful. Yes, I am your friend. I've always been. But don't forget, babe, no matter what, I love you." She has to know she's the love of my life.

"Parker."

"I can't help it, Rain. That's my truth. So, are we having pasta and wine?" I ask, forcing myself to slow down. I don't want my girl upset with me.

"What else?" she asks. Her smile is bright and wide. I feel relieved to be here with her.

I take out my phone and order something from her favorite restaurant. I have the restaurant on speed dial. I join her on the couch.

"Okay, Rain. Spill it. What do you want to ask me?"

"Are you dating?" I'm shocked at how the words roll off her tongue with ease.

She has got to be fucking kidding me. I try my hardest to stifle the laugh of disbelief begging to come out. I can't, and it slips out anyway. She looks at me and starts laughing, too, and it's uncontrollable.

I take a deep breath. "Rain, are you trying to break me? I profess my undying love for you, and you ask me if I'm dating? I would be dating if only you'd say yes. Skip that. I would never have to date again if you would marry me. Is that what you want? Do you want me to ask the question, Rain? Because you know there's only one answer to that." Her eyes widen because she knows she can't deny me anything and vice versa.

"Parker, stop." She puts up her hand, and I grab it.

"Then Rain, honey. Please don't joke with me about that again. I'm all yours. All you have to do is say yes."

"I'm sorry. I'm still stunned you're here."

"No, you're not, Rain. You know me. What did you think a man like me was going to do? Have I not shown my dedication and love for you?

You've seen the extent I'll go to protect you, to ensure you want for nothing. You've witnessed the wrath I bring to anyone who disrespects you. How could you not know I'd be here?"

Rain knows the power I wield. The power to put my foot down and stop this charade. I only took a step back for her. I won't disregard her feelings or that she's trying to heal herself in her own time, in the only ways she knows…without me as her man.

"You're scaring me, Parker."

"Is that the truth, Rain? Are you afraid of me? That's not us. We were never that couple. There were no misunderstandings between us. Our relationship was always layered in love, respect, and honesty. The last time you said those words, you weren't honest with yourself or me. Shall I ask you again? Is that what you want? For me to ask you the same question I asked you all those years ago? For you to take me as yours like you did before and swallow those words? This 'let's just be friends' ends now if you do. I will claim you as mine, and you renege on asking me to walk away. Because the day you give yourself to me, and I come inside you again, you will be mine, Rain…forever. I promise you that."

"You're right. I'm not afraid of you, but I won't take you like I did before. However, I will do this." She comes to me, sits on my lap, buries her face in my neck, and hugs me tight.

She's tired of fighting. It's Rain's version of an olive branch. Loving. Gentle. Honest. My eyes fill with tears. I wish I could stay strong. Strong enough for her to find her way back to me, one breath, one moment, one tear at a time. This is the beginning. The start of us. A long journey to a promise of forever.

"I'm so sorry Parker. You'll always be in my life." She sighs against my neck. "Let's figure out how…together."

CHAPTER 52

Fear of Forever

Rain

It's six in the morning, and my brain already hurts. Last night was too much. Parker professed his undying love, and I fought to keep my walls up, protecting my heart. I can't hurt him again the way I did before. I'm not ready to receive his special kind of love. I can't. I won't. He deserves more—someone whose life is not a mess. Someone who's had an example of a functional family. Whose brain is not a wreck. He needs someone whose body doesn't fail them. The one good thing I can claim is my work, worth, and will to be the best.

My phone buzzes, and I know who it is before I look at it. I just answer.

"Good morning, Parker."

"Uhm, good morning." The woman's voice on the other end jerks me out of my morning haze. "You can talk with Parker, but not me?" Her voice is laced with resentment.

"Mom. What's wrong?"

"Nothing. I'm calling to check in on you, to see how London is."

"Um, it's fine. I'm fine. London's fine." At least, I was until she called.

"Well, seems like everything is fine. Why haven't you called?" And here we go.

"You know, I'm not sure. It's not like we have the best relationship.

We don't really talk, do we? If my perfect recall ability serves me right, the last time I called, you had a nail appointment that was rather pressing."

"Don't—."

"Don't what, Mom? Go there? I just did. Now, tell me why you called."

"To talk."

"Great. So, tell me. Why did Dad really leave in the middle of the night when I was eight?"

"That's not why I called."

"Okay. As you may have noticed, I was expecting another call. I need to clear the line for that. Unless you have something else you want to say?"

"No, Rae, I don't have anything else to say. You stay well," she says before hanging up.

I don't know what my mom is doing. This love-hate relationship needs to change. I've tried to get her to talk to me, but unless she plans on telling me the truth, we can't resolve what's between us.

If there's one thing I've learned being with Parker for the past eight years, it is that a real relationship can only stand on solid ground, no matter what kind of relationship it is: friends, family, or lovers. A solid foundation involves honesty, unconditional love, and trust. As much as I don't like it, Parker did what he did because he loves me. It's pure and absolute. He trusts in our commitment to each other, to be honest and never deny each other anything. Almost a year ago, I asked Parker to let me go. He did, but he didn't leave me. He only did what I asked, nothing more. Last night, he called my bluff when I told him I was afraid. I am not afraid of Parker Page. I have never been. I'm afraid of taking him like I did then. Being consumed by him. I have a fear of… forever.

I wasn't ready then; I'm not prepared now, but my connection to him led me to respond five years ago when he asked why I was afraid.

"Because I don't know what this is. Why do you want me? Why…?"

"Why what, babe?"

"Why me? I'm not from your world, Parker. If we never had class together, we never would have met. I wouldn't be here in your arms."

"Maybe. Maybe you wouldn't be here right now, but that doesn't mean you would never be in my arms because the gravitational pull I feel between us feels like forever, like it's been there my whole life. I know we would have met at some point now or in the future, and we would be locked like we are in each other's arms…together. I've never wanted anything, Rain. You're right about that part. I never wanted anything, that is, until I met you. And right now, I have you, and I'm happy, and you're all I need. So don't be afraid of me, Rain. Just let me give you everything you need. Let me make love to you. Let me hold you. Let me make coffee. Let me protect you. Let me be your everything. Because I'll never do anything to make you afraid of me."

He pulled me into him, and just when I thought he was going to kiss me, he didn't. His lips hovered, his breath mingled with mine in the air, warm with sex and sweat rising between us.

"Show me you're not afraid of me," he said, and I knew exactly what he wanted. For me to close the distance, take what he was offering, take what was rightfully mine, to give myself to him freely without fear.

I leaned forward and licked his lips like he did mine. Then I tasted him, pressed my lips to his, and opened my mouth to welcome him. He licked into me, and that was all it took. I was his.

"Show me you're not afraid of me," he'd said back then. I did. Last

night, Parker was right when he told me that if I take him again, I can't go back and say I don't want him. This is not a game. I still love him. But I'm not ready to fall under his spell again. And if I were to take him that way, I'd lose myself all over again. My love for him runs that deep. One night in bed, we bound ourselves to each other. I won't deny the significance of that moment. I felt at my core its implications—marriage, commitment, forever. I'm not ready.

My phone buzzes…this is him.

"Hey, how's your morning?" he asks. The sun is barely up. I notice from the street signs that he's walking outside somewhere.

"Well, it would have been better had I woken up to a call with you."

"What do you mean? Aren't I the first call of the day?"

"Unfortunately, not." I sigh.

"You want to talk about it?"

"Yeah."

"You up for company?"

"How soon can you be here?" I ask. The doorbell rings.

"Hold on…not sure what neighbor needs what." I open the door, and it's Parker. He hangs up the call, takes my phone, and hangs it up, too.

"How's that for soon?"

I shake my head and let him in. He returns my phone, hugs me, and heads past me.

"What are you doing?" I call behind him.

He stops and holds out his hand to me. I take it, and we walk into the kitchen together.

"I'm going to make you some coffee and breakfast. You okay with that?"

I take a seat at the counter while he goes about his business of fixing things. "Yeah, Parker. I'm okay with that."

I watch him maneuver around my kitchen, and he's lovely to watch. It's surreal having him here after months apart. I should have never done what I did, the way I did it. But here we are, and I'm determined to repair our friendship even though Parker doesn't seem to think it needs fixing. When he's done making coffee, he sets a cup in front of me. He dips his head and kisses my cheek.

"Good morning, babe."

"Good morning, Parker."

"Have a sip and tell me what happened this morning."

I take a sip and tell Parker about my mom calling while I watch him toast bread and make us poached eggs. Then he washes strawberries, cuts an apple, and mixes them in yogurt to make parfait. When he's done, he sits next to me.

"Okay, your mom called. Do you think she's trying to build a relationship with you or just curious about your whereabouts?"

"That's the thing, I don't know. Mom calling is so random. It makes me think she's building up to ask me for something."

"What do you have that she needs?"

"That's the thing—nothing."

"Let's play it by ear. If she reaches out again, press for more information. Try to be neutral when she calls. Get her to open up. Use your lawyer training."

"Yeah, I guess you're right. We'll see if she calls again." I eat breakfast and wash it down with coffee. Parker does the same. In between eating and drinking, he watches me. He always watches, checking to see if I'm okay. "So, Parker."

"Babe."

"Last night's conversation was heavy."

"I know, Rain. It was heavy for me as well. I may seem tough, but parts of me are fragile when it comes to you. Being here in your presence is…well, let's just say it takes a lot of restraint not to pull you into my arms, take you into the bedroom, and make love to you."

"Parker."

"Rain, you need to hear this. We can't sidestep our feelings. My feelings. I know yours—you made it clear we can only be friends. I'm trying to understand and accept that, but I don't plan to turn off my feelings, so you need to listen. Hopefully, I can curtail the desire to say or act out the things in my head over time. But you're still the love of my life."

I close my eyes and blow out a breath. This is hard. "I understand, Parker. I'll listen, but first, can I shower and put on clothes so I look decent?"

He laughs. "Yeah, babe. Go. Do your thing. I'll clean up in here."

CHAPTER 53

The Hardest Part

Parker

RAIN TAKES HER TIME IN THE SHOWER AND GETTING READY. SOME things never change. I remember when she would drag me out of bed in the morning to shower with her because she liked how I would bathe her. She said she enjoyed the feel of warm water washing over us when I was inside her. She said she felt alive, knowing my seed was rolling down her legs. Sometimes, the simple act of me washing away evidence of our love between her legs made her come again. Rain is beautiful that way. Everything has meaning for her. God, I need to push those thoughts from my head.

I'm sitting on the couch in her living room when she finally appears. She's wearing oversized jeans and a T-shirt that has David Bowie on it. She loves his music. She loves music in general: jazz, R&B, pop, all of it.

"Rain, babe, you look comfortable. Come and sit with me," I tell her, and she does. That is another thing about Rain. She's loyal. Even though we've been apart, and I randomly show back up in her life, she honors our commitment to each other. We won't hesitate to do what one another asks.

"I am, Parker."

"Can I talk to you now?"

She looks at me curiously, like she can't believe I'm asking. I am, because what we have right now is fragile. Our conversation can either strengthen what's between us or shatter it completely. My heart is already broken enough for both of us, so I'll do whatever I can to heal us and our relationship.

"I can't do this like this," she says.

"You want me to go? I'll go. We can talk later."

"No, that's not what I mean. It's too hard to sit here like I don't know you. Like you're a nobody that doesn't mean anything to me. Like I'm having a random conversation about the weather."

"How do you want to do this? You have to tell me what you want, Rain."

She walks over to me. She sits on my lap with her legs across the couch. Like she's done many times before, she puts her arm around my neck, turns to me, and kisses me on the cheek.

"Parker. I don't know how to do this. For so long, all I've known is you. You know there can never be any distance between us when we talk. Even if we're not a couple. I can't help myself. We started this way, we loved this way, we ended this way. And so, we begin again." I lace my hand in hers. "Whatever you say, I promise never to leave you again. I never want to hurt you like that. I want our friendship to last forever, whatever form that takes. We promised to listen without judgment, to tell each other everything, and that it would always be the truth. I told you my truth yesterday. I want to hear yours. Now, tell me what you have to say. I'm listening."

I feel a powerful sense of relief when I hear her words. It solidifies that she'll be there for me in some form. That on the basic level, our friendship has a chance to survive. I take a deep breath.

"Rain. Hearing what you said makes this a little easier. Well, I still need to control myself if you insist on being this close, because you know it's hard for me to concentrate when you're around. And it's been a while."

"Get over it, Parker," she blurts out in her not-so-subtle attempt to rein me in. That's my girl.

"You know I love it when you do that, but I think that will be the hardest part, Rain. All the things you do are things that I love about you. They're the things that made me fall in love with you. You're asking me to shut off the part of me that wants to haul you off to the bedroom. I'll try, but I cannot deny that those things set me off. Your scent wafting around me, the way you look at me, the warmth of your arm around my neck, and the weight of your body against me. It's hard, honey. I'm hard. I know you feel my body responds to you. But I need to dial that part of me back even though I don't want to." I pause and blow out a breath.

Rain doesn't say a word. She watches my every move, and I know she sees and hears me. She's processing it all. I know my girl will never forget and that my confession will wrap around her heart and live there forever. No matter who she's with, wherever she goes, Rain will never forget that I am the man who professed his unconditional love to her, and that's all I can ask for now.

"Rain, when you walked out of my life…when you told me we couldn't be together, it was the second worst day of my life. The first was the day we lost our child. I don't want to bring up this trauma for you, but you need to understand it was traumatic for me, too. You need to know that I planned to propose that day."

She gasps. "Parker. I—."

"You don't need to say anything, Rain. Today is the present. I need to say this. When you said you were pregnant, I was elated. I saw the future I dreamt for me, you, our child, our life together. That's all I've ever wanted. What I still want. I know you're not ready for that. Asking me to be your friend comes with this knowledge. I'm going to be here patiently waiting for our day. I don't believe you're afraid of me. You're pretending to be afraid of me, Rain. Intentionally pushing us aside for fear of something else: the things that cloud your head. Whatever it is, we can solve it together, and when we do, you will come to me when I hold my hand to you. Right now, I'll give you whatever you need. You say that's friendship. You have it. It's a package deal, though. It comes with our pain, passion, connection, and love. When I say I love you, I do. I don't know how not to love you, Rain."

"Oh, Parker."

"Let me finish, babe. I can only bear this if I know you love me. When you say those words to me, what do you feel?"

I hold my breath, waiting for her response.

"I love you, Parker. It's pure and honest. But I don't know how to be what we were before. My head, heart, and body won't allow me to give in to the love while I'm broken. You're all I've ever known. All I've ever wanted. But I need to be me. I need to be me without you, but not separated from you, if that makes sense."

It does. Although I don't want to hear it, I understand Rain's point. She's asking me to wait for her, and I will.

"I get it, babe. I promise I do. Do what you have to do. But never forget that I love you." She tightens her arms around my neck and buries her head, and I pray she won't cry again because it breaks my heart, especially when I'm the one making her cry.

"Can I tell you something?"

"Yeah, babe. Anything." Anything to take my mind off my heavy heart.

"Okay, so I think I've developed some type of quasi-codependency thing with you."

"Babe, we're connected. That's a given."

"I know, but what I'm trying to say is that when I think about you, when I see your face, hear your voice.... It's pretty much the only thing.... I don't know how to say this...."

"Rain." I lift her head, cup her face, and restrain myself from kissing her. "Look at me. Say what you have to say, babe. Like you said, it's me. I've never seen you fumble your words—that's not you, so tell me."

"That's just it, Parker. You just have to say, 'Tell me,' And it flows out. The sound of your voice cuts through the fog. When I'm about to lose myself in my mind, I think of you, and it pulls me out right away. Sitting entangled in your arms gives me the courage to tell you everything. It's stupid, but I don't know how not to do this. I need space to wean myself from these things. To stand on my own two feet. To take charge of my life. If I can." She shakes me, and it's funny, and she smiles to match mine. "I'm serious, Parker."

"I know you are, babe. That's one of the things I can't stop, calling you babe, telling you I love you. Like you said the other night, we'll figure out how to do this new thing together. Although it pains me, I will honor your request just to be your friend. To give you time to figure it out. But also, like we talked about—we can't cross the line because we are all in or not. You can't toy with my feelings. Not like that. I love you too much. I hear everything you're telling me. I just want you to remember there are two of us in this and that every second we're apart, I die a little inside. You didn't know that part, did you?"

"No, Parker. I didn't."

"Because on the surface you see the power, privilege, and everything else that comes with being an elite. But there's more to me beneath the surface. Passion for a woman who wants something else for now, pain for losing the love of my life and our child, plans for a future with my family. You see, I've envisioned you as my wife and the mother of my children for so long that at times it's hard to breathe. Then I stop and think about how amazing you are. The strength it took for you to walk out the door that day. How much courage you demonstrated coming to London alone. Although, as long as I'm alive, you'll never be completely alone. I'd wait a lifetime for you. And I'm not saying all this for any other reason than it's the truth of our love. So babe, if you need to hear my voice to help cut through the fog—I'm here for you."

"You make this difficult."

"What?"

"The things I like about you most. Your power, your privilege, your passion, your love. Your determination. You make it hard to resist you."

"Then take me when you're ready. I'm all yours. Now get off my lap, babe, before I take back what's mine," I tell her. She jumps off my lap like I shocked her. I laugh because I know that we'll be okay. I have a lot of fucking work ahead of me, but we'll be okay. One day.

"I love you, Parker. Thank you."

"One day," I whisper.

CHAPTER 54

Fire in His Eyes

Rain

BUILDING A LIFE WITH PARKER AS ONLY FRIENDS HAS BEEN GOOD AND exhausting at the same time. I've been doing my best not to be so clingy, and he's been doing his best not to confess his undying love for me and talk about our future lives together. Parker envisions me as his wife. I'm not ready for that. Not now. Not yet. I need to figure things out for myself. I need to rid my head of the things that lurk in the shadows. I need to stand on my own two feet.

It's been one month since Parker walked back into my life. The cling factor is still there, and Parker is uncomfortable with me instinctively grabbing him, and rightly so. It's hard for me not to be close to him, especially when discussing difficult topics. We put parameters in place to help us navigate our new normal.

We continue our morning calls. Parker felt it was not a good idea for him to come over early in the morning on weekends because mornings for me remain challenging due to my memory issues. His natural instinct is to hold me in his arm of protection. When we were a couple, mornings were my favorite time to make love to him to push the bad memories out of my head. So, between it being his favorite time to be with me and mine, we agreed to video calls. I also had to decide to stop jumping in his lap to talk for obvious reasons. Additionally, I'm doing my best not to touch his hair because I want to bring his mouth to mine as soon as I slide my hands into it. Needless to say, we have a lot of things to work through.

On a positive note, he seems to understand why we can't take our relationship further. He suggested we go to therapy, but I refused. I'm afraid. What new monster will therapy bring to the surface? Will it reveal I was wrong for what I did to Parker? This past month, we also decided to limit our time together. We meet for lunch once a week and have dinner every other week. I'm really hoping he'll find someone. Because although he talks about his commitment to me and how much he wants me, he needs to release the pent-up energy he has. I can't be that person for him, and I know from experience that he has a strong sex drive. When we were together as a couple, we spent a lot of time connected to each other in the biblical sense. Ugh, I need to get that out of my mind. Because I have needs, too.

My bell rings. It's Parker. We planned to hang out today since it's the weekend, and he wanted to show me something around London. That's another thing. We aren't supposed to walk in on each other's houses unless there's an emergency like last time.

"Parker, you look good," I tell him, stepping aside so he can enter.

He dips his head to kiss my cheek. "So do you, but you always look amazing, Rain."

"No hug today?"

"I don't know if I can handle it. It's been a while since I've seen you." I open my arms to him, and he hugs me anyway, because he can't deny me anything, and I want this hug. I want to smell his sweet, woodsy smell. I want to be comforted for a moment. But as soon as it starts, it's over.

"Thanks, Parker. Where are we headed today?"

He sits on my couch, stretches his arms across the back, and crosses a leg over his knee. "We have reservations for brunch."

"Works for me. I'm ready when you are."

The place Parker chose is within walking distance of my apartment. I should start calling it my building since Parker put it in our names. It's strange owning my first place. Even more so because it's in a foreign country. Back in the States, I rented all through college. Parker suggested that I purchase a house when I move back. He still has his home in Atherton but is considering selling it upon his return and buying a home in the heart of San Francisco. We were both born in San Francisco and plan to establish ourselves there.

When we arrive at the restaurant, we're seated at a table that provides a nice view. It has a cozy, modern vibe, which is hard to do without over-indexing one or the other direction.

"You can order for me, Parker."

"Sure, babe."

That's the great thing about being with Parker. He knows my situation. The fact that I can remember everything means everything, including menu items. It sucks, but when he wasn't around, I avoided trying new places because I had read the menus, knew the locations, and read the reviews. Ugh. It's too much information that I unnecessarily hold in my head. After eight years of knowing me intimately, Parker knows everything I like and dislike. So, going to a restaurant I've never been to before, he can look at the menu and decide what to order for me. Not because he's trying to be the dominant male, but because he's thoughtful and understands me.

"Have you tried anything new that I can add to your list of likes?"

"No. They're the same."

A wait staff member comes to the table, and Parker shares our order. When he's done, the person disappears into the back of the restaurant.

"Rain, tell me about returning to the States. What's the plan?"

"It's simple: the Adlers think I should join June's team, learn from the senior counsel who'll also be working on the team, and do what I do best. They think I made the right decision to focus on real estate. Andrew says I'm a natural. Alex and Aaron agree."

"That's great, babe."

"Are you returning, too?"

"You know you don't need to ask. The answer is always going to be yes. I'm here because of you. Not that you asked me to be, but because wherever you are, I'm going to be there."

"That's one of the things I wanted to talk about today."

The waitress comes with our order and places a dish in front of me and the other in front of Parker.

"Thank you," I tell her.

"Is there anything else for now?"

"No," Parker responds. Then she disappears again. I eat my meal. Parker doesn't eat his. He watches me until I stop chewing, then speaks.

"Talk to me, Rain. Tell me what you wanted to tell me."

I inhale, filling my cheeks with air, and blow it out. "Parker, you have to start seeing other people," I say in a rush and look at him. His penetrating stare and furrowed brows tell me he's pissed. "Don't look at me like that. By people, I mean women. Or a woman. Somebody."

"Why are you telling me this, Rain?"

"Because I know you. You have needs, and I'm not your person to satisfy those anymore."

"I've never seen you dance around a topic before. It's cute but irritating at the same time." I look at him curiously. "You're telling me to find a woman to have sex with because I can't have you."

"We're not together."

"That's easily rectified."

"No, it's not, Parker. You need to move on from me."

"I'll never move on from you. We never talked about moving on. What you're asking me to do is have meaningless, protected sex with someone else. Is that what you are saying?"

"Parker, do you have to put it that way?"

"Our agreement is to always to tell each other the hard truth, Rain. You are my forever person. That's not the first time you've heard me say those words, so don't pretend it is. So yeah, you are not asking me to move on because you know I won't. You are telling me to seek sexual satisfaction from someone other than you until you come back to me. Because Rain, as certain as I am that the sun will rise tomorrow, I know you will come back to me. That was your promise." He lifts my hand with the ring on it. "This signifies my promise and your acceptance."

"It doesn't matter what you call it. You have my permission to be with someone else."

"Are you seeing someone? Is that what you're trying to tell me?" I see him tense up; his eyes feel like they're piercing my soul. This is too hard. I can't breathe.

"No, Parker, but you need to brace yourself because if I'm not with you, I will inevitably end up with someone else. You need to accept that." I take it a step further. I know he won't accept my words until I say this. "I am asking you to let me live a normal life that doesn't involve you as my man. I plan to date other people. Not now, but eventually. I need you to accept that."

Parker's mind is racing. His rage is building. His eyes are darting back and forth, searching mine. His need to possess me overrides his brain, but he's my Parker. He will agree—he can't not. Because it's me.

Then, for the first time since we reached the restaurant, he looks away from me. He hasn't even touched his food. He looks at the patrons and the décor, and then his eyes shift to me. There's fire there. I just don't know what kind.

CHAPTER 55

Lessons in Love

Parker

I'M SITTING ACROSS THE TABLE FROM RAIN, TALKING ABOUT OUR FUture, not us together, but apart. I loathe this. The heat emanating from me is enough to burn this damn building down. Rain has no idea what she's asking me to do. To stand by and watch her be with someone else. Is she fucking kidding me? The only woman to carry my seed. The only woman whose entire body I've claimed as mine. The only woman I've ever wanted. The woman with whom I plan to build a life is asking me to let her loose to explore. Because that's all it is. Whether she realizes it or not, our connection tells me we are a forever couple, that I was born to be with her, and that she was born to be my wife. I can't fucking look at her now. I want to kiss her and lock her up at the same time.

She reaches across the table and touches my arm, attempting to control the flames consuming me, using a cup to douse the raging wildfire she lit, which has spread across a million acres. She wants an answer, but I don't have one because she didn't ask a question. She delivered a command for me. One I can't deny because it's her.

My eyes shift back to Rain. I tilt my head to one side and then the other. I take a deep breath. "You will introduce me to any man you decide to be with. You will tell them I am your former lover and an important part of your life. You will never have unprotected sex. No other man's seed will enter your body other than mine. You will never commit to forever with another man. And lastly, Rain, there will be consequences for any man that slights you."

"Parker. This is insane."

"What did you think I was going to say, Rain? You know who I am. How I am. You promised me your love, your body, then gave it to me freely. Only my seed will enter you."

"We're not together like that anymore."

"Because you asked for a time out, and I gave it to you. Time-outs are temporary unless that's not what you really want. You have to tell me what you want. You know how this works, Rain. We're both adults. Don't treat me like the enemy. I've never wronged you. If you don't want me, say the words. Tell me you were lying when you said you wanted me in your life. Tell me I'm waiting in vain. Tell me saying you had to fix yourself was all a ruse. Tell me I got it wrong. Tell me to leave right now and I'll go, and you'll never see me again. One word—is all you have to say. I promised never to deny you *anything*. I meant it." My voice is harsh, but I don't care. She initiated this conversation—she'll take the consequences it brings.

I take a deep breath. Pulling a power move on the love of my life is not what I had intended to do today, but Rain has overstepped. There's only so much I can take. I can end this entire conversation by taking her home, holding out my hand, and telling her to come to me, to let me love her as her husband. We promised never to deny each other anything, and she would never deny me that. I only have to ask. But even in my anger, I wouldn't do that. I hear her. Even in my fear of losing her I won't back down from my promises to her. I listened to what she said. She has to come to me willingly in her own time. If ever.

"You're not eating. Can we go?" she asks, ending the discussion.

"Yes, Rain. We can go." I stand, take her hand, and help her up.

I don't need to settle the bill. They have my card on file. I chose this place because they have all her favorite foods. I thought the past ten months were the hardest, being separated from her. But this, navigating life and living separately with her moving forward without me, is unbearable.

As we exit the restaurant, I give Rain time to think through my response. Rain wants time to figure herself out, to explore. I disagree with that approach. When we lost our child, I asked Rain to go to therapy with me. The loss of a child layered on top of her childhood trauma is a lot to bear for anyone and more so for someone doomed to relive negative events daily. I didn't tell her I'd been getting help since that day. It's the only thing keeping me from putting my foot down and putting an end to what Rain is attempting to do on her own. Because I learned this is not just about me. Living her life how she wants—if that's without me, she has to tell me. She's in control and she knows it.

Instead of calling the car to pick us up, I decide we'll walk to the park before heading to where I wanted to take Rain before she unloaded her bombshell. She's walking quietly by my side, and I'm straining not to take her hand.

"Do we have far to go?"

I lift my chin. "We're heading to the park just down the street."

As we're walking, I hear someone calling out. "Excuse me. Excuse me."

I turn around carefully, shielding Rain from whomever it is.

"Do I know you?" I ask.

"No, I was talking to her."

I turn toward Rain. "Do you know this man?" She looks past me.

"Hi," he greets. "You remember me from the coffee shop on Holborn? You're the triple shot latte."

"Babe," I say.

"Oh, hi. I remember seeing you a few times, but we've never talked."

"No, we haven't. You were rushing in and out those times, and I figured you were heading to work or something."

"I don't recall you mentioning your name," I tell him.

"Max."

"Max." Rain repeats. "It's nice to meet you formally. My name is Raven. This is Parker, my friend." My jaw clenches when she says the word "friend."

"Parker. Nice to meet you."

"Max, was there something you needed?" I ask. "We have to go."

Max looks me over, and then he looks at Rain. The urge to punch him is pressing. This adds fuel to the fire that's already ablaze.

"No. Maybe I'll catch you next time at the coffee shop, Raven. It was nice seeing you again."

"Have a good day." Rain doesn't confirm or refute his advances, and I'm fuming. But I will hold my peace because our conversation isn't over, and Rain needs to learn a lesson.

We walk silently until we make it to the park. Rain sits on a bench, and I sit beside her. Trying to control my anger, I focus on the crunching sound made by people jogging on the decomposed granite path and the laughter of children playing in the grass.

"I want to talk about what you said back there," Rain says with a clip indicating her mood.

"We can talk about anything you want," I say, even-keeled.

"I won't agree to do what you said."

I don't respond right away. Rain needs to think about what she's saying. Think about our promises and our commitments. She needs to remember who she's talking to. My eyes are focused on the people in the park going about their everyday lives while I do my best not to control my girl. I love her so much. I'd give her the world.

"I know you heard me, Parker."

"I heard what you said. And know what that implies."

"I'm not yours, Parker."

"Hold my hand, Rain." I hold out my hand, and Rain doesn't hesitate to take it. "Come sit here." I pat my lap, and she sits on it because I know that's her favorite thing to do. She can't resist it. I brush her curls over her shoulders and look up at her. My girl is beautiful, and as much as I love her, I must make a painfully brutal point. "Do you love me, Rain?"

"Yes, Parker. I never stopped."

"I love you too. You are everything to me." I say the last part slowly to drive home my point.

"I know."

"Do you trust me?"

"With my life."

"Have I ever hurt you?"

"No. You never would."

"Straddle me." Her eyes widen in surprise. I know she's torn between doing what I ask or denying me. She ponders a few seconds, then positions herself over me so I can no longer see the people ahead of us in the park. If only she knew how badly I want to take her right now. Rain's a smart woman. I suspect she does. But this is not about me. She didn't tell me to leave. I want to know why. This is about her showing me what she wants. "Kiss me."

"We're not that way, Parker."

"It wasn't a question. You don't have to be here. The car's across the street."

I lock eyes with Rain until she lowers her lips to mine and kisses me. I allow her to guide the kiss, to take it to whatever level she wants. Her kiss is gentle and chaste at first, and it feels like bliss because it's the first time we've kissed like this since we parted. I want to lick into her, but that's not the point. I reach my hand between us and unzip her pants, then break the kiss.

"Lift your body for me," I whisper.

She lifts a little, then, on instinct, crashes her lips back to mine. I reach my hand beneath her underwear and between her folds, and good god, I have to hold back a groan. My girl is fucking wet. I close my eyes and sigh because it makes this lesson worth the pain it will cause. Her breath hitches as I rub between her folds. She doesn't resist me or try to take my hand out. Her hips move in rhythm against my hand as her body craves more friction. She pushes her tongue past my lips, and I let her suck my tongue. My baby wants me, and I take it all in momentarily. I push two fingers into her while I caress her clit with my thumb. She's so wet my fingers slide in and out with ease. I feel the first wave of contraction and increase the rhythm and pressure as she devours my mouth. She fucks my hand.

"Come for me, Rain. Give it all to me." And like I knew she would, my woman comes on my hand hard as I capture her moans in my mouth. My hand stays in place as I coax her through her climax until the pulsing stops. Until my fingers are soaked. Until she stops chasing the feeling of finally having a part of me in her. She breaks the kiss, panting.

"Parker. What are you doing?"

I take my fingers from between her legs, put them in my mouth, and lick them clean. Then I zip her pants. I brush her hair over her shoulders and look her in the eyes. She's so beautiful. So perfect.

"Proving a point." My voice comes out sternly.

"What?"

"Rain. If you want to see other men, you'll do what I asked. Don't challenge me again unless you mean it. I know you well enough to know you're toying with me, and I don't like it. You got what you wanted. It's time to go."

CHAPTER 56

The Man of the Hour

Rain

PARKER PAGE, ESQUIRE IS POWERFUL, PRIVILEGED, PASSIONATE, AND A pain in my ass. I was stunned silent when he made me come on his hand in the park last month, shutting down my stunt in the restaurant.

I pushed him too far. I regrettably played off his vulnerability and could have handled the conversation better. But I didn't. He's not to blame for my mess of a life, but he did emphasize one truth. Parker and I are inextricably linked. I can't deny him anything and vice versa. I don't want to. Because the truth is I want him as much as he wants me. *Hmph.* But I can't act on the love between us until I get myself together because I'm not strong enough to say no to him. He proved that.

After we left the park, something changed between us, a bigger shift than any I've ever experienced with him. Beyond our connection, I learned something important about us. That I'm just as stubborn, if not more so, than Parker. He was right. I will do what he asks, but now I know he won't ask me for anything more than I'm ready to give. And he will have to wait a long time to get it.

There's a knock at the door to my room. I already know who it is. The most handsome guy in the world coming to collect me to see the second most handsome guy. I open the door for Parker. He's dressed in his black tux. It's been a while since I've seen him in a tux. When we were dating, after events, we'd return to his place or mine, and he'd let me undress him. I smile and remember those days. I couldn't keep my hands off him.

Now, we're back in San Francisco for the weekend to attend Josh's event to celebrate the opening of a private school. They already had a grand opening. This is a private celebration amongst his peers. It'll be the first time in a while for me to see many familiar faces from their world. Parker's parents will be there, too. I'm nervous because although we are going together, we're not a couple, and people know it. This is our new normal. But when I committed to loving Parker, I committed to being a part of his world, his life, and these people are a big part of that.

"Rain, you're not ready. The event starts at six. Josh wants us on time."

"I couldn't decide on this or this." I hold up two silk dresses.

"Blue," he says. I excuse myself and put on my blue maxi slip dress. When I go to the living room, Parker is there, holding my coat out, waiting for me to slip in, which I do.

"You're so efficient. And you look handsome."

"Thanks, babe. The car's here. You ready?"

I take a deep breath. "Yeah."

He puts his hand on the small of my back, walks me to the car, helps me in, and slides in beside me.

"I'm nervous," I admit. Parker reaches his hand across the seat and takes my hand.

"You'll be fine. You know most of these people."

"Yeah, but our situation is different."

"You haven't stopped loving me, have you?"

"No, Parker. I'm just trying to find me."

He turns away from me and looks straight ahead. "You'll be fine.

Make sure to give Josh a big hug. He misses you—won't stop hounding me about you."

"I still owe him a kick in the butt for not telling me sooner you were sick that time." Parker laughs at that.

"He'd enjoy it coming from you. Anyway, when are you gonna see your mom?"

"I'm going to stop by in the morning and say hi. Nothing formal."

"You need me there?"

"No."

The car stops in front of the white three-story mansion. Parker helps me out, and we walk up the white marble walkway to the entrance. Someone takes my coat. Parker and I walk into a large space that looks like a ballroom. A pianist plays classical music, and people walk around with champagne glasses in hand, talking and greeting each other. That is what these events are like. An impressive group of people enjoying themselves, catching up on their important work, and discussing how their family has been. I know all too well since Mrs. Page insisted I attend every event Parker was required to participate in. With people this powerful, you don't refuse a request.

A gentleman approaches. It's Mr. Rathbone. He takes my hand. "Ah, the beautiful Raven. How are you, my dear?" he asks. I've met him twice before. Mrs. Page told me he has a keen eye for art. She doesn't buy any without his input.

"Good, thank you. I haven't purchased any new art, so that you know."

He winks at me. "Good. You reach out to me should you have the urge."

"I will." He releases my hand.

He pats Parker on the shoulder. "Parker, it's good to see you. How's

London treating you?"

"I'm good. London has been great."

"That's good to hear. It's awesome to see you and Raven again," he says and then moves on to the next person.

We walk further into the room and spot Josh encircled by people talking and congratulating him. He's so freaking handsome in a dark, mysterious, broody way. He is confident but not cocky, and I know all this attention is not his thing. He can be shy in certain settings.

"Do you want any champagne?"

"Not now. Look. I think Josh needs rescuing."

"You think?"

"I think."

"Well, if you're up for the challenge. Let's go."

Parker leads me toward the crowd. When people see us, the greetings start. Finally, we get to the last layer. Josh sees me and smiles. It's warm, and he's so handsome, and it's good to see him again. He walks away from the others and toward us.

"Hey, the man of the hour," Parker greets.

"Raven?" Josh calls my name, and I nod. He's seeking my permission to greet Parker because their protocol requires him to greet me first.

"Man, it's good to see you. Welcome back." He pulls Parker into a shoulder bump. Then he looks down at me, and I swear his green eyes light up.

May I?" He's always a gentleman, asking my approval to do something that comes so naturally to him, like hugging me. Parker winks at me.

I nod. Josh wraps his arm around my back and pulls me into a tight embrace like I might perish if he lets me go. He smells good, like spiced sandalwood and honey. If I hadn't fallen in love with Parker first, I could easily fall for Josh. He's that good of a guy.

"You look beautiful," he whispers. "I've missed you. And my boy looks better than I've seen in a year. Thank you," he says before releasing me.

"Thank you, Josh. And congratulations are in order. I don't know how you manage to do all that you do. You seem to be living the life of five people."

"Maybe when you find me a woman, I can slow down." He gives me a half smile and locks gazes with me, and I know there is truth behind his eyes.

"Have you seen my parents?" Parker asks.

"Yeah, right behind you." Josh lifts his chin.

Parker and I turn and see the Pages heading toward us. As soon as they reach us, Parker's dad embraces him, Janis embraces me, and then they switch because this is how it works with family.

"Raven, darling. I've missed you. You have to come to visit while you're in town."

"Yes, Raven. It's been a while. Your absence leaves a gaping hole in our lives. We'd love to have you over before you head back to London. Do you have plans of resettling in the States?"

"I'll return in the new year. As for this trip, we're slated to fly out Monday morning." I suspect he knows since we're flying on their private jet, but is being discreet, or maybe he doesn't know.

"We'll be by tomorrow afternoon. Rain has somethings to take care of in the morning," Parker tells them. I had no idea we were planning to spend time at their house. Parker previously told me it was hard for his mom to accept we were no longer a couple. I thought she would be upset with me for what I put him through. I'm learning that of all the things Janis is, she is not superficial. She's smart, confident, considerate, and very even-keeled. Most of the women in this elite group are. So, I guess I shouldn't be surprised by her welcoming response. Parker is a good mix of his mother and father.

"What about you, dear?" Janis turns to Josh. "You come by, too. Let's make it a late lunch."

"Of course," Josh tells her and kisses her on the cheek. "It'll be good to catch up with this guy." He lifts his chin to Parker.

"Then it's settled," Mr. Page says. "I see your dad. I need to chat with him about something," he says before taking his wife by the arm and leaving.

More people head toward us to get access to Josh. Parker pats him on the back before we leave him to his business of celebrating. The event isn't as stressful as I expect, and I realize it had to do with the caliber of people I am surrounded by. These are not people who do drama. Nor do they have a reason. Tension happens when people are fighting to be seen and heard. These people don't need to do that. They have a level of freedom that is extremely rare.

When we return to Parker's house, he takes my coat, puts it away, and we go into the kitchen for a nightcap. Since it was my first time back in the presence of the elites, I didn't drink so I could have a clear head. With my likeliness of fainting, I didn't want to risk it.

"Red?"

"Sure."

Parker opens a bottle of red wine and pours us both a glass. He hands me a drink, then leans against the counter with the sink, crosses his legs, and watches me.

"You were stunning tonight. Did you have a good time?"

"Thanks. Yes, it was better than I expected. I was a little freaked out when we first arrived, but...."

"Everyone was cool," he says.

I take a sip. "Yeah. I'm learning that's the norm with this group. Josh seemed to be having a good time."

"He did well for someone who doesn't like attention."

"Being the second most handsome man in the world, he better get used to it."

Parker's eyebrow raises. "I'll let him know. Who's the first?"

"You."

"Do I need to take your drink away?"

"No. I promised to tell you the truth no matter how difficult it is to hear." He blinks and closes his eyes for a second before opening them. He's checking himself. I take another sip of my drink and study his face. He hasn't touched his wine. He picks up the glass, tips it over the sink, and pours it out.

"We have an early day tomorrow. You want me to help you out of that before I go to bed?"

"Sure." I gulp down the remainder of my wine and follow Parker upstairs to the guest room where I'm staying. His mood changed when I called him handsome. He's the most beautiful man I've ever seen, whether he wants to hear that or not. I turn my back to him. He lifts my hair and places it over my shoulder to access my zipper. His hands are warm on my skin as he grabs the top of the zipper. He pulls the fabric away from my skin and then slides the zipper down. His scent wafts around me. It's moments like this when I wish I were whole. I wish I were put together enough to turn around and accept the love this man desperately wants to give. Even now, my sex clenches, craving him.

His tone is resigned when he says, "Done," before stepping back. I turn before he walks away.

"Parker."

"Yeah, babe."

"Thank you." I lift on my toes and kiss his cheek because I still need help reaching him, even in heels. He smiles and leaves.

So much for maintaining boundaries. I start the night sleeping in the guest room, but I eventually make my way to Parker's room. He doesn't balk when I slide beneath the covers at one in the morning. He opens his arms, and I nestle in. That's how I wake up in the morning. In his arms.

Our agenda today is full. As soon as Parker drops me at my mom's, he'll make his rounds, catching up with folks in the community who benefit from his foundation. Then he'll retrieve me from Mom's before we head to his parents' for lunch.

He reaches across the seat and takes my hand. "Hey. You okay? I can go in with you."

"I'm good, Parker. I doubt I'll be long. You have a lot on your plate. I'll send for the driver when I'm ready."

We pull up outside the modest two-story house where I grew up. Like most houses in the city, the homes share an outside wall. I remember learning how to ride my bike and peddling up and down the sidewalk as my dad looked on. One day, after I thought I had the hang of it, I figured I'd try riding it after school. My dad wasn't home yet, but my mom was inside. I opened the side door near the garage, got on my bike at the top of the driveway, went down the driveway, across the sideway, into the street, and didn't stop until I crashed into the parked white car across the street. I don't know what I was thinking. I was going so fast that I momentarily forgot how to use the brakes. My neighbor came out. He was more worried for me than mad. Story of my life—always trying to do things on my own.

The door opens to the house. My mom looks beautiful, but the light in her eyes is dim. I wonder what's really going on with her.

"Hi Raven. Is he coming in?" Her head tips toward the car, but it pulls away.

"No. How are you?" I say, stepping past her into the open-plan living room-slash-dining room. I pull out a chair and take a seat.

"Good. Bill and I'll head to Vegas in a few days."

Vegas. It's not on my list of places to frequent. People seem to love it. Not me. I'm not a gambler, I don't smoke, and I hate to shop, so Janis ends up buying me dresses. I prefer the opera over ostrich feathers and rhinestones.

"Sounds fun," I say.

"How long are you here?"

"I leave tomorrow morning, returning to London."

"You said you wanted to talk. Is this the same conversation about your dad?"

"Yeah, Mom. There's a gaping hole in my life, not knowing what caused him to leave. Whatever happened between you two, I understand that it might be difficult to discuss, but I'm your daughter. It's only right that you fill in the missing pieces for me. Don't you want me to be a normal, healthy, functioning adult?"

"You seem to be doing fine."

"You don't care enough about me to know how wrong that statement is."

"What your dad and I had is over. I've moved on. I don't know anything more about him."

"You know why he left, and you know more. You're just not saying. I can handle it. Just tell me."

"Raven, if you want to talk, we can talk about something else. How are you and your friend, Parker?"

"We survived me being dysfunctional because my family life is screwed up. I don't know where I'd be if I didn't have him. That's how it's going," I say, pulling out my phone and texting the driver. I already know this conversation is going nowhere.

"Raven, don't say that. You graduated from Stanford and Berkeley. You work at one of the most prestigious technology companies in the world. You're doing fine."

Fuck. She doesn't get it. I mentally extracted myself from the world to get through it. If I hadn't met Parker, I'd be a zombie functioning on autopilot. I need to get out of here. My phone buzzes.

"I have to go. That's my driver. I have a luncheon to attend. I'll text you when I get back to London."

I stand and touch the table instead of my mom, then turn to leave. Patience is not one of my strong suits. Neither is holding my tongue. If I stay any longer, we would end up in a heated discussion.

When I step outside, the rear window rolls down. It's Parker. I half smile as he steps out of the car. I get in. He slides in beside me. I bury my face in his chest.

PART 6

"The truth is not always beautiful, nor beautiful words the truth."

— Lao Tzu

CHAPTER 57

My First Date

Rain

Two Years Ago

Being back in the States is incredible. I feel a little more like myself every day. Well, as much of myself as I can. Parker keeps insisting I try therapy. I keep telling him I need to try and figure this out on my own. My judgment regarding my personal life hasn't been the best, but I'm getting better. This is why I agreed to meet Jason, a guy I met at a conference earlier this year, for dinner.

We've been out a few times, once for lunch during the weekday, which was nice. We discussed his role as Chief Technology Officer for a global company that recently went through an initial public offering. He seems passionate about his work and the people that work for him. I like that. It says a lot about a person. At the end of the lunch date, Jason walked me back to my building. Before I went in, he grabbed my hand, told me how much he enjoyed our time together, and asked if he could see me again. I should have been taken aback when he bent and gave me a chaste kiss, but it was lovely. His lips were soft, and the kiss was everything it should have been for a first kiss near the office.

Needless to say, I agreed to meet for dinner and drink. In the back of my mind, Parker's words hung like a bell ringing, reminding me of my commitment to inform him if I plan to have relationships with other men. I have to tell him.

"You will introduce me to any man you decide to be with. You will tell them I am your former lover and an important part of your life. You will never have unprotected sex. No other man's seed will enter your body other than mine. You will never commit to forever with another man. And lastly, Rain, there will be consequences for any man that slights you."

I was so pissed at Parker that day after he took me to the park and taught me a lesson. Instead, he reminded me of how connected we are. I wanted so badly to fuck him that day—to give in to my desire to have him inside me again. But I think that's all it was. Parker is so amazing in bed that I honestly think he's ruined me for everyone else. Damn, Parker Page, Esquire. I'm doing this. At least I'm pumping myself up to do it. But my first hurdle is walking in the door.

"Jason."

He walks up to the table with his perfectly chiseled face and banging body in a blue suit and no tie. I love a man who works out. I can imagine myself clinging to those muscles in bed. But I'm getting ahead of myself. His six-foot-two frame bends to kiss my cheek before taking his seat. He's so fine.

"Raven. You look spectacular."

"Thank you."

"I hope you haven't been waiting for long."

"No. I just arrived."

The server comes to the table.

"Hi, I'm Kate. I'll be your server. Would you like a drink to get you started?"

Jason looks across the table at me. "What would you like?"

"I'll have red wine to start. You choose." When Jason doesn't look at the menu, I know he either frequents this place or reviews everything online before coming.

"The lady will have Silver Oak, and I'll a Macallan 18 neat."

"Do you need more time to review the menu?"

"Yes, thank you," he responds. The server disappears to get our drinks.

"I hope you're okay with the selection."

"Absolutely."

"Do you have a preference for dinner? I remember you telling me you dislike reading off the menu."

"Yes, a pasta dish or salmon will be fine."

"Great. So, how was your week?"

"It was good, Jason. I've been making serious strides since returning to the States. It feels good. Like this what I should be doing."

"There's nothing like the feeling of firing on all cylinders. Have you considered whether you'll be attending the upcoming Tech Force conference?"

"I've been thinking about it. It depends on whether I get to a place in my current project to break away. What day are you speaking?"

"Day two. I'm on a panel about the future of technology and AI."

The server returns with our drinks and takes our order. Jason relays what we're having. She takes the order and disappears again.

"Shall we?" Jason holds up his glass. I repeat the gesture. "To the most beautiful woman I've ever met, Raven."

"Wow. I'm unsure if I should top that, but thank you. Cheers." I clink my glass with his and sip my drink.

"Raven." I hear someone call out my name and immediately know who it is. I turn in the direction of the voice.

"Tina. Nice to see you here." She flips her blond hair over her shoulder and bends to kiss my cheek. Tina is Parker's old high school fling and peer elite. "And who is this?" Subtle. Not.

"Tina, this is Jason, a friend of mine."

"Jason, this is Tina. Tina, did you just arrive?"

"No, I'm on my way out. It's good to see you. I hope to see you and Parker at my upcoming fundraiser. I recall seeing your RSVP."

"You did. I'll be there."

"Great." She touches my shoulder. "Nice meeting you, Jason. Have a good dinner," she says and leaves. She's stunning, but Jason doesn't track her with his eyes—thank God. However, he looks at me curiously, and I know why.

What do I do? What do I do? Can I go through with this? If he wants more with me, I have to tell him about Parker. If I don't, Tina will. Tina's going to tell him no matter what, so fuck it. Oh, my god, I hate this. Why do I have to have a freaking umbilical cord connection to a man? Ugh.

"Raven." His voice pulls me out of the dumpster fire in my head.

"Jason."

"Should I be worried about this Parker person?"

"About that…Parker is my ex."

"Your ex…." He pauses, and I can only imagine all the thoughts streaming through his head. If he only had a glimpse into what's in mine, maybe he'd understand—maybe not. Sometimes, I'm not even sure I understand it.

"Yeah. He also happens to be my best friend."

"Like a best friend with benefits?"

"No, God, nothing like that. However…" This is embarrassing. But it speaks to just how messed up my life is. Now I know exactly why we both agreed to this—I want to make sure Parker knows I'm not seeking forever in another man, and he wants to protect me. It feels impossible. I always had the option to walk away from Parker like I did before. I don't intend to. Fuck it. I blow air into my cheeks and just let it out. "Jason, Parker is very special to me. Although we don't date, we are extremely close—there's not much we don't do together, and meeting anyone I date is important to both of us. So, if this..." I gesture between me and Jason. "Were to go further. You'd have to meet him. No questions asked. He and I are a package deal."

"How long have you been separated as a couple?"

"A little over two years. I've known him nine years."

"Raven, that's...I don't know what to say."

"Just be honest. I've spent most of my life with a man who's only told me the truth no matter how difficult. I can't accept anything less. I know this seems odd, but he's my best friend."

"Listen, I think you're amazing. For any man to want to be around you like that says a lot. I'd love to continue to see you. It sounds like if I do, and if you're interested, I have to meet Parker. I think I can handle that."

Whew. I breathe a sigh of relief. This is the first man I've had to explain Parker to since that day in the park. The day I learned a big lesson over an even bigger orgasm. Now for the second hurdle. I can't date or sleep with a man until I tell Parker. Sometimes my life sucks the big one.

"So, who is Tina to Parker?"

Yeah, that's a story all to itself. Our food comes, we eat it, and I relay what I know about Tina, which isn't very much since I only briefly met her twice before. Usually, when I'm at the elite functions, I'm with Janis, who makes it her business to introduce me to all their connections and to ensure I am stoking previous connections to maintain access to their world.

After dinner, Jason helps me with my blazer, and we walk outside. His arm is wrapped around my waist. My car is already waiting.

"Rain." He stops and turns me to face him. "I'm serious. I want to continue seeing you. You're smart and beautiful, and I think we get along. Don't we?"

"Yes, Jason. You're easy to be with, and you know some things about tech." My lame joke earns me a smile and him some brownie points.

"May I?" He dips his head until his lips hover over mine. His breath brushes my lips, and I get a hint of whiskey mixed with his scent of amber and cardamon. I nod. He presses his lips to mine, and he's surprisingly sweet. The kiss is soft and gentle initially, then I lean into it and put my arms around his neck, inviting him to deepen it, and he does, parting my lip with his tongue and mingling it with mine. He pulls my body to him, and I feel everything he wants to do to me in that kiss. He's hard. I pull back, breathless.

"Jason. Yeah. That's working."

A slow smile forms on his face, and he licks his lips. "That was nice, Raven." He dips his head and gives me a slow, gentle kiss like he's confirming what he already knows. He wants me. "Well, lady, you have me all heated. I sincerely hope we get to do that again."

"It was lovely, Jason. I'd like to see you again. That is, if you can handle meeting Parker."

"No problem." If he were the wrong type of man, this would be his cocky cue to challenge whether Parker can handle meeting him. I would walk away if he said that because no one outside the elites can handle Parker. Not even me. Instead, I reward him, get on my tiptoes, and kiss him again.

"Thank you for a lovely evening, Jason. I'll have a discussion with Parker and get back to you."

He hugs me, puts me in my car, and I leave.

CHAPTER 58

What's His Name?

Parker

RAIN TOLD ME SHE WAS ON HER WAY OVER TO TALK WITH ME. I SWEAR, if this woman sits on my lap again, I will have to lay her out on the bed. I love Rain, but she's too much. My natural reaction to her whenever she's in my presence is a state of arousal. When the day comes to reclaim my woman, I hope I don't break her because my need for her is off the charts.

How am I supposed to get on with my life? I can't. I love her—we promised ourselves to each other, and I'm never giving up. I shouldn't feel this way, but I want my woman back. The waiting process is unbearable, yet I need to trust and believe she'll be mine again one day. If Rain is coming over to come back to me for good, I'll be the happiest person alive.

In anticipation of her arrival, I have her favorite things ready—wine, snacks, treats. She mentioned she had an early dinner, and so did I. Just as I set the wine bottle on the coffee table, my bell rings. I don't know why she doesn't use her keys. When I answer the door, she stands there looking stunning.

"Come in, Rain." I kiss her cheek and take her sweater.

"Parker, how was work today?" she asks, heading into the family room with me in tow.

"I spent most of the morning in court. You know how that goes."

Rain sits on the couch. Once she's settled, I pour wine into her glass and hand it to her. Then, I pour myself a drink and sit on one of the oversized chairs. She gives me a "what are you doing?" look.

"You don't want to sit next to me?"

"I'm good over here, Rain."

"Suit yourself." She sips her drink, eats a piece of cheese, and washes it down with another sip of wine. Her movements are measured. Now, she has me curious.

"Babe, you said you need to talk. What's on your mind?" She takes a big swig of wine. I stand, refill her drink, and retake my seat. "Talk to me," I say the words that will pull whatever it is out of her.

"Remember the discussion we had in London about me dating?"

Fuck, this is not the conversation I want to have. Fuck, fuck, fuck. "I remember."

"The lesson you taught me."

"Rain, if you have something to say—say it." I rest my arm over the armrest. My fingers instinctively curl in on themselves. Rain blows air in her cheek and releases it in a sigh. I uncurl my fingers—this is my girl. I need to rein myself in and listen. "Rain," I urge.

"Okay. I think I should be sitting over there with—."

"No." I cut her off. My tone is clipped and harsh, but I can't help it. "Tell me," I snap.

I can see something resembling fear mixed with confusion in her eyes. "I met this guy, and I want to date him." Her words come out in a rush.

I close my eyes, take a deep breath, open them and stand. I can't look at the woman I love sitting across from me. I turn my back, take a few steps, and turn back. To say I'm angry is a colossal understatement. I'm ready to burn the town down.

"What the fuck is this about, Rain? Sex? If you want that, get upstairs and get in my bed already. I'll give you whatever you need. Whenever you need it. What are you doing?" I hate what she's unleashed in me—that I have to harden myself to listen to this. That I have to talk to her this way. Oh my god, Rain, what are you doing?

"I told you. I need to find myself. To be me without you."

"Rain, babe. For fuck sake, you've been doing that for almost three years. You're not lost. And getting under another man is not how you find yourself. What are you looking for? We can work this out another way. We can go to counseling. Fucking another man when the one you love and who loves you at his core is right in front of you is not the way. We can get help."

Rain is not herself. I know her—she's running scared, running from love. From pain, from I don't know what—all while putting someone else in harm's way. But why? She knows I will destroy this man when he's done with her. Any man who agrees to what he just did is only after one thing. Rain and I knew that the day we made the agreement. It's why she's waited so long to do this.

"Don't. You told me what I needed to do if I wanted to see someone else. I did that. I told him about you. That you are a permanent fixture in my life, and if he wanted to date me, he had to meet you."

"My god, woman. What have you done? This is not a game. Why are you gambling with someone's life by bringing them into this? This is not the way."

"I want this."

"Rain. Are you sure? You don't forget a thing. You know exactly what I told you—this won't end well. You intentionally put a target on someone's back. Why? For sex? You don't want him. You showed me what you wanted that day in the park." I watch Rain's defiant expression soften, and her eyes widen when she remembers everything I told her. The day she came on my hand after I told her that I would ruin any man that slights her. She's not herself—whoever this fucking idiot is, he can't handle her, and he won't tolerate us. Because there is no Rain without me by her side. Ever.

"Parker, please let him be. However this goes—let him be."

"No. That wasn't the deal. When's the meeting? What's his name?"

PART 7

"You can only lose what you cling to."

— BUDDHA

CHAPTER 59

A Pair of Soft Lips

Parker

One Year Ago

San Francisco is so lovely in the summer. Even at night, it's beautiful. It's been two years since we've been back. Rain and I have finally found our rhythm together. It hasn't been easy seeing her with other men. The only thing saving me is that I get to ruin anyone who dares hurt her.

Rain came to me once to tell me she had started dating. Eventually, like I knew he would when he was done filling his needs, he ended it. He told her this was not what he signed up for—that building anything more with her was impossible. Out of commitment to me, she told me. I suspect now he's rethinking his choices. Well, his options are slim when it comes to women. Because not many women want a destitute man, which is what he is now. I knew what I was doing when I told her she couldn't date anyone unless she introduced them to me. I've met everyone she's dated. Subsequently, anyone who hurt her, I destroyed. Rain won't listen to me when I tell her any man serious about her won't tolerate what she has with me—and rightly so. I expected her to stop wasting her time on them, but she's determined to do this. I told her there were consequences—I meant it.

"Hey, Parker, you're early." My high school friend Tina says when she arrives at the bar.

She comes from my elite world. We used to date, but that was a long time ago when I was young and exploring women. Right away, I knew we didn't have a connection, but she was cute and fun and could easily navigate my world because it was her world, too. When we reconnected at one of my mom's parties, I took advantage of her wanting to hook up. Not to date, because I won't date anyone. All my affection is reserved for one woman, Rain. No, Tina is a distraction to provide me what I need…release—a pair of soft lips.

"Tina. Good to see you. How's your mom? Did she finally settle on that property she was thinking about?"

"Yeah, she did. It's in the south of France. It's beautiful. You should come with me there sometime."

"Thanks, but I need to stay close to Rain."

"Rain. Is she on her way?" she asks with a twinge of sarcasm.

"Yes. Play nice."

"Of course. What do you think I'm going to do?"

"I don't know. You're unpredictable at times."

"I'm everything you want me to be," Tina says. She is. Tina's a temporary fix—soft lips to solve a raging hard-on. And in return, I satisfy her, but not with my length because that's only reserved for one woman…Rain.

"Can I get you something?" the bartender asks Tina.

"Ice water with lemon." She doesn't drink. Many of the young women in our world don't. They're trying to stay young and pretty, preserving something genes often don't offer. She's lovely to look at. However, my girl Rain is stunning.

"I'll have another one of these," I tell the bartender.

"So, Parker. What are you doing later? Are you coming over?"

"No. Tina. We're here to take care of this, and then I need to go," I tell her. This isn't a fun outing; I hate what I'm about to do. That I'll need to provide Rain and myself time to process it. That *this* is one hurdle I must overcome to get to forever.

The bartender brings our drinks. Tina picks up her glass and clinks it with mine.

"To old friends," she toasts.

"Salud." It is the only thing I can offer a woman I don't feel anything for. I take a sip, and Tina throws her arm around my shoulder. I turn toward her. "Don't," I say. Then I see Raining coming through the door.

CHAPTER 60

Boundaries

Rain

THE MOVE BACK TO SAN FRANCISCO WAS BITTERSWEET. I LOVED MY experience of getting to know the people in our London office. It was the start of a career I'd been dreaming about for the longest time. It was also where I restarted my relationship with Parker following our traumatic breakup. It's been two years since we returned, and Parker and I are moving into our eleventh year together. It's been a hard road, with several failed boyfriends and a new job, but we survived. We found our rhythm. Despite not being a couple, we spend a lot of time together. It's unconventional, but it is ours.

Now, I need to meet Parker at Tavern, a restaurant owned by our friend. It's Friday, and I'm ready for a drink. He sent a car for me because when I leave, I'm spending the weekend over at his house so we can get up early and attend a function for his mom. We seem to do that a lot—attend functions, mingle, and ensure the younger elite have an example to follow. It's a society that once you're in, you're in—and by proxy, I'm in. I shouldn't say that because the Page family is biding their time, waiting for me to be one of them. I'm not ready for that. I don't know if I'll ever be.

I leave the car, walk into the restaurant, and spot Parker immediately—who wouldn't? He's stunning. I stop when I notice the back of a blond woman beside him putting her arms around his shoulder. I know her. I'm shocked at what I'm seeing. Parker in the arms of another woman is foreign to me. But then I hear his voice, and at that moment, he looks over and sees me.

"Don't." I recognize the harsh timbre in his tone. That's not affection. She has overstepped some boundary they have.

She removes her arms. He gets up, comes to me, puts his arm around my waist, dips his head, and kisses my cheek. My body doesn't want to move forward, but his pull compels me. He takes me over to her. Tina Bahler, his former girlfriend from high school, is part of their elite circle. I met her at several of Janis' many events. She came over to say something to Parker and was all clingy even then. She was also the catalyst for me telling Parker about my first date—this feels like some kind of revenge.

"Rain, babe. You met Tina before."

"I remember, Parker."

"Hi Raven. Nice to see you again." Tina holds out her hand to me. Like the professional I am, I take it and give her a sturdy handshake even though I want to punch her in the throat. It doesn't get past me that she calls me Raven. Only Parker calls me Rain. I'm sure he told her she could never use that name with me.

"Tina. I hope your evening is going well."

"Yeah, it is."

I look up at Parker, whose face I can't read, and I know he's up to something.

"Parker, why am I here?"

"I wanted you to meet Tina formally." Parker is still holding me, and I try to pull away. He tightens his grip. It's my signal. I need to let him do whatever he came here to do.

"It's nice to see you're dating again," I say.

"That would be nice," Tina says. Parker shoots her a stern look.

"No. We're not dating. Tina and I have an arrangement."

"Parker." My voice is admonishing.

"You need to hear this," he tells me, with a voice that's strong but calm. But it doesn't mean I don't want to bury my head behind his back because this is too much even for us.

"It's okay. I know what I am to Parker. He told me you are the love of his life and that I will never be that. He told me I would never have access to the things you shared. That I can never feel his length between my legs. That my lips can never touch his. That there are things reserved only for *you*." The daggers in her eyes as she stares at me are unpalatable.

I press my lips together to keep them from falling open. Parker can feel me stiffen beside him. This is outrageous. I can't believe he's doing this. I can't believe *she's* doing this. She wants him bad enough to accept this from him. To be his relief and nothing more. I feel sick to my stomach.

"I need to go, Parker," I tell him in a secret plea.

"We'll leave when we're done."

"Seems I've heard all I need to."

"Raven, I'm no threat to you," Tina says.

That's it. "Tina." There is a bite in my tone when I call her name. I need to shut her down right now. "I know you're not. That's the reason you said what you did with such precision. No one needs to tell me what I am to Parker. I wake up to that hard truth daily. I'm not trying to leave here to get away from you. I want to leave because I am embarrassed for you. Because the bile is rising from my stomach because there are women like you." I turn toward Parker, who hasn't let me go since I walked in. "Parker. Take me home."

"I'll see you next week, Tina," he says. Then he lifts his chin to the bartender—a signal I've seen over the past eleven years. The tab is settled. We're done.

I look up at Parker. He drops his hand from my waist, places it in mine, then walks me out to the car. We don't speak until we get to his house.

CHAPTER 61

Piss and Vinegar

Parker

It's done. Rain knows. Now, it's time for me to deal with the aftermath. Sometimes, when you love someone...you'll go to extreme lengths to prove it or do what it takes to get them back. Rain will forever be in my life. That's a fact. My heart was shattered into a million tiny fragments when we broke up. But I'm putting the pieces back together. Since the day Rain allowed me to video call her in London, small fragments have reattached themselves. Each small victory puts me on a path to healing my heart. Each tender moment, each chaste kiss or loving glance from Rain is building back up my heart. Now I know the slash of her tongue in defense of her position beside me has the same effect. The way she spoke to Tina is what I needed to hear, what my heart needs for repair. It sickened me to do it, but now I know. Rain, the love of my life, is still fighting for us—finding her footing. Somehow, one day, we will be together again.

I open the door to my house. Rain walks in and puts her things in the foyer. I take her coat, and she heads straight to the kitchen with me following behind.

"Parker Page, that was atrocious," she scolds me, voice laced with irritation.

"No, it wasn't, Rain. It was necessary."

I go to my wine fridge, retrieve a bottle of wine, open it, and pour us a glass. Rain sits on the opposite side of the counter, and I join her, but I don't sit down.

"Look at me," I tell her. She looks at me with piss and vinegar in her eyes, and I want to fuck her right here.

"What do you want with me, Parker? You just introduced me to your relief. Why aren't you with her? Why am I here?"

"Don't ask me questions you already know the answer to."

Although Rain anticipated I'd do something like this one day. She didn't realize how she would respond when it happened. She also didn't understand that I'd never be with anyone like I was with her and that I was saving myself for her.

"You're a single guy. You're free to do what you want." I stand between her legs and lift her chin so she's looking at me. So that what I say is etched like glass in her memory.

"No, Rain. I'm not free to do what I want to do. Because what I want is you."

"Get away from me, Parker."

"No. That's never happening again."

"I hate this part."

"Which part is that?"

"Our connection, the memories...." She tries to move her head away from me, but I won't let her.

"Stop fighting me, Rain. We need to talk."

She slides off her chair, and when she does, her body is pressed to mine, and I have to hold my breath like I do every time she touches me. She doesn't even try to solicit a reaction from my body—it just responds. It's instinctive. Our connection doesn't allow us the space to free ourselves from each other.

I remember the second time she stayed overnight here when we returned from a night of drinking our first year back in San Francisco. I set up the guestroom for her when she returned to my house. I had all her things ready. She fell asleep in the car, and I carried her in. I removed her clothes, put her to bed, and then went to my room. I went to bed but wasn't tired, so I scrolled through the email on my phone, getting some work done to quiet my mind. A movement caught my eye. Rain.

She stood at the threshold, rubbing her eyes, looking sleepy, leaning against the doorway. She was waiting for my permission to enter. I know Rain well enough to know that she wasn't offering me her body. She just needed to be near me, to be close, to hold me. I held my hand out to her, and she came to bed, pulled the covers back, and made me move from my warm spot. I did, and she slid in, covered us both up, and turned her body to mine. She wrapped her legs around me, tucked her head into my arms, and fell asleep.

I was rock-hard the entire time. To this day, whenever she's here for the night, that's how we sleep. Fifteen other fucking rooms in my house, and Rain sleeps with me. When I'm at her house, it's the same. She won't let me sleep in the guest room. And when she awakes to her sleep terrors, we get through them together—her in my arms.

She's so close and smells so good. I sigh. Talk about the hard part—this is that for me. The closeness, but I'll take every soft bit of it. I grab our wine glasses and bring them into the family room. I place them on the side table and sit on the chaise lounge. Once I'm settled, Rain sits on me, facing me the ways she's done all our lives. It doesn't matter how mad she is at me. She's incapable of not doing this. I'm okay with that, except I just want to pounce on her every time, but I'll get through it. I have to.

"Talk to me," I tell her.

"How you treat Tina is not okay." I don't say anything. I need to hear her out. I tip my head and wait for her to continue. "Parker, she's a woman with feelings…for you."

"Rain, do you have a question for me?" My tone is clipped, and I want this conversation to be done.

"Why? Why are you doing this?"

"I guess I got tired of using my hands. I'm not interested in other women. Tina wants to be with me. I told her I love you, that no one could ever be with me the way I am with you. That she could never have anything with me other than sex in the manner I dictate. She agreed. She got on her knees and proved herself to me. I told you to meet me there so you knew about her."

"It's none of my business."

"Everything about me, my life, what I do, where I go when I'm not with you is your business. If you don't want me to have what I have with Tina, then Rain, get off my lap, take off your clothes, and get in my bed already," I say the last words hard and with conviction because Rain has to decide to do it or accept it until she's ready.

"Parker Page, I should slap you."

"Make it hard. Because your anger already has me rock hard. Feel me." I take her hand and place it on the steel between us.

"Parker, you're insufferable."

"Get off me, Rain. This conversation is over."

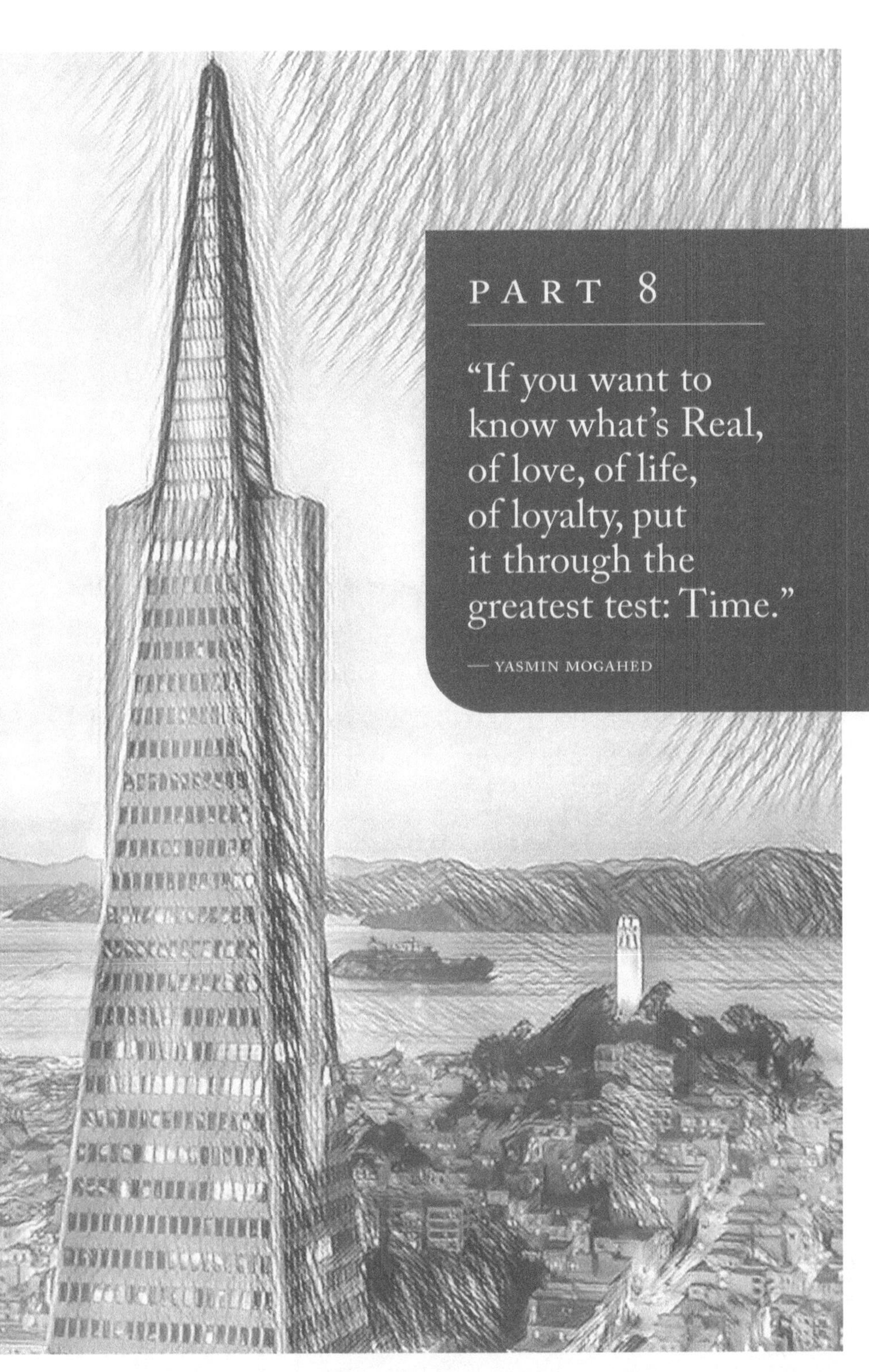

PART 8

> "If you want to know what's Real, of love, of life, of loyalty, put it through the greatest test: Time."
>
> — YASMIN MOGAHED

CHAPTER 62

Searching for Rain

Parker

Two Weeks Ago

IT'S BEEN FOUR YEARS SINCE RAIN AND I STOPPED BEING A COUPLE. Although that was the second worst day of my life, the first being the day our baby died, it's not the end of our story. Our connection still survives. Our twelve-year relationship has had its peaks and valleys. Having her in my life daily is great; however, waiting for her to find herself so we can be together again is the worst part. I want the love of my life back. I need Rain.

This week, Rain is in Seattle. I was dreading dropping her off at the airport the other day. She's fresh on the heels of a breakup with Blake. It hit her hard—they all do. That's always the most challenging part and makes me wish I didn't love her so much. It makes me regret promising never to deny her anything. Watching the love of my life be with someone else is as devastating as the day she walked out on me. But I promised Rain I'd step aside and allow her to find herself. As hard as this is, I know she'll find her way back one day. She has to. Rain is running from me, our love, commitment, past, and pain. But she can't run past our connection. We're tied together by a thread that can't be severed. However, as I've watched her over the years, I see it was the right thing to do.... She's stronger and more beautiful than ever, and I love her even more. We will be together one day soon when the time is right.

Recently, Rain has been struggling more with her sleep terrors and getting up earlier than usual. I need to leave earlier this morning, so I'll call her after showering.

"Hey, handsome. I was just about to call you," she says as I plop down in my occasional chair. Studying her face, I search for signs that she's okay. She's beautiful. Her hair is pulled into a ball at the top of her head, and she is wearing a t-shirt.

"Hey, beautiful. I need to head out early today, so I figured I'd call you. How are you?" I ask, holding her gaze. Years ago, Rain tried to mask her distress with a brave face. Although she doesn't do it often, and I know her face better than mine, she still tries to hide behind a forced smile. She's okay because she's studying my face to hide from her memories, but I know the sleep terror is lurking in the back of her mind.

"I'm ok now that I'm talking to you." My eyes shift from her face to the setting. A boat passes by in the background, catching my eye.

"Where are you, Rain? I don't recognize the space you're in. I can see the cityscape in the background."

"I'm at a lake house with a friend," she says. I feel my temperature rise. I don't know where my girl is. She turned her locator off years ago, after we broke up, and I haven't pushed her to turn it back on. Until this week, there hasn't been a reason to force the issue. I've always been near her. Even when she ran away to London, unbeknownst to her, I followed. She'll never be entirely out of my reach.

"Lake house where? Text me the address," I say, trying to restrain myself, but my words come out as a command.

"It's nothing, Parker. I'm just here for a few days. I'll be fine," she tries to reassure me. Attention diverted, she peeks over her phone to something in the distance…someone. My fingers curl. She's with another man. This part grates my soul every time.

"Was that him?"

"Yes. Parker, it's nothing."

"Rain, I'm worried, is all. You just got out of a situation. I don't want to see you hurt again. And I'm surprised to see that you've left the city. You usually keep me posted on things like this. Text me the address where you are or turn on your locator."

"It's not a big deal, Parker. Everything's fine."

God damn it, Rain, don't fight me on this. I hate it when I have to put my foot down with her. I try to calm myself.

"Rain, I don't know this person. It'll make me feel better if I at least know where you are. What if something happens? I need to be able to get to you. We've been down this path before. I'm just looking out for you." She looks away again, and I'm two seconds away from getting on a plane. "Rain?"

I'm watching her face, trying to read what is happening with her. This is unusual behavior for her. We have a commitment. I need to calm down and trust her…trust in us. Because the last thing Rain wants me to do is get on a plane and come after her. I inhale to put myself in check and hold her gaze. She forces a ridiculous smile, clearly battling whatever's in her head to return to me.

There she is. I shake my head. "Babe, you can do better than that, but it'll do. Now, swipe your screen and send me your location." She breaks away from our call briefly. I hear my phone ding. She's on Lakeside

Drive. Got it. "We have a little time before I have to go. You want to talk to me and tell me what's happening?"

Rain settles down and tells me how she met Nik at a bar the night she and I talked. He's British-American and has two brothers, but she doesn't know anything more. Based on those brief facts, I know who she's talking about. But I don't tell her. I need to confirm my suspicion. I try calming down and listening as she speaks, but I know I'm not doing well. How can I? Rain is with another man. Another man. Fuck. She and I will need to discuss ending this philandering of hers once and for all. I want my woman back.

"You know I disagree with what you're doing. I need you to promise me you'll be careful, Rain. You say it's just good times, but you can get hurt. I want you to come home whole."

"I will," she says unconvincingly.

"You know you mean the world to me."

"Yeah. You've told me. Parker, isn't it time for you to get ready to be brilliant?"

"Yeah, I like to think I'm brilliant whether I'm dressed or not. Which reminds me, Mom will call you this week to discuss the birthday party she's throwing me. It's more like a private gathering than a party. There'll be some people there that she wants us to meet."

"She'll use any reason to have a big party. Why call? She can just text. Besides, it's a few months away."

"It's a themed party, so I assume it's to talk about what you and I should wear, brief you as usual on the crowd. And I think she wants to hear your voice. Although I keep reminding her that we're no longer a couple, she's in denial. You can't blame her, though—she loves having you around. You're like the daughter she never had." My mom fell in love with Rain the first time she met her. She's so magnetic that you can't help but be attracted to how naturally curious, engaging, and thoughtful Rain is.

"I suppose the way we behave doesn't help. Don't worry. I'll be ready for her call. Hey Parker, I'm sorry for being so difficult."

Her apology provides me with a bit of relief in knowing my girl is still there. She might be confused, but she's trying to figure it out. I need to get her away from these distractions once and for all.

"You don't have to apologize. Now I need to get ready. I'll talk to you in the morning. Love ya."

"I love you, Parker Page, Esquire," she says before ending the call.

When I hang up, I call my friend Niall King, head of King Enterprise security company. It's run by him and his older brother Aedan King. Although their company is headquartered in Belfast, Ireland, they have global operations. He's either in the States with his woman or back in Belfast. We've known each other since grade school when our families attended a special function for the elites around the globe.

"Parker. How are you, mate? You must know I'm in the States."

"Hey, Niall. No, I was taking a chance. Got a minute?"

"Yeah, mate. What's up?"

"Can you have your guys give me everything on a man named Nik, who lives on Lakeside in Seattle?"

"I can give you that right now. You good on time?"

"Let's do it."

I give him a second and hear him type something on his phone. He starts reading the screen.

"Your man is Noah Ignatius Knight, son of Elisiah Knight, the billionaire property developer. He's British-American. Noah's name is associated with a trust tied to properties in multiple countries. The address you gave is a property Noah acquired recently outside the trust."

"So, it's his private home."

"Yeah."

"The digital footprint shows Wade Wallace is actively monitoring him."

"Wallace.... My family financed most of the buildings on California Street where his building is located—I own Wade Wallace."

"Bingo."

"Anything else?"

"Yeah...you won't believe this. That's not the only company monitoring him. So is my lady's company, Ross Enterprises." And my woman's client. Fuck. Rain doesn't know she and Nik work together. Rain, what the hell are you doing? I hear Niall type something else. "There's a meeting Monday at nine in Seattle between the two companies."

"Will Rose be there?"

"No. Her cousins, June, Jake, you're boy, Noah, and..."

"My lady," I finish his sentence.

"Right."

"You could have a career in this security stuff, man."

Niall barks out a laugh in the background. "Yeah, I guess you can say that. You good, mate?"

"I'm good. Let's grab drinks while you're in the States."

"Let's do it," he says, and we hang up.

My next call is to Wade Wallace.

CHAPTER 63

The Short List

Parker

IT'S THURSDAY. TYPICALLY, I'D LOOK FORWARD TO THURSDAYS because it's the day Rain routinely comes to hang out with me after work. The following day, I take her to work, or sometimes, if neither of us has to go to court or see clients, we work from home. On the weekend, we spend time in the community, hang with friends or my family, or both. I suppose it's our way of expressing our deep commitment to each other in ways others can't possibly understand. It works for us, but she's not here tonight because she's still in Seattle. Therein lies my dilemma. With each morning call, I'm increasingly worried about her. She seems to have a sudden unhealthy attachment to Nik so soon following her breakup with Blake. As her friend, I want to help her get through this week to land the contract she's worked so hard on.

My phone rings. It's my mom.

"Hi, Mom. This is unusual for you to call me this late in the evening. Is everything okay? How's Dad?"

"Preston is fine. He'll be looking for you this weekend."

"Is this about those documents he wants me to review?"

"You can handle that with him when you get here. That's not what I wanted to talk to you about."

"Then what is it, Mom? Are you okay?"

"Raven called me today."

"I spoke with her and told her you wanted her to attend my birthday party."

"Yes, dear, we had a chance to speak about that. She confirmed her attendance. I invited her to meet me when she returns from Seattle."

"Seems you two have things under control."

"That's not it. Before we ended our call, I heard a man's voice call out her name."

"Mom, you know Rain and I are not together that way anymore. She's free to be her own woman. You shouldn't be surprised."

"Parker, honey. I don't like this. You and Raven were designed for each other. She should be with you, not a random guy. Do you even know who these men are that she's been with?"

"Mom, I have this under control. Rain needs to work through some things, like when I went to therapy. The difference is that she wants to work it through on her own and not as a couple. I'm sure you can see I need to respect that."

"No, Parker. I can't accept that. From my experience of being with your father, I know she's scared. She's running."

"I know, Mom. She is afraid, but not of me. Rain is struggling with her past trauma, which affects her ability to commit."

"Then what is your plan? I know you have one or you wouldn't continue to stay so close to Raven."

"I do, Mom. I'll handle this. For now, Rain says she has things under control."

My mom is worried about me and is doing her best to facilitate a reunion. I get what she's doing, but Rain is complicated. My concern now is the man Rain is with in Seattle. She doesn't know that Knight Development Corporation is run by Noah and his brothers, who happen to be clients of Ross Enterprises, Rain's client.

I received information about Noah. He's the president of capital markets for his family's business. His brother, Roman Knight, is CEO and president, and the younger Knight, Mark, is President of their investment management division. My concern is how Rain will respond once she discovers his real identity in her Monday morning meeting.

Noah is also on the short list of bidders for the Wade Wallace building in San Francisco, a property where my family trust owns significant shares. Which is why I'm on my way to have lunch with Wade. I decide to meet him at a restaurant my family financed where I can guarantee anonymity. Upon arrival, I sit near the back of the restaurant. There will be no patrons here this afternoon because I arranged to have the restaurant clear for our lunch. As I expected, Wade is punctual. He heads toward me, and I stand and extend my hand to shake his.

"Parker. It's good to see you. How's your family?"

"Good, Wade. How about yours?"

"Good. However, I'm sure you've heard my boys are focused on their own company."

"I heard. How are you handling that?"

"It's disappointing. Handing the rein over to them has always been my plan. Now I need to move to plan b."

"That's what I came to talk to you about."

"I suspect this is important since *you've* come to see me."

I nod in agreement. "You're selling your business."

"I am. After a lengthy discussion with Jude and Jayden—it's my only option. I can't convince them to step in."

"Thus, the curated list I heard about."

"You seem to have a vested interest in this, which is rare from a man of your wealth and status. Let's cut to the chase. What exactly do you need from me?"

"I want to know your plan for these bidders."

"I've shortlisted three developers I believe have the right mindset to take the business forward. I'm meeting with them this week to outline my requirements and request they deliver a proposal."

"Making them jump through hoops."

"In essence."

"Don't sell."

"Why would I not?"

"Pause a minute."

"I've already started the ball rolling and set up a meeting. I'll outline the plan and then request proposals for them to showcase their vision of the next iteration of the business."

"Get what you need from them and hold on to it. How much time do you think you can handle staying put?"

"I want to be out next year at the latest."

"I don't think what I have in mind will take a year."

"Parker, you're overstepping. Why are you here?"

"Because I own this block. Anything that happens here is my business."

"What else do you need to know?"

"Of the three developers you're considering, which one is at the top of the list?"

"The Knight Development Corporation. I have my eye on Noah Knight."

"Don't commit to anyone. Hold off."

"I need to—."

"As the majority stakeholder, you know I can pull the rug off from under everyone on this."

"But you won't. A man with your level of wealth has no interest in my building, nor do you need it. Listen, I'll keep my process going. You handle your business with Noah, who, gauging by the tick in your jaw when I said his name, I suspect you have an issue with."

"Perceptive."

"I've known your parents for many years. You are your dad's son. You have his temperament, and I suspect Noah is the cause of some angst. So, I won't make you pull rank over me. Do what you must and let me know when it's done. Now, are you leaving, or are we eating?"

Lunch with Wade went well. He's right. I don't need the building, but I will purchase it from underneath Noah if he oversteps my boundaries. Because one thing I know for sure is that a man like Noah is not the man for Rain.

CHAPTER 64

He Doesn't Know

Rain

It's a few hours before sunrise, and I can't sleep. My mind is reeling with thoughts of this week and the potential end to whatever Nik and I are doing. I fall into my morning routine and sneak to the safety of the sitting room to call Parker.

"Hey, Parker. Good morning."

"Morning, Rain. What are you doing? It's five o'clock. This is early even for you." I can hear the irritation in his voice. He closes his eyes, reopens them, and focuses on me, reading me. "What's on your mind?"

"I just need to hear your voice. I miss you, Parker." If only he knew how much. I would curl into him and tell him everything I'm feeling if he were here right now. He'd tell me that everything would be okay. That whatever these feelings are, they will dissipate in time. That he's there for me now and forever. But I'd also have to admit I'm a mess and don't know what I'm doing.

Parker's looking at me like he's searching my soul, and I know he sees more than I'm telling him—because he always does.

"I miss you too, but Rain, I don't like the look on your face. Are you okay? Tell me what's happening in Seattle between you and this guy Nik."

The way he says Nik's name reminds me of the first time I had to tell Parker I wanted to date someone who wasn't him. By then, we had been apart three years, but the deal Parker and I struck years ago is not something anyone will ever understand. It was a deal between two inexorable people who loved hard and lost even harder. *"What's his name?"* Parker asked me. Those three words sealed the deal, and the dominos fell. Anyone I dated would have to meet Parker. But Nik is exempt because I'm not dating him. After Monday, I'll never see him again, and he'll never have to come face-to-face with Parker. I'll never have to explain who Parker is to me—that he's the only man I've professed my love to.

"So far, we've been enjoying ourselves touring Seattle, spending almost every moment together except when we step away for work."

"That's a lot of time together. You mentioned previously that this tryst would end this week. Has that changed?"

"No."

"You say you're enjoying your trip, but you don't sound like yourself. Have you developed feelings for him? Talk to me, Rain. I need to know what you're thinking. I promise I've got you no matter what."

Parker wants me to open up to him, but I don't know how without the floodgates breaking and every thought from a lifetime of storms spilling out. Even now, I feel unshed tears fighting their way to the surface. Focus, Rain. Look at his beautiful face, closely-trimmed beard, and piercing blue eyes you used to get lost in. I focus on Parker and use all the tools in my arsenal to pull myself out of the kaleidoscope of memories. It's enough to help me center my thoughts so I don't completely lose myself. But it's hard to tamp down my feelings. My face is hot, and although I stare into his eyes, they blur and become crystal blue waves before I feel the water run down my cheeks.

"Ah, honey. It's okay." He reins in his tone. "Please talk to me," he pleads, watching my distress unfold. If I can't pull myself together, he'll be here within hours. I need to focus, but memories of the past flood my mind, and everything feels like it's happening in the present all at once. I see my family, my dad, and my days with Parker, Blake, and Nik. It's too late—I'm spiraling. "Rain. Close your eyes, honey." His words cut through the noise in my head like a knife, and I close my eyes and concentrate on his voice. "Take a deep breath, Rain." I take a deep breath. "That's it. Again." I take another. "Good. Now, concentrate on my voice. Can you do that for me?" I nod, unable to find my voice. "Rain, I'm here. You're safe in the house overlooking a lake. Visualize the water, how it's sparkling under the sun's warm rays."

Parker continues describing the scene outside the window, guiding me through it as if he were here with me. His voice is like a beacon guiding me out of a heavy fog toward a clear path. When he senses my breath coming under control, he stops.

"Okay, open your eyes when you're ready and look around." I take a minute, then open my eyes. "Good. Now, tell me five things you see."

"I see you on my phone. I see a blue pillow. I see a beige throw. A painting on the wall. I see an unlit fireplace."

"That's great, Rain. How about four things you can touch around you?"

"My phone. The pillow," I say and pick up the pillow. I rub my hand on the chair. "The lounge chair. My chest." I touch my breast.

"Okay. Enough of that. I think you're doing just fine." He laughs. It's warm, and I feel a sense of calm come over me. "Take another deep breath, then tell me how you feel?" I take a deep breath. "Are you okay to talk?" he asks again. I take another breath, wipe away the tears, then try to focus on what I want to say.

"Parker. I don't know what's happening. I think I'm developing feelings for Nik, but I don't understand them. Our time together is winding down, and I'm trying to enjoy the activities and not focus on feeling. We agreed to just this week, but I want more time."

"Time for what, Rain?"

"To see if there is more between us. To not feel alone. I don't know. When I arrived in Seattle…well, I was still reeling. Still stewing over Blake's BS. I shouldn't have come here until the day before my meeting."

"Tell me what you need."

"I should have come home, Parker. The minute my sister bailed on me, I should have come home. When I said goodbye to you at the airport, I felt like I was being torn away from something." Torn away from what? Parker? A sense of security? I shake my head because I need to pull myself together. This is why I should have taken his suggestion to go to therapy. To better arm myself with the necessary tools to deal with these heavy emotions on my own. To help me wean myself from calls like this.

"What are you saying?" The softness in his voice is gone. It's a valid question because I'm all over the map with my feelings and don't have a good answer.

"I don't know, Parker. Maybe I needed to talk through it with you. To figure out why I can't seem to make these relationships work. To focus on myself. To have time to heal."

"Do you feel you went into this thing with Nik as a rebound?"

"I feel a lot of things. Lonely, missing you, conflicted about saying yes to Nik. He's easy to be with, but how he is with me is not how he is normally."

"What's his normal state?"

I tell Parker about how Nik initially approached me like he was looking for a one-night stand, how he came across then, and how he's different now.

"Tell me he hasn't hurt you."

"No, Parker. He hasn't hurt me. I don't know if the player in him is real or if the way he is with me is real. But he's intentional about how he is with me."

"Which is?"

"Respectful, thoughtful, caring. Nik is completely focused on me when I'm with him like he's enamored." I tell him about how Nik told me to let him know if he does something I don't like because Nik doesn't want to create negative memories for me.

"Rain, it doesn't sound like you two have discussed seeing each other beyond this week. What's your plan?"

"I don't know. I've been asking myself a lot of questions."

"From what you said, you two behave differently together than you normally would. If this were to go beyond this week, would he eventually be frustrated for becoming someone he's not? You said he's not this way with other women. Okay, you're the first. What are the other things he's learning about relationships he's yet to experience? Is that the role you want to play, Rain?"

"I'm not sure."

"But you should know these things, Rain. What emotional support are you receiving? Would you receive? What does he know about us?"

"Nothing." He doesn't know anything about my twelve-year history with the man I called the love of my life. Whose heart I broke because I can't get my act together. He doesn't know about the one I compare every man to and who they all pale in comparison to.

"Does he know why you leave him every morning?"

"No, Parker."

I haven't told Nik that my brain can't handle the trauma from accidentally witnessing my dad leaving us without a word. The man who was my world. The one I looked up to, who I worshipped as a child. He doesn't know how he left in the wee hours of the morning when he didn't think anyone was aware. I knew. I can't unsee his step falter when he figured out that I was there…watching. "Dad?" I called out to him. He didn't even turn around. He just walked out of our lives like we never existed.

No, Nik doesn't know that I get up early to avoid sleep terror and that even then, there's no hiding. I can't stop the tape from replaying the scene every morning, marking the hour he left while I sit paralyzed, seeing my former self. That was the last time I ever saw him. No. He has no idea about that or other traumas that are triggered by reliving that one moment. He doesn't know how messed up my mind is. How every blip in my life feels like the searing poke of hot steel branding my brain. How every negative thought brings forth a wave of bile that I have to force down.

He doesn't know the relief I find in the sound of Parker's voice.

"Rain, I didn't mean to upset you."

"It's okay. You're right. If this continues, there's a lot to talk about."

"I'm concerned about you. This is insane. Does he even know you're on the heels of a breakup with Blake?" When he says Blake's name, my stomach turns because I haven't told him about what Blake did, but I need to before he discovers it himself. The situation with Blake needs to end, and even though he walked away from the party, it doesn't mean it's over.

"Can we talk about him?"

"About Blake? Why? What happened, Rain?"

"He was at this party I attended with Nik last night and—."

"Jesus, Rain. He what?"

"He was at this party and approached me upset about his exchange with you. I didn't ask about it. I told him I wasn't having a conversation with him."

"Oh my god. I'm sorry he approached you because of something I did."

"That's not your fault. That's how he is."

"Did he listen to you?"

"No. Blake was persistent, but Nik's brothers handled him, and he left without another word."

Parker closes his eyes a second before reopening them. "Nik's brothers? Where the hell was Nik?"

"He was there meeting with someone to discuss business," I tell him, and the look on Parker's face, like he's about to punch someone, is one I haven't seen since college. The night Kevin dared approach me, reeking of beer at a party and trying to make me leave with him, I learned the extent to which Parker would go to protect me. I realized just how powerful his family was and the extent to which they'd go to take care of their own. That was the day many people's lives were forever changed for the worse.

"Listen. I'm going to solve this once and for all. You're going to get a call from Blake today with an apology like he was supposed to give you before. After that, I promise he will never show his face around you again. Take the call, and this will be done."

"But I don't want to talk to him."

"Take the call, Rain," he insists. "You don't have to talk. Just listen. I promise it's done after that."

"No, Parker. I can handle this. If you asked him to apologize, then fine—I agree, he needs to follow through with that. Before I left, I told you that's what I wanted. Will you step aside after that? Don't take any further action."

He takes a deep breath. This is hard for him because he can't deny me anything. "If that's what you want." It's what I want. To stop allowing Parker to step in and handle this myself for once. I can do this.

"It is." I don't tell him he's the reason I want to be the one to set Blake straight. That I sense Blake's beef with Parker is not over. He's had one ever since I introduced him to Parker and he realized that Parker's family is the majority shareholder controlling the Wade empire. Parker could shut this down within seconds—but I want to do that.

"Okay. I'll let you handle it, but Rain, what are your plans with Nik?"

Shutting down my emotions for Nik may prove more difficult than I can manage.

"Honestly, Parker, I don't know. We promised to go our separate ways after this week. I walked away the first night. Even then, it felt difficult. I've asked myself the same questions you're asking: what's the attraction besides the power, the confidence, and the attention he gives me? I just want to feel like I'm needed, and I feel that way with him—like there are things I give him that no one else has. That no one else can."

"But what is he giving you? You said this is his first time doing anything like this. Did Nik tell you he wants to continue the relationship?"

"No," I say, and the tears start to fall again.

"Ah, Rain, say the word, and I'll be there in a few hours." His words are a promise that if I ask for the comfort of his arms, he'll give it. And

I desperately want what his promise will bring, but I won't ask.

"I...." I can't bring myself to say the words. To tell Parker to come to me because he will...he'll drop everything to be here in a heartbeat. He's done it before, but it's unfair for him to continue picking up after my mess. I made a mistake. I should have walked away from Nik before it became too much. Before I caught feelings.

"Hey, don't cry. You're not in this alone. I've got you," he assures.

"I should have listened to you. Come back to me whole, you told me." But I was too determined to do my own thing versus looking objectively at what Parker was telling me—to realize he was protecting me from myself. It's been a constant battle, thinking I've got the situation under control when sometimes I need to settle down and listen.

"It's okay. When you get back, we'll talk and figure this all out. Don't overthink it. Listen, you still have your upcoming meeting, so you need to pull it together. I dealt with the media company, and they've retracted their claims. I'm forwarding you the confirmation statement now just in case you need it," he says, breaking away from the screen. When he returns, my phone pings with an email alert. "All you need to do now is lock down your clients at the meeting and show them what you're made of."

"Parker, I don't know what I would do without you."

"I'm committed to ensuring you never find out. So, this is the plan. Review what I sent so you can update your clients and close this deal for Monday. Take the call from Blake today. Like I said, I'm only telling him he owes you an apology. When you return, we can continue this conversation and discuss the next steps for both of us. Because, Rain, if I have to fucking put my thumb down on another man, I'll end up in jail, a psych ward, or both. I'm backing off, but this is hard," he admits, and I can't help but laugh. "Seriously, Rain. I heard everything you said, and we need to talk. This stops here. We'll figure this out. Regarding Nik, I'm going to rein myself in for twenty-four hours and leave him to you to manage. Just note that it's a very short rein." He emphasizes the last sentence. "You know I have no issue securing the jet to get you. Say the word—I'm there."

Parker's alarm buzzes in the background. It's Sunday. I know his routine by heart. When he gets off this call, he'll go downstairs to his gym and work out for ninety minutes. Cardio. Hydrate. Strength. Stretch. Then he'll take a shower, after which he'll check messages before making something healthy to eat. He'll fit in time to be brilliant and work before going to his parents. I watch as Parker shuts the alarm clock off.

"You have to go."

"The only thing I need to do is talk to you. Nothing else matters right now. How are you feeling?"

"Better, because you make it seem so simple."

"It's not simple. I'm taking the emotion out of it. You think you can handle the next twenty-four hours?"

"Yeah. I think so. Thank you for the work you did for Ross Enterprises. This is a big deal for me."

"I've got you, babe. Get your day started, get some breakfast, and don't hesitate to call me if you need me," he says, and then we say our goodbyes.

I mull Parker's words over in my mind. I've got you, babe. Despite everything, the heartache, the headaches, the men, the memories, the mess—Parker has me. The question is, given the circumstances, would Nik do the same?

back and forth, she has time to take a call from me. I press video.

Rain is sitting in the back of a car. "You're stunning, Rain."

"Parker, it looks like you're at your mom's house." My mom is in the background talking to Dad.

"I am. Now tell me how you're feeling."

"Fine now, but when I took the call from Blake, I wanted to throw up."

"That's a natural response considering the circumstances. However, I'm sure you didn't. But he apologized."

She doesn't have to tell me. I know he did. I made sure he had no option but to. These men who walk around thinking they can treat women any way they want just because they have titles and positions have no clue what real power is. They're just pawns for those of us pulling the strings, watching the show as they go through this thing they think is life. Blake has no idea that having his boss on his tip is only a fraction of what I could have done. I could have ended his career, but Rain asked me not to ruin him, and said she wanted to handle him. I hope whatever she has planned is enough to stop him in his tracks. Before he ended the call, he said I'll pay for it. I'm already paying for it—the woman I love is sick to her stomach because of Blake's inability to be a real man.

"Yeah, he did, but I didn't say anything to him."

"Good. That's over. You ready for Monday?"

"Is that Raven, honey?" Mom gets up and walks over to me. I shift the phone so Rain can see my mom. "Raven, darling. I trust you received all the details for when you return."

"I did, Mrs. Page. I'm looking forward to it." I move away from Mom before she takes over the call. When I do, I'm immediately chastised by

Rain. "Be nice to your mom."

"She was one second away from taking over the call. You didn't answer my question. Are you ready for Monday?"

"I am. I revised the agreement and sent everything to the in-house counsel. They were excited you resolved the media issue."

"That was a small fraction of the work. The rest was you. You know you're brilliant."

"Well, thanks all the same." Rain's eyes shift from the screen to something out the car window. "Parker, I have to run a few errands."

"Okay, babe. I just wanted to see your face. Let me know if you need me for anything. Come home soon. Love you."

"I love you, too."

I love you. Those words still hold weight for me when I say them to Rain. There was a time when Rain said those words to me, and I knew she meant it to her core from the look in her eyes. Even now, she loves me, but I feel her slipping away as other men continue crashing into her life, chipping away at her protective shell.

Most of Rain's trauma stems from her dad walking out, obliterating her former family dynamic, and losing our child. I've repeatedly asked Rain to attend therapy with me, if not by herself. We have a chance if Rain can find her way back from the pain of loss. It scared her. It scared me. But unlike Rain, it made me feel more strongly about building a life with her as my wife. I can see a home filled with our children. Mini versions of ourselves running around, occupying our time. I want that so bad I can taste it. I need to help Rain find her way back to us. She needs to stop running.

Finding her father and helping her get closure in that situation is a start to healing. She tried to get her mom to tell her the truth behind her father's departure, to no avail. I promised not to overstep Rain's boundaries and initiate an investigation into his whereabouts without her approval. I sense she's already pushed past where she can take her self-healing. Facts and therapy could help her the rest of the way.

CHAPTER 66

Shards of Glass

Rain

Things with Nik are heating up. I have feelings I never thought I'd have for any man other than Parker. When we agreed to spend the week together, we promised to maintain our anonymity, that it would be sex, no feelings, no strings attached. We said that on Monday, we'd go our separate ways, and Nik wouldn't try to claim me like he was my man. I don't know what Nik thinks about our time together. Whether he has feelings for me or sees this as an extended one-night stand.

When I compare Nik to Parker, the similarities are apparent. They're both powerful, passionate, and protective. Parker is committed to me. Sometimes, I sense his irritation when I get clingy, but I know it's a defense mechanism to keep me off him. I can't help myself. When he's near, my body is pulled to him like the draw of a magnet. With Nik, the sex is excellent. He's serious yet funny at the same time. I feel a sense of family when I'm around him and his brothers, like I belong with them.

This is all too confusing. Like Parker told me, I need to focus on my work. I have a meeting to run, clients to impress, and a deal to make. Becoming a partner under Alejandro's leadership is my dream. A life with Parker was what I wanted—if I could find my way back. I don't know if I can get there alone. My dream was to be raised by a mom and dad in a loving household. Sometimes, dreams get shattered. Like glass, you need to be careful not to cut yourself with the shards as you clean up. That's where I am now—shifting through shards of glass, trying to pick up the pieces. To see whether what's broken can be salvaged or if I will have to throw it all away.

CHAPTER 67

Chasing Train Wrecks

Parker

When I spoke with Rain yesterday, she was in distress. It feels like she's regressing to how she was right before we ended it. Four years ago, she told me to walk away to give her time to figure things out so she could live a life without me as her partner. But she promised to return. So, I stepped away to allow her space to find herself and rid her mind of the shadow lurking between us. Our physical time apart lasted ten months, but the tie that bound us prevented us from staying separated. The gravitational pull between us is too strong to resist, and she called for me I didn't think she would, but she did.

Even after that day in London when I told her I would leave if she asked—she didn't. When I asked her to show me what she wanted—it was me. I asked her not to toy with me—she did. When she gave me permission to have other women—I save myself for her. When she told me she wanted to see other men—she did. I did my best to help her make a better decision. Despite my advice, she chose who she wanted, and they hurt her badly. I would never hurt her—yet they did so easily. Afterward she came to me, and I picked up the pieces. I held her while she cried her eyes out.

Last week, when Rain told me I couldn't do anything to the man who cheated on her, I bit my tongue—that is after he apologized. For twelve years she wouldn't let me research the situation with her father, something I knew from therapy could help control the darkness in her mind. She finally gave me permission. Now, she says she's handling the situation with Nik. I trust her. Still, she calls me. The one thing I know for sure is that Rain can walk away from me at any moment without hesitation, but she hasn't.

That is confirmation that we're meant for each other. But I need Rain to complete the journey to becoming whole. To realize that although times may get tough and things may not always go our way, we can get through it together. I told her I had her back, and I meant it. I'll do whatever it takes to protect her, to clear a path for her to find her way back to herself. That means I'll do whatever it takes to help her forget the man she knows as "Nik"...Noah Knight.

With thoughts of Rain guiding me, I call my pilot. "Perry."

"Mr. Page. What can I do for you?"

"I need to be in Seattle by eight tomorrow morning."

"I'll have everything cleared and ready to go. How many passengers?"

"One to Seattle, two on the return flight. Me and Raven Nichols."

"We'll see you in the morning."

When I last spoke with Rain, I told her I'd see her soon. There's a reason for that. When she realizes who Nik really is, it won't go well for him. Rain is an intelligent woman, but she's still hurting due to past trauma. The last thing Rain wants is to walk into a train wreck intentionally. Especially one she'll have to ride for the rest of her life. Will walking away from Noah hurt? Yes, but she'll do it. As sure as I know that the sun will rise—she'll leave. And like she always does, she will seek out comfort and love. And she'll find exactly that...in my arms. Because the first face my woman will see when she walks out of her meeting is mine.

To be continued....

Want a taste of what's next for Parker, Raven, and Noah? Subscribe to my newsletter at **https://www.ritaagordon.com/subscribe-page** to get special excerpts and stay updated on the *Let It Rain* series, which concludes with Book 3, "The Fall of Us."

Scan me

BLURB

The Days With Rain

Their love was supposed to last a lifetime. Fate had other plans.

What happens when you meet the love of your life, but you're not ready?

The moment Rain met Parker, they became inseparable. They shared everything, from their lawyer dreams to their deepest secrets.

Parker came from a wealthy, loving family and wanted to give Rain the world.

Rain came from a broken and distant family, and Parker was the only one who could calm her down and make her feel safe.

They fell in love and planned a future together, but life had other plans.

After twelve years of heartbreak, pain, and drifting apart, they finally decide to try and save their love. But is it too late?

***The Days with Rain**, a contemporary romance, is Book 2 of the "Let It Rain" series.*

Praise for Rita A. Gordon

Seven Days In Seattle

Book 1 of the *Let It Rain* series.

"Readers will connect with the realistic banter whose humor and subtlety is worthy of a Hollywood script."

— *BookLife Reviews, Editor's Pick*

"In Seven Days in Seattle, Rita Gordon weaves a swoon-worthy story that kept me riveted until the end."

— *Kenya Goree-Bell, Bestselling Author of The Blood Legacy Series*

"…intriguing story with a complex protagonist that flouts convention."

— *Kirkus Reviews*

"One thing Rita Gordon will do is write a[n] FMC who is strong and powerful [and] who also lives by the motto "YOLO" when it comes down to men! Whew. Once I picked this up, I couldn't put it down."

— *Brianna, Goodreads Reviewer*

BLURB

Seven Days In Seattle

Book 1 of the *Let It Rain* series.

One week. No strings. No names. No feelings. What could go wrong?

Rain

This Seattle meeting will change my life…just not the way I expected.

Instead of focusing on my presentation, I'm dealing with a cheating boyfriend and sister who bailed on me. The only good thing to happen is when a stranger at a bar offers a pretty distraction: a one-night stand, no strings attached, no questions asked. A distraction from my mess of a life is exactly what I need….

But our one-night stand turns into a week-long affair. He only wanted sex, no feelings, no last names, no talk about business, nothing personal. And I was fine with that. Until I wasn't.

Nik

I don't have time for relationships. I have a company to run, a legacy to uphold, a reputation to protect. I only care about power and success. I don't do dates and I don't do tomorrows. I only do one-night stands with women who know the rules and don't ask for more.

But then I met Rain at a bar. She's beautiful, smart, and sassy. And suddenly, I want more. The more time we spend together, the more I want from her. Her name. Her story. Her dreams. And I was fine with that. Until I wasn't.

Fate is about to punish us for staying anonymous…by throwing us into each other's lives in the worst possible way.

Seven Days In Seattle*, a contemporary romance, is Book 1 of the "Let It Rain" series.*

Available in eBook, paperback, and hardcover.

EXCERPT

Seven Days In Seattle

Book 1 of the *Let It Rain* series.

Chapter 1
The Way We Were

Raven

Sometimes, there are moments when you have to laugh hysterically just to keep from crying. Then, there are moments when you just want to scream.

"Parker Page, I swear I'll kill you if you don't give that back to me," I yell across the kitchen counter, then dash to the other side where my soon-to-be ex-best friend Parker clutches my phone, scrolling through the contacts. When I'm directly behind him, he lifts his arm and holds my phone above his head. He's a six-foot-four-inch-tall wall of muscles. I'm a five-foot-six piece of brown paper and have to jump in my bare feet to try and reach it. "What are we, twelve? Give. Me. My. Phone." I jump up again and miss. When he extends his arm over the counter, I do the only thing I can in a moment of desperation. I jump on his back. "Woman, if you don't get off my back. Let me handle this situation." He leans over the counter and turns to the side to get me off his back. Gravity takes over and I swing to his front, and like a koala, I cling to him, bringing him down to the counter, hovering over me. My shoulder shoves a fruit bowl that tips over. Oranges, apples, and lemons roll the length of the counter, and one after another, I hear them collide with the delivery bags containing our dinner. A wave of uncontrollable laughter washes over me when I think how ridiculous we must look. And it feels good to laugh after sulking the last two days. I pull Parker's arm forward until he's forced to lean over me on the counter. Still straddling him, I lick his face to distract him and manage to grab the phone from his hands.

"Got it," I say triumphantly, but it comes out more like a pant. Parker is still leaning over me, arms on either side of my head. "Now you back off *me*." I reach up and muss his curly dirty blond hair. Our faces are so close that I get a whiff of him. It's deep, woodsy, and sweet, and I'm tempted to dip my nose in his neck, but I don't dare. "This is sexy, but you really need a haircut. Now get off," I tell him.

The look Parker gives me is a mix of surprise and seduction. He touches his wet cheek. "What was that?" He straightens, grabs me by the waist, lifts me like I weigh nothing, and gently stands me back on the floor. I walk across the kitchen and sit on the opposite side of the counter.

"What?" My lips spread into a sly smile.

Parker retrieves a bottle of wine from his wine fridge, opens it, and fills two glasses. He hands me a drink across the marble counter. I lift it to my lips and sip. Parker always has the best wine. He must have been a sommelier in another life.

"The woman with perfect recall is asking me *what*."

He has a point. I don't forget anything. It's both a blessing and a curse that I can recall in detail what I've seen and heard. It helped in my profession as a lawyer, but unfortunately I could never utter the phrase, "I forgot." Only my closest family and friends and my boss, Alejandro, know about it. It's not something you talk about. People either pick up on its existence or don't. Parker picked up on it when he became my best friend at Stanford University. We had almost every class together since we both studied law. Parker knew everything about me and vice versa, so there was no pulling the wool over his eyes.

"That's me, using my feminine wiles to get what I want," I tell him.

"Be careful," he growls. "I may be your best friend, but I am all man."

"Yeah. That part I remember."

It's etched like glass in my memory because, for five years, Parker Page was my man in every biblical sense of the word. And he's right. He is all man. Just not mine. Well, not that way anymore. We're very much alike. Both stubborn. Both opinionated. Both passionate. And if I'm honest, we're both a little wild, which is how I ended up on his back on a Sunday night at the age of thirty.

As I watch Parker move seamlessly through the kitchen, I reflect on that time of our lives. In all appearances, we were the perfect match. Young, beautiful, intelligent, determined...unstoppable. And for a while, we were, in essence, perfect...for a while. We tried to make it work as a couple. We really did. But in life, there are obstacles you can't move on from. Well, mainly one I couldn't move on from. However, we found our rhythm as friends; it just works better this way—we're inseparable. And right now, my best friend, my confidant, my protector, has latched on to a bone named Blake Wallace, my ex. The man I discovered was cheating on me.

Parker opens the food delivery bags and plates our pasta. Then he carries both plates to my side of the counter and sits beside me.

"That's what I thought," he says and hands me a fork. "But seriously, let me deal with Blake."

"That's not necessary. I've already dealt with Blake." I twist the fork into my pasta until a large roll of noodles forms, and then lean in and eat the entire thing. "Hmm," I moan. "I swear pasta and wine are my love language."

"I know," Parker says, then picks up his napkin, puts a finger under my chin, and turns my head toward him. He wipes the corner of my lips. "You're such a mess."

"I know." It's the story of my life.

"So, tell me. Did you confront him before or after dinner?"

This is not a conversation I want to have. To stir up bad memories that lay rancid in my mind like the stench of sauce that's gone sour in Tupperware. It's a lid that's best left unopened. But I always tell Parker everything, so I prepare myself and down the rest of my wine in one gulp. I think about that moment in the restaurant as Parker refills my glass.

"Mr. Wallace, it's good to see you again so soon. I trust you and your lady friend had a good meal last night?"

"Yes. Everything was great. The ribeye was perfection."

"Will you be having the same this evening? I can go over the specialties if you like."

"Let's wait for my girlfriend to return. She's in the restroom," he said. I waited for the manager to leave before returning to the table. I don't know if I waited out of embarrassment or whether I was trying to help him save face. I should have outed him in front of the manager, but that's not how I operate.

When the manager left, I returned to the table.

After I was seated, Blake reached across the table to touch my hand. I pulled my hand away like his touch had burned me.

"Is everything okay?" he asked, and my blood began to boil. My mind started racing, and every disappointing interaction I'd had with Blake flashed through my head. I felt dizzy as the scenes played on repeat in my mind.

"Rae, is everything okay?" he repeated, pulling me out of the dumpster fire he'd started.

I took a deep breath. "Did I hear the manager correctly? Oh wait," I snapped my fingers. "We both know I can't misunderstand something I can recall verbatim. You lied."

"I—."

"I'm talking. You need to listen. You said you were with 'the boys' at the gym last night. Mr. Manager here says you were with a woman that wasn't me. So, I can assume three weeks ago, when I asked you to go with me after work to have drinks with Parker and our friend Josh, and you said you had to work late—you didn't really have to work. Two weeks ago, Thursday when you couldn't break away for lunch, when you, and I quote, 'never miss a lunch,' you really didn't miss lunch. You just didn't want to go with me."

"Rae, let me—."

"Explain? No, let me explain. Your actions speak louder than words, Blake. So, I'd say you've said enough. I'm not that woman. I don't need to settle for less. You should have said something four months ago at the charity event if you didn't know what you wanted. But you didn't. You know why, Blake? Because you are a pathetic excuse for a man and a colossal waste of my time. When I walk out of here, don't call me, don't text me, and as a matter of fact, lose my number. When you see me in public, pretend you don't know me because that's what I'm going to do. I don't have any more room in my brain for trash, Blake. Goodbye."

I grabbed my purse and left the restaurant. I wandered into the bar next door, ordered a drink, and called Parker.

"Rain. Hey, babe."

"Parker, come get me."

Once again, Parker came to my rescue and I'm here walking him through another one of my failed relationships.

"I couldn't stomach the thought of sitting through dinner with him after overhearing his conversation with the manager. The fact that he didn't have the guts to tell me to my face that he didn't feel our relationship was working makes me feel cheap and unimportant."

"You're right. He should have been man enough to talk to you. He should have apologized."

"He should have, but he didn't. So, I confronted him before he could order, then left him sitting there. You know me, there is no retort once I lay out all the facts."

I eat more pasta. When I notice Parker isn't eating, I raise my chin toward his plate. He twirls his pasta and takes a bite. I scrunch my nose. He rolls his eyes. I put my fingers to my lips and blow him a kiss. It's silly, but we have a way of speaking without words. We've had that ever since we met in our contract law course at Stanford. One day, our professor was upset because some students did poorly on the test, and he admonished the entire class. His German accent was so heavy that he was almost unintelligible as he ranted, *"You're not going to get this by divine inspiration. If only I were a brain surgeon."* Our professor's voice boomed in the lecture hall. I had an urge to turn to my left, and Parker turned at that exact moment. Our eyes locked and I pursed my lips. He raised his eyebrows and he shook his head. We held a whole conversation without saying a word, using only body language, as our professor continued ranting in the background. Once we were out of the class, we huddled outside the door and laughed like old friends.

"I'm Parker." He held his hand out to me between laughs.

"I'm Raven. People call me Rae."

"What's your full name, Raven?"

"Raven Rain Nichols."

"Rain. I love the sound of that. I'm reminded how essential it is to all life. Can I call you Rain?"

"Yeah. You can call me Rain."

That was twelve years ago, and although we're no longer a couple, we've been inseparable ever since. And now, the way Parker looks at me tells me how deeply he still cares. We've been through too much together. Whatever *this* is between us, it's good, it's precious, and I'll do everything within my power to protect it. Sometimes, I think that's why it was better that we stopped being a couple, to hold on to what we have—to conserve *us*.

"It wasn't your fault," Parker tells me. "I can't believe the audacity of that man. I hate that this happened to you, but I'm glad you weren't with him long."

He's right. One second is too long to be with anyone who doesn't treat you as you deserve. I was with Blake for four months. Early in the relationship, he was attentive and seemed interested in my work as a real estate attorney. But over the past few months, he became preoccupied. Thinking back, I feel so stupid. I should have read the signs. I've been focused on proving myself at work, and rightfully so, but it sucks how this went down. I never would have learned about him cheating if I hadn't stepped away to freshen up in the restroom before dinner. I was stunned to hear the restaurant manager mention seeing

Blake the previous night with a woman. He had told me he was at the gym. That wasn't the truth. He was having dinner with another woman at that restaurant.

"I get it wasn't my fault, but you can't just call him up and give him a piece of your mind. I understand you're only protecting me, but you and I are attorneys. We have reputations to uphold. This could go sideways."

"You may as well hand over your phone because I'm calling him whether you like it or not. I can guarantee that he'll rethink doing this to anyone again."

"I'm not giving you my phone. If you want to call Blake, do it on your own." I shake my head, resigned that my best friend won't take no for an answer regarding something like this. Because even though we're no longer lovers, Parker is still protective of me. I get it. We're both invested in each other.

If I'm being honest, it goes much deeper than that for Parker. In the past, when my relationships went sideways, I ended them first. If I didn't, once Parker found out that they were heading downhill, he'd take matters into his own hands. He's not a mean guy, and he'd never hurt anyone unless they hurt me, but they undoubtedly wished they'd never met me when he was done. Parker Page is powerful, privileged, and used to getting his way. He comes from one of the most elite families in California. His family is part of a group you'll never hear about in the media—they're that rich. So, if he tells Blake to do something, then Blake would be wise to proceed with caution.

"Okay. I'll handle this. But not like I did the others. I'll talk to him. At a minimum, like you said, he owes you an apology, Rain."

"Fine. I'm done with this conversation, and I'm done with men. Anyway, I need to focus on my career. This meeting in Seattle could be my ticket to becoming a partner."

Being an ambitious overachiever has done wonders for my career, but it hasn't afforded me time to nurture relationships with men. That is, except for Parker. But I needed to break free of him to prove I don't need a powerful man in the room to validate or protect me. That despite everything, I can stand on my own merit. I've been so focused on this that I haven't put the time into getting to know the men I've dated. I would have noticed signs that Blake wasn't all in sooner if I had.

"You will, Rain. You have one of the most brilliant minds in real estate law. And don't be so jaded regarding men. I wasn't so bad, was I?"

"Oh my god, Parker. I didn't mean—." I don't finish. Instead, I hop off my stool, throw my arms around Parker's neck, and hug him dramatically. I kiss him on the cheek and muss his hair again. "The fact that you are still in my life says everything, and don't you forget that."

Parker untangles me from his body and glares at me, reading my face. After a second, his brows unfurrow, his expression softens, and he seems satisfied with what he sees. "You have everything you need for the week?" he asks. The mood lifts and I return to my seat.

"Yes. Thank you for volunteering to drop me off at SFO tomorrow. Car service is so impersonal—there's no one for me to hug before I leave. I think that could be awkward for the driver," I whine, and my admission gets a chuckle.

"Depends on the driver. Well, at least you get to see your sister. It's been a while. Tell her hi for me."

"Yeah. Let's see how Robin is. You know she can be finicky at times." Rather, all the time, I should have said. We're so different that sometimes I wonder whether we're even from the same parents.

"It'll be fine, Rain."

"It would have been better if you had some time off to go with me. This is my first break in a year."

A year ago, Parker saw that the demands that I was putting on myself were taking their toll and suggested we drive down the coast for a three-day weekend in Carmel. He was right; I needed the break. It allowed me to momentarily clear my head of men, my memories, my work—it was the best weekend ever. I should have listened to him when he suggested I take a break from dating. If I had, I never would have given Blake a second look. I wouldn't be in this position: scrubbing the recesses of my mind, remembering the time wasted on him. Ugh, stupid Blake Wallace.

I don't need this mess in my head. I need to focus. Focus. Focus, Rain. I direct my eyes to Parker's mouth as he speaks. I trace the curve of his lips with my gaze.

"My calendar is set for the next month, or I would fly out for a few days. And my parents need me to review some contracts for them."

"They have people for that."

"That's what I told them. Anyway, I'm sorry I can't be there. Hopefully you get time to see some sights before you dive in with your client meetings."

"I have a list of things to see and do. Let's see how far I get. It's not all fun and games, in any case. I still plan to work a few hours after I arrive tomorrow. And of course, I have to check email throughout the week to stay on top of things. Also, Alejandro wants to brief me before I get into vacation mode. He says this could be the biggest deal of my career."

My boss, Alejandro Rodriguez, is the founding partner in the law firm. A top international attorney, he is outside counsel for some of the most prestigious corporations in the world, Ross Enterprises being one. A year and a half ago, he poached me from my firm to focus on building out his real estate division. Our client, Ross Enterprises, is expanding their company to more locations and needs an attorney who specializes in real estate development to review real estate contracts and advise their legal counsel. That's where I come in. Structuring real estate contracts to protect Ross Enterprises is right up my alley. If I nail my next few projects, I could potentially make partner, which makes next Monday's meeting a big deal.

Parker begins clearing the counter and putting away the food containers. I return the spilled fruit to the bowl, then wet a towel and wash down all the marble counter surfaces. That's another thing we share—we're both neat freaks. When the kitchen is clean, Parker goes to the sink to wash his hands. I stand beside him and wash mine, too. When I'm done, I hold them out with my palms up. Parker gives me the "you're something else" look, shakes his head, and dries my hands. I bump him with my hip.

"Thanks, Parker."

He pulls me to his side and kisses the top of my head. "I have to prepare for a brief. I'll be in my office for a while. You want to watch TV or something?"

"No, I'm good. I'll plop on the sofa in your office and catch up on my reading. But first, I'm changing into my PJs."

It doesn't take long for me to shower and change. I wander through the house, taking in the space that's become my second home. Parker and I share the same taste in modern design. His grey-toned walls, mahogany furnishings, and brass fixtures reflect our shared aesthetic. As I walk toward the office through the narrow hallway from the main bedroom suite, a photo on the wall catches my eye. It's a picture of me and Parker throwing our caps in the air on graduation day. Seeing the image brings back fond memories of our time together in college.

We were two people figuring out what it was like to be adults living on our own. First as classmates and friends, then as lovers. Even back then, we were inseparable. Like an addiction, the need to be near one another was all-consuming—we loved each other that much. Whenever Parker was near me it was as if the world fell away. I don't know if I was prepared for that kind of love, having come from a broken family. It scared me. It still does.

It wasn't until our third year of undergrad that we formally started dating. We continued dating while working on our juris doctorates, even though we went to separate schools. However, something shifted during our time away from each other. I used to think it was the stress of school, the distance, or the fact that we were getting older and growing into our own. But that was me playing tricks with my mind. Truth is, Parker and I were speeding down a path to becoming…more. Then, one night, our relationship took a terrible turn that threw us off track—if I'm being honest, me more so than Parker. I think I used the situation as a catalyst to refocus. To try and become my own person. By the time we received our JDs, we were no longer a couple, yet despite pushing past the passion and the pain, our friendship was preserved.

When people ask why we're so close that we seem like more than friends, we have a standard response. We say we've talked about it numerous times but can't explain our connection. We don't try anymore. We just know this is the way we are. At least that's what we say. But it's a lie. I know exactly why. I made a promise to Parker a long time ago. A commitment that became the ultimate tie that binds us, one I don't know if I can ever satisfy. When we broke up, I said the thing you say to someone who can't stop loving you no matter how bad you are for them. We all have our secrets, and the promise I made to Parker is mine. So yeah, if anyone asks, that's the way we are—inexplicably tied together.

When I reach the study, I find Parker on a call. I lean against the door frame, watch his beautiful face be all business-like, and pause before entering.

"Yes, I need that case cited. Don't forget all the corresponding notations. Right. Are you ready? Great, I'll see you tomorrow," Parker says to someone in an authoritative voice I seldom encounter.

After he ends the call, I walk into his study and stand beside him at his desk. He pulls me to his side. "Rain." My name slides off his tongue like silk, and I smile.

"Why haven't we created our own firm?" I ask. My hand instinctively slides up his neck and into his hair. It's soft. Silky.

Parker takes my wrist and flips it to check the time on my watch. I remember the day he brought it for my birthday, the year we started dating. He told me to wear it always as a reminder that our time together is precious. I thought walking around with a gold Rolex every day was silly, but I got used to it. He kisses my fingers and then releases me. He reaches across his desk, picks up my iPad, and hands it to me.

"Honestly, babe, I don't know. Don't we already spend so much of our lives together?"

He's right. Although we don't live together, we share meals at least four times a week, whether we meet for coffee before work, have lunch together, or have dinner. And when we don't see each other, we communicate by phone, typically via video call. We even use our friendship as a litmus test for people we date. If they can't accept that

Parker and I are best friends, they're out.

Catching his hint, I take my iPad and move to the sofa facing his desk. I prop pillows on one end, lay back on them, and open my email. My eyes automatically shift to Parker when I feel him watching me, waiting for a response.

"I suppose you're right. Don't forget to set the alarm for six, and don't you dare leave me lying on this couch if I fall asleep. I swear I'll kill you if I wake up here."

I hear the crunch of a paper before I feel it bounce off my head. Then, as if on cue, we laugh.

~

Seven Days In Seattle

BLURB

The Fall Of US

Friendship wasn't enough.
Book 3 of the *Let It Rain* series.

To what extent would you go to reclaim your life?

In the pulsating heart of a city where power reigns supreme and passion ignites, Raven Nichols finds herself torn between two magnetic forces: Parker Page, her constant friend and first love, and Noah Knight, a captivating stranger who challenges everything she thought she knew.

Grappling with her own demons, Raven is drawn back into Parker's sphere, his allure as potent as ever. But promises made in the heat of youthful passion may not withstand the weight of time and trials to transformation.

Enter Noah Knight, a man who thrives on the thrill of conquest and the rush of control. Like Parker, the command and confidence he conveys are her catnip. Yet, beneath his formidable exterior lies a vulnerability Raven can't resist. Their fleeting connection leaves her breathless, but the clash between her heart's desires and sense of duty leaves her reeling.

With each passing day, Raven's world grows more tangled as she navigates the treacherous terrain of love, loyalty, and self-discovery. In a landscape where power is currency and every choice has consequences, she must confront her own truth and decide which path to follow.

Will she honor her promise to Parker and reclaim their lost love, or will Noah's allure prove too powerful to resist?

***The Fall of Us**, a second chance romance, is Book 3 and the highly anticipated conclusion to the "Let It Rain" series.*

EXCERPT

The Fall Of US

Book 3 of the *Let It Rain* series.

PROLOGUE

The First Time I Saw Her Face

Mark "Mak" Knight

THE FIRST TIME I SAW HER WAS WHEN MY OLDER BROTHER ROK AND I video called Nik to razz him about canceling dinner with us. He never cancels. He did that night. More surprisingly, was when we discovered the reason he canceled. We soon realized why when he pulled a woman close to him and positioned the phone for us to see her—she was stunning.

That was the first time in years that I'd seen something in my brother's eyes that resembled pure happiness. It was also the day I saw someone standing beside him who could be a sister, a friend, a future family member, someone who could be the solution to helping my brother be human again.

Yeah, that was the first time I saw her face. Rae.

"Rok. Was that you blowing up my phone? This better be good." Nik said before I took the phone away from Rok to see what was happening on the other end.

"We told you to take time away from work, not from us. What's the deal, man?" I asked as Nik pulled a woman to his side, angling his phone so they were both on the screen. I positioned the phone so Rok and I were on the screen together.

"Well, shit," I said. Rok took the phone from me.

"Hey, I'm Rok, with a K, Nik's older brother. And this one," he pointed his thumb at me. "The one with a potty mouth is our baby brother, Mak." I held my fingers up, forming the sign letter for K. Rok elbowed me in the side. "I see now why our brother canceled dinner plans with us," he said.

Nik turned and smiled at the woman still watching us on the phone screen—that's when we knew she was the one. His face relaxed as he briefly scanned hers—he had a gleam in his eyes like he had finally found what he was searching for. She turned to look at him briefly, then back at the screen.

"Hi, Rok, with a K, and Mak." She held up her delicate fingers, signing the letter K when she said my name, mirroring me. "I'm Rae, with an E. It's nice to meet you. Is Baby Mak potty trained?" she asked, and we couldn't suppress our laughter.

That was a week ago. Their story was only supposed to last one night. That's my brother's MO. But I discovered the next day they were still together. Nik told me she wouldn't be in town for long. *"She's only going to be in Seattle for seven days,"* he said.

A lot can happen in one week. It was enough time for my older brother Rok and I to fall in love with her over brief calls with Nik and at our cousin Chase's birthday celebration. At the party, I ran off Rae's cheating ex, who happened to be in attendance, and she introduced me to a beautiful woman named Melanie. That's a story for another day.

By the end of the week, we were all hooked. One week was enough to discover Rae's that special type of woman—the smart, sexy, sassy kind that would fit wonderfully into our world like the missing centerpiece of a thousand-piece puzzle you thought you'd never find.

That's what Rae is. The perfect find, the perfect fit—the woman who first captured our attention with her wit. The perfect woman for Nik.

PRAISE FOR RITA GORDON

30 Days In Belfast

***Publishers Weekly* Indie Spotlight February 2023 (Romance & Relationships)**

"An addictive, rollicking tale of friendship, love, and lust."

— *Kirkus Reviews*

"Gordon's debut offers readers a winning combination of intrigue and romance, revealed slowly through the lens of opulent travel and luxurious living."

— *BookLife Reviews*

"I loved the relationships between the characters, the storyline was heartwarming and after a while, I couldn't put it down. Would definitely recommend!"

— *LoveReading, Indie Books We Love (starred review)*

"…It's the best book I've read, period."

— *Sana Aubuliel, Author of Letters to The Person I Was*

"A[n] easy, beautiful, knowledgeable read!"

— *Goodreads Reviewer*

BLURB

30 Days In Belfast

JUST ONE DISTRACTION COULD LEAD TO FAILURE—SEVERAL MAY SPELL ruin.

As the daughter of the wealthiest Black man in the country, Rose Ross struggles to make a name for herself as the COO of her father's tech company. She's even forced to let go of a promising relationship to focus on her career, but still cannot seem to escape her father's legacy. Rose fears that if she remains at Rick Ross Enterprises, she will never rise above the vast shadow his name casts.

When her ailing friend reaches out to her for help, Rose doesn't hesitate. She has just thirty days to curate the most important charity art exhibition in Europe and break into a field she is truly passionate about. However, just before she leaves for her flight to Belfast, her father informs her that she has only three weeks to decide whether she will succeed him as CEO.

With her concentration already split between one life-altering decision, Rose is stunned when she meets her friend's handsome and overprotective brothers. Right away, she recognizes an undeniable, yet different, attraction to both.

Her mind in turmoil, Rose's focus is now fractured among love and business. If she cannot make a decision—or if she makes the wrong one—she will lose everything she has worked for and, perhaps, more.

30 Days In Belfast *is a standalone contemporary romance.*

Available in eBook, paperback, and hardcover.

EXCERPT

30 Days In Belfast

PROLOGUE
We Have Time

"If you love somebody, let them go, for if they return,
they were always yours.
If they don't, they never were."
– Kahlil Gibran, *A Tear and a Smile*

"I'LL RACE YA," SHANNON CALLED AS SHE RAN PAST ROSE TOWARD THE foam remnants of a forgotten wave on the shoreline.

Rose stopped scribing her initials in the sand heart drawing, a covert confession of love to her celebrity crush. She jumped up and headed toward the water. "Wait for me," she shouted to Shannon, who didn't see her. The glare from the sun dancing on the waves mimicking a million miniature mirrors distorted her view. Rose chased a wave and jumped in the water, pushing through the powerful current. When it subsided slightly, she popped up. "Shannon!" she called over the waves, but didn't see her friend. Rose continued to push through the currents, shoving the waves back with her arms that were growing sore by the minute. With each breath she took, she became more panicked, still unable to spot her friend.

Rose looked toward the shore to see if Shannon had made it back. "Shannon, where—" Rose called out before being sucked under by the current. Before it all became a faded memory.

Fifteen years later, the aftermath was fuzzy in her head. She remembered eventually getting herself to shore. The shock and overwhelming sense of loss she felt when she realized Shannon was not by her side finally came into focus as people crowded around her in the sand. An endless stream of questions rushed through her. The sudden end of a forever friendship stolen by sun, sand, and sneaker waves. Rose felt her face grow warm as memories of Shannon flooded her mind. Her heart started to race. Panic washed over her as she relived the day her friend died. All she wanted to do now was run.

"Rose, talk to me. I know it feels like it came out of left field. Tell me what you're thinking." The sound of Alejandro's voice sitting across the table pulled her out of her head. He was staring at her with a mix of concern and longing in his eyes. Shelved was the swoon-worthy smile that usually greeted her. The smile that made her melt after spending weeks away from her man. He reached his hand across the table.

Rose averted Alejandro's gaze and looked around his London flat, where they had just spent the last three evenings wrapped in each other's arms. Where they had made love for hours until they were both sore, satiated, and spent. Where they had shared rare stolen moments between their busy schedules. She was the one who convinced him to get the flat since he spent so much time traveling between New York and London. He was busy building his career as an international attorney, and Rose was recently promoted to COO. A reward for endless hours helping her father build his business and developing new technologies to innovate the company. Living on the west coast, paired with the busy travel schedule that came with her new position, meant they spent more time on video calls than in person.

Rose focused her attention on the modern, muted earth tones of the room. Her eyes were drawn to a painting she commissioned: A Black woman with a crown of flowers blooming from her head and partially covering her face. Rose remembered posing for the portrait with her chin turned toward her bare shoulder. "Think about your man," the artist had instructed her.

Now, she was sitting across the table from the man she thought she could build a life with. His words washed across her, pulling her down like the sneaker wave that snatched her childhood friend from her life forever. Stirring within her was the same sense of shock and sudden loss.

Rose sucked in a breath. "You sure about this?" she said, sounding as if negotiating a business deal—placing a wall around her heart and tamping the need to reach across the table to take his hand.

"No. But I do know we're both committed to our work. The time in between when we finally get together keeps growing. I'm torn between you and the job, and I don't want to ask you to bend for me. I respect that you're building your career, too. I want to make it work but can't see a way. You just got promoted and want to make a name for yourself away from your father's shadow. That's a tall order, and I'll use all my resources to support you in that effort. But trying to build something more between us is no small feat. Think about it. How many things did you and I have to shift to get these three nights together?"

"Quite a bit," she answered, hesitant to strengthen his argument.

"That's exactly the point. You and I know that you had to rearrange twice as much as me. I won't continue asking you to do that. Your father is my largest client. I know the demand he puts on me. I can only imagine how exponentially higher that is on you. I care about you, but I won't be the one to stifle your success. Let's take a step back and focus. Let's give ourselves a year." Alejandro leaned back in his chair and ran his hands through his hair.

Rose knew he was rethinking his words. But they were out, weighing heavy between them.

Was he right? Should they take a break, allowing time to establish themselves? Could they walk away and get back when the time was right? Would it ever be right?

The idea of them not being a couple made Rose feel like she did when she lost her best friend. The same emotions flowed through her all over again. She paused to think, unaware of what was keeping her from ending the conversation, putting her foot down, and refusing his suggestion.

Rose closed her eyes, inhaled, and opened them. Alejandro's gaze was still locked on her. "This isn't about something else. Or is it? You—" she started.

Alejandro stood, rounded the table, and pulled Rose to her feet and into a tight embrace. He planted kisses all over her face before touching his forehead to hers.

"Oh, Rose. Don't ever think that. I…I'd be hard-pressed to believe I could be with anyone other than you. You are the center of my universe, but I know I'm not yours. This is me setting you free—giving you time to do what you need to do. To be you without me interfering."

Rose listened intently, her breath becoming synchronized with his.

"I'm not saying it's just about you," he continued. "I also need to figure out why I haven't moved heaven and earth to be by your side.

And for that, I'm at fault." Alejandro swallowed, then turned to look out the window. Rose held onto his hand, walked up behind him, and pressed her chin to his back.

"Okay." Rose paused. "We'll give it some time."

~

30 Days In Belfast

ACKNOWLEDGMENTS

THE THIRD TIME IS A CHARM, OR SO THEY SAY. I'M THRILLED TO BRING you the story of Parker and Rain's twelve-year journey in **The Days with Rain**. Behind the scenes, there are so many people to thank. Thank you, Cassandra, for continuing to help me polish my books with your editing skills. To the Beta Readers who have committed themselves to the series thus far, LaToya and Kim—thank you for helping me stay true to my characters. Thank you, Kenya Goree-Bell, for all the online late-night writing sprints. I couldn't have done it without you rallying writers together and helping us be accountable for writing consistently. As always, thank you, Deborah, for your friendship. Every writer should be so lucky to have someone like you in their corner cheering them on. And lastly, to my sister Bess, who understands that I have these stories in my head that need to come to life on paper.

Thank you all,
Rita

Discussion Questions

1. In Book 1, *Seven Days in Seattle*, we learn that Raven has paternal issues that fuel her propensity to walk out as a defense mechanism. When do we get our first glimpse of that in *The Days with Rain*?
2. Raven and Parker fall in love and quickly become tied almost at the proverbial hip. Do you feel this kind of love is real? Do you believe it will last?
3. Parker goes to London, unbeknownst to Raven, to be near her. She learns about it following a sudden illness and is upset with his reemergence in her life. Her immediate response is to distance herself from him. How would you have handled the situation?
4. In the *Chasing Trainwrecks* chapter, we learn Parker will pay Raven a surprise visit. Four years have passed since he last pulled a stunt like that. Their relationship has evolved since then. How do you think Raven will respond this time?
5. How do you think Raven will resolve having feelings for Noah and Parker?
6. Which scene stuck with you the most?

Interested in facilitating deeper book discussion? Scribe to my newsletter and receive a link to my free resource, Romance Book Discussion Guide. https://bit.ly/ritasnews.

ABOUT THE AUTHOR

Photographed by Abigail Huller

Rita Gordon is a California native living in the Bay Area and is a San Francisco State University graduate. As an emerging voice in the contemporary romance genre, Rita brings a fresh perspective to storytelling. Inspired by the power of love and the beauty of cultural exploration, her writing captures the essence of human emotions, leaving readers spellbound with each page turn. In addition to writing, Rita is an avid reader who's amassed an extensive collection of books that fills the rooms of her home. When not reading and writing, she travels, draws flower designs for her coloring books, and volunteers in her community.

To learn more about the author, visit **ritaagordon.com.**

CONNECT WITH RITA

Let's stay in touch! You can find me here:

Subscribe to her newsletter:

https://www.ritaagordon.com/subscribe-page

Follow Rita on:

X | Instagram | Pinterest:

@rgordonshaw

TikTok:

@authorritagordon (ritagordonwrites)

Facebook:

https://www.facebook.com/authorritagordon

Goodreads:

https://www.goodreads.com/author/show/21524163.Rita_A_Gordon

ALSO BY RITA A. GORDON

Standalone Novel
30 Days in Belfast

Let It Rain Series
Seven Days in Seattle (Book 1)
The Days with Rain (Book 2)
The Fall of Us (Book 3, coming 2024)

Coloring Books
Little Flower Garden
The Big Flower

Inspirational Books & Journals
The Book of Love
On A Positive Note
Grateful

www.ingramcontent.com/pod-product-compliance
Lightning Source LLC
Chambersburg PA
CBHW020249030826
48979CB00030B/2670/J

* 9 7 9 8 9 8 5 3 5 6 6 7 0 *